By the same author:

Belfast Girls

Danger Danger

Angel in Flight:

the first Angel Murphy thriller

Johnny McClintock's War:

One man's struggle against
the hammer blows of life

Cover photo & design:

Raymond McCullough

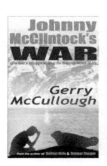

Angel
in Belfast

Gerry McCullough

Published by

Precious Oil
PUBLICATIONS
www.preciousoil.com/publications

ISBN 13: 978-0 9525785 9 8

ISBN 10:   09525785 9 X

First published **2013**

10a Listooder Road, Crossgar,
Downpatrick, Northern Ireland BT30 9JE

Thanks to my husband, Raymond, for cover design, editing, proof-reading and general encouragement.

Chapter One

It was the howling of wolves. Grey, hungry, vicious wolves, ready to tear the flesh of any living thing in their feeding frenzy. Frankie Fitzgerald shivered and turned the music up louder. But although he was listening with his earphones plugged well in, the noises from out-side the cottage kept creeping up on him.

He had come home to Northern Ireland for some peace. This little cottage in the Glens of Antrim, just above Cushendall, was perfect. It was whitewashed, in all the best traditions, and the small front garden, fenced off from the road (road? – it was more of a track!) was full of roses and sweet smelling honeysuckle and many coloured sweet peas.

This wasn't home as Frankie knew it. He'd picked the cottage not because it was the familiar place he grew up in, but because it was the other side of the coin, the Ireland that Americans and other tourists dreamed of. A real place. One he'd heard of all his life. One he'd occasionally known on brief childhood holidays. One he wanted to experience for himself.

Frankie had grown up in the backstreets of Belfast, surrounded by small houses, streets full of noisy children enjoying themselves at play, a main road, the Newtownards Road, nearby, where the big red buses would take you into the heart of Belfast's shopping centre.

Or on the Newtownards Road itself you could buy anything from a cheap saucepan to a smart pair of 'designer' jeans or homemade soda bread. And some of the best homemade ice cream Frankie had ever tasted, before or since. Other parts of the city, Frankie found out later, were brighter, with trees growing along the footpaths, and gardens in front of the houses. The city centre itself was lined with trees. But Frankie's own home was bereft of that sort of beauty. Which didn't mean that he didn't love it.

The song which he had written, and which had hit the heights and pulled up his band, *Raving,* to reach the pinnacle of success, was the story of Belfast and its increasing wealth and renewal since the end of the Troubles – *Snowball.*

Angel in Belfast – *Gerry McCullough*

Frankie had found it hard to believe how successful *Snowball* had been. He had poured all his love for his city into the words and music, and had somehow hit a chord worldwide. Something in *Snowball* had meant a lot to the people who heard it. It had sold by the millions and had hoisted *Raving* to the top.

> *Rolling on, rolling on,*
> *Growing lovelier each day,*
> *Picking up the pieces.*
> *How I love you,*
> *My shabby town...*

Frankie pulled out his earphones and hummed the tune softly to himself.

Chapter Two

Monday morning

Angeline Murphy ran lightly down the steps at the front of the huge yellow bricked BBC building which led out onto Ormeau Avenue. The hot summer sun beat down on her face and she raised her left hand to shield her huge dark eyes from the dazzle. A light pleasant breeze lifted her long fair hair and sent it floating round her face.

'Angel!'

Angeline turned her head.

A small girl with curly blonde hair darted out from the crowd of people passing by and seized Angeline by the arm.

'Mary! Mary Branagh!'

Angel smiled at her friend. Then her face changed as she looked at Mary more closely. Mary's normally cheerful face was white and pinched looking.

'Mary! What's wrong?'

Mary choked back a sob. 'Come and talk to me, Angel. Or have you got time? I was just coming to see you.'

Angel frowned. 'Actually, Mary, I'm on my way to have a meeting with Nathaniel Deane – you know, the painter? His exhibition is on next week at the *Grafton Gallery?* I'm intending to interview him – this is just a preliminary link-up. It won't take too long. I'm meeting him in *Made in Belfast* for lunch. Should be free by 2.30 at the latest. Can I ring you then? Will you be okay if I leave you?'

Angel felt anxious. She'd never seen the normally calm Mary in such a state before.

'Yeah. I'll be okay.'

Angel looked doubtful. She glanced at her watch. Time she was away.

'Go and have a coffee or something. In fact, make sure you eat some lunch. I'll see you in an hour or so, right?'

Mary nodded. 'I'll be in *Clements*, just round the corner from you.'

Mary gulped back the tears which were trying to force their way out and headed for the nearest *Clements*, in Donegal Place West, on one side of the City Hall. As she sipped at her latte, she hoped fervently that Angel wouldn't be too long.

Angel sat opposite Nathaniel Deane, the up-and-coming artist, in *Made in Belfast*, the restaurant in Wellington Street. All round them the walls were covered with mementos of old Belfast, deliberately written graffiti, and different coloured hangings. Angel's shepherd's pie had come in a white enamelled dish edged with blue, of the sort she remembered from her granny's kitchen. Nathaniel's upmarket burger and chips was served on a breadboard.

'So, Nat, what do you especially want to talk about in this interview?'

Nathaniel groaned, and ran one hand through his curly dark hair. His good looking face took on a rueful look.

'Hey, Angel, I thought you'd have all the ideas yourself.'

'Well, I have, Nat. Just wanted to give you a chance first.'

They both laughed.

'I suppose,' Angel went on, 'that your portrait of Frankie Fitzgerald will be the main attraction? People will be coming to see that in their hundreds?'

'Thousands, I hope.'

'Yeah, if you get a lot of his fans – and I should think you will.'

'Right. Ever since *Snowball* hit the Number One spot, *Raving* has been big news. And since Fitz is their lead singer, he's been the focus for the paparazzi and really big on the news both here and in the good old US of A. So I've every hope that they'll show up in their thousands – millions? – to see my portrait of Fitz. I've had offers already from a major company to buy the rights in it to turn it into a poster.'

'Hey, you'll be a millionaire, Nat!'

'Well – maybe. And then will you go out with me, Angel?'

Angel coolly shelved the familiar suggestion. 'So, Nat, are you fine with focussing on Frankie Fitzgerald? Wouldn't you rather talk about your art? Your other pictures? How you've come up with a new style, an advance on Damien Hirst or Jasper Johns? The new Lowry for today? And the rest of the stuff art critics have said about you?'

Nathaniel Deane laughed and pushed a falling lock of dark hair back from his face. 'Sure, Angel, I'd like nothing better than to centre on that. But will it bring people along to the show? A bit of that, great. Of course I love having all these nice things said about me. But, sure, I know right well Fitz is going to be the big draw, and I'd be an eedjit not to talk mainly about him and my portrait of him. Now, take that last remark as off the record, sweetie, won't you? I don't want to be seen as a commercially minded grabber!'

'Sure, Nat, you'd be the last person I'd label that way.' Angel's mobile tinkled. 'Sorry, I meant to turn this thing off while we were chatting.'

She took a quick glance at the screen as she pressed the off button. A news update from her Twitter account. She said, 'Okay. So where were we?'

The mobile went back into her bag. She'd wondered for a second if she'd tell Nat the news headline she'd just read. But she didn't think so. Time enough for him to hear it later.

Chapter Three

Sunday night

In the cottage at Cushendall Frankie Fitzgerald listened to the howling outside. He knew he shouldn't have pulled his earphones out. The noise outside had grown and swollen until he could bear it no longer.

Not wolves. Jackals.

He stood up and drifted over to the window which looked out on the back garden. The temptation to pull back the concealing curtain grew on him. He was pretty sure he'd recognise a good many of the people out there. They'd been following him around, refusing to give him any peace, for weeks now.

He twitched the curtain gently to one side, making a slim bright line of light at the edge of the window where he could peer out at his persecutors. Without them seeing him, he hoped.

There was Stanley Dougan from the *Daily Globe*, camera slung round his thin, geeky neck, mini recorder held high in his left hand, his right hand ready to grab the camera at the first chance to use it.

Behind him, pushing forward, was Cindy Baron, the gossip columnist from *Hi* magazine. A pretty girl if it hadn't been for the avid, greedy look in her bright eyes and the protruding teeth which should have been corrected in her childhood. She looked like a vixen herself, if not a jackal, he thought suddenly.

And further back in the crowd – was it? Yes, he was nearly sure. If that bald man, someone local whom he didn't recognise, would just move his head a bit to the right – yes, it must be Robbie Mallet. DJ, columnist, panel member on more than one reality show, known for his vicious flaying of the miserable contestants. Fitz's fellow musicians, people doing their best, Fitz thought. Robbie Mallet was the one among this horrible crowd whom he disliked most.

He must have moved the curtain too far in his efforts to see if it was really Mallet.

A sudden roar increased the noise by 100%. A flash went off in his eyes, blinding him for a moment.

As he dropped the curtain instinctively and dived backwards from the window he heard the shouts.

'Fitz!'

'He's there!'

'At the window!'

'I was right! Told you he was here!' That was Cindy Baron's high squeaky voice.

The crowd were surging forward, pushing against the doors, forgetting everything in their compulsion to get the exclusive news, the personal interview. *Did they really think this sort of behaviour would get them anywhere?* he asked himself bitterly.

The doors were secure. Locked and bolted, alarms switched on to connect with the nearest police station. Proof against this sort of attack, he was pretty sure. If they weren't, he'd fire his security expert, he told himself, grinning for a second. But it was no joke. He felt his legs trembling, his stomach heaving.

Staggering slightly, he moved away from the window and sank thankfully into the huge comfortable armchair beside the turf fire. Not much turf left, he noticed. No way he was going out to the shed for more. So the fire would be out before morning. But there was efficient central heating. Nothing to worry about. Just a pity. He'd looked forward to building up the turf fire and relaxing in front of it until sleep overtook him.

A crash against the nearest window roused him abruptly from his thoughts. Surely they weren't mad enough to try to break in?

If there was any more of this he would have to phone for help. The last thing he wanted was to drag the police into this. But he couldn't sit back and let these scavengers break into and wreck the cottage.

Perhaps he could compromise. Phone, not the police, but Seri. Talking to her always had a calming effect on him. She would advise him what to do.

He picked up his mobile from the table beside him and punched in Seri's number.

'Hi, pet,' said her soft beautiful voice. Immediately he felt the comfort flow through him.

'Seri.'

'Are you okay, sweetheart?'

'Yeah. Well, sort of.'

'So?'

'They're outside, Seri. Like a pack of raging wolves. What should I do?' In spite of himself, he knew his voice quavered on the last few words.

'Do you want me to send Billy?' Billy Patterson, his P.R. agent. Billy's job was handling the media. But did he want to run to Billy like a helpless child?

'No,' he said at last. 'No, they're a pain, but all I have to do is keep inside with the doors and windows shut. They won't actually break in.'

There was a questioning in the last sentence.

'I don't see it,' Seri said. 'They'd be in big trouble if they actually broke the law that way. No, just ignore them. Put on your head phones and listen to something.'

'Yeah. I was doing that earlier. Best idea.'

They talked for a few more minutes, short loving words which brought him peace and assurance. Then the phone began to break up. It wasn't the best area for reception. Finally it cut out.

He'd have liked to talk to her for longer. Hearing her voice made all the difference.

Crossing over to the worktop against the far wall, at the kitchen end of the large open plan room, he took down a glass and a bottle of Bushmills whiskey from the wall cupboard and poured himself a slug. He left the bottle on the worktop, deliberately. It was possible he'd want another drink later. Back in the armchair by the gradually collapsing turf fire, he sipped the amber liquid slowly. Where were those earphones?

Plugging them back in, he heard the last lines of *Snowball* again.

> *Picking up the pieces*
> *The broken pieces*
> *Making something big*
> *Something beautiful*
> *Beautiful...*

The dying fall of the last line mixed the melancholy note of Irish music with the hard pounding beat of rock.

He didn't want to listen to it right now. Where was Seri's latest? Her beautiful voice promising love and safety was what he needed. He found it on the player and settled back to listen.

> *Never again*
> *Never again*
> *Will I leave you...*

This was the one, he thought, that would make her a major star. They'd written it together, when they had first met up again. They'd known each other as children, but things had drawn them apart for a dozen or more years. Now here she was, back in his life.

But as he sank deeper and deeper into the words and music, his eye searched out and found the forgotten container of pills, partly hidden behind the glass door of the wall cupboard above the Bushmills bottle. Should he? Or shouldn't he?

A gentle knock on the front door of the cottage brought him back to the present. A voice he knew. The voice of a friend.

'Fitz? It's me. Let me in!'

He sprang up and went over to the front door, relief flooding through him. He would have to be careful opening the door. He couldn't afford to let any of the avaricious crowd in. But it shouldn't be impossible They seemed to be mostly round the back, trampling down the garden.

And so, pulling the door open only enough for one person to squeeze through, Frankie Fitzgerald made a major mistake.

He let in the night. The night and the darkness.

Chapter Four

Monday

'Try the lavender ice cream, Angel.'

'Hey, you want me to get fat, or what, Nat, boy?'

'Sweetie, you can easily afford it, you're as slim as a magic wand.'

Angel laughed. 'TV adds pounds to what you look like, darlin' don't you know that? I want to keep my job!'

'Coffee, black and sugarless, please,' she told the waitress.

'Okay, but I'll have mine with cream and heaps of sugar, right?' Nat told her in turn.

'So, let's move over to that sofa,' he suggested. 'The people there are going.'

'Okay.'

Made in Belfast provided a number of large sofas and chairs with coffee tables in between, as well as more orthodox tables where meals could be eaten in comfort. When the waitress delivered their orders, Angel and Nat lifted their coffee cups and moved over to grab the momentarily vacant spot.

Leaning back in his soft chair, Nat grinned. The preliminary interview cum lunch had been going well. They had covered a lot of ground in the last half hour.

Angel had begun by asking, 'Tell me about your background growing up in Belfast, Nat?'

'I was a young teenager by the end of the Troubles, Angel. No fun, right?'

'And do you think it influenced you – your emotions, your painting, all that?'

'Well, yeah. We could probably talk a bit around that sort of stuff.'

'But you moved on when you were eighteen? Scholarship to the prestigious Slade art school in London. Were you glad?'

'Bouncing off the moon, sweetheart. I thought I was made for life.'

'Just as long as you didn't bounce back too hard, tough guy. Then there was your time in New York, meeting up with Andy Warhol's followers for instance?'

'Yeah, wow, that was something. I could talk about that, certainly.'

'And then all your numerous successful exhibitions and your various famous paintings. Starting with the horrific early work reflecting your experiences in the Belfast of the Troubles? That one, *Legless*, with the drunk in the foreground and the bomb going off?'

'Right. You'd want me to talk about that?'

'Yes. The details, right? Just enlarge on what exactly you wanted to get across.'

'If it isn't obvious without me talking about it, then it's a failure,' Nat said drily. 'But, okay, I could say a bit. The comparison between the leg-less drunk – out of control – and the legless – literally legless – victims of the bombers, with no control over what's happening to them. And the terrorists, drunk on violence till they're legless, out of control, too. Okay.'

He looked down for a moment, covering up the emotion the discussion had so quickly rekindled in him. 'And then I moved on to the second war in Iraq. If you want to know, that was even worse. So much suffering on such a large scale – and carried out by people claiming the moral high ground – but, hey, what's new about that?'

Angel felt the need to move on. This was going to be a tremendous interview – but she couldn't bear to take it to the limit here, in the brief preliminary.

'So then came the portraits?'

'Yeah – portraits of the rich and well known and of the poor and obscure.'

'Including one of the poor and obscure, *Beggar in Subway*, which was bought and hung by the Tate. 'The skull beneath the skin', one of the critics called it. The beggar's bones protruding, the skull he holds out as a begging bowl. It really knocked everyone who saw it for six –including me.'

'That's good to know.' Nathaniel was obviously growing embarrassed by Angel's praise.

'So the portraits – particularly that one – brought home the same theme as the Iraq pictures – the war of the rich and powerful, the satisfied, against the poor and helpless?'

'I suppose. I'd be happy to talk about that.' Nat looked up at her, his big, sad eyes gleaming. His mouth was twisted in pain, a pain he wanted to put aside.

'So, Angel, is that enough about the interview?' His long curly dark hair fell forward round his forehead. Bright greeny-grey eyes watched Angel carefully from a strikingly attractive face.

He had been in love with Angeline Murphy for years, since before her disastrous marriage to the abusive husband, Mickey Murphy, who had almost destroyed her. It was good to see Angel picking up the pieces again, emerging as a strong woman able to run her own life. But Nat hoped very much that he might be able to contribute something to her recovery.

'Sure, it'll be fine, Nat. Some good stuff there. Ought to go well.' Angel glanced at her watch. Nearly time to catch up with Mary. 'So, can you come in sometime soon and record the interview?'

'No problem, Angel.'

'And we'll send out a crew to get some cut-in stuff of the exhibition, okay? What time would be good? Maybe tomorrow afternoon – Tuesday? And Wednesday for the crew to visit you at the exhibition?'

'Great. And, of course, you know the opening is on Thursday night? Hope you'll make it! Free glass of fizzy wine and some really nice cheese and biscuits – worth taking the time!'

'I'll certainly make sure I get along sometime, Nat. I definitely want to see these paintings. But no promises about the opening, I'm afraid. I really don't know where I'll be on Thursday.'

For a moment Nathaniel Deane looked disappointed. But he brightened up again. 'Then, changing the subject dramatically,' said Nat, 'how'd you like to come for a meal and cabaret at *am/pm* with me on Saturday? Would you be free then? Sort of thing you ought to keep up with for your programme, right?'

Angel supposed it was. Her recent promotion to the new TV Arts programme, *Belfast Shout Out*, where she was expected to suggest topics as well as interview celebrities and the up and coming in the world of local creative people, had her on her toes, eager not to miss anything important. The cabaret in this local restaurant had so far included both music and drama – possibly something she should report on. The whole conception of a meal and cabaret was something new in Belfast.

'Sounds good, Nat. Okay, next Saturday it is – if nothing else urgent comes up. Give me a ring and we'll get together.'

'Ha! I've finally done it! Got you to come out with me!' Nat said triumphantly.

'Thought you said it was business, Nat?'

'No way! This is going to be a special evening, gorgeous.'

Angel laughed. 'Hope so, darlin'. Now, I need to settle the bill here and rush on. I'm due at *Clements* round the corner in ten minutes.'

Nat tried to take the check from her, but Angel was firm. The lunch, as a preliminary to a formal interview, would be covered by her expenses. No way was Nat going to pay.

On her way to the door, she remembered the text message she'd ignored earlier. Nat ought to be told, she thought. She opened her mobile and glanced at it again.

'Nat, some bad news – sorry. But I'd better pass it on. Did you know Frankie Fitzgerald took an overdose in the early hours of this morning?'

Nathaniel's shocked face gave Angel the answer.

'Fitz? No way! Impossible!'

'Oh?'

'He's stopped all that stuff – right off it!'

'Well, you know him and I don't,' Angel said. 'All I can tell you is they found him unconscious and rushed him to *The Royal* by helicopter. Apparently they're doing everything they can. But it's pretty serious. They don't know if he'll live.'

Nat stared at her, horror stricken.

'I can't believe it, Angel,' he said again.

Chapter Five

Monday

Seri had begun ringing at eight o'clock that morning. Her last call to Fitz, the previous midnight, had gone unanswered.

'Sleeping,' she thought. 'Good. He needs it badly.'

She'd been careful not to try again until a reasonable hour. But by eight o'clock, awake herself since six, the longing to hear his voice had overcome her and she had punched in his number.

No answer.

Restraining herself, she'd given him another hour, then tried again.

No answer.

Seri began to worry. It wasn't like Fitz to sleep so late, except after a gig, when, drained and exhausted, he'd been known to tumble straight into bed and sleep the clock round. Regardless of his possible need to sleep on, she rang again. And again.

His last call to her, unhappy and worried about the massed crowd of paparazzi outside, had left her concerned. Now, as her calls went repeatedly unanswered, the worry swelled until it finally burst the damn and Seri, unable to bear any more, phoned the local police.

'Serena Smith speaking,' she began. 'I'm worried about a friend of mine. I lent him my cottage and he isn't answering his phone.'

'Well, miss, I wouldn't worry. Maybe he's just gone out for a walk – it's a beautiful morning.'

Seri pulled herself together. She hadn't explained properly.

'He'd have his mobile with him. But you don't understand, officer. I'm talking about Frankie Fitzgerald – Fitz, the lead singer of *Raving*. You were asked to look out for him, weren't you, by his security people? Last night the cottage was surrounded by paparazzi. I'd be grateful if you'd check on him – before anything bad happens, right?'

The magic name woke the policeman up. 'Fitz – wow! I didn't realise that was who you meant. Okay, we'll go up there and check. We have the details here, address and so on.'

'And you'll let me know if everything's okay?'

'Yeah, yeah, don't worry. I'm ringing off now, heading up there.'

Seri paced up and down her room, frantic with worry in spite of the policeman's advice. It was at least half an hour before her mobile rang. She seized it at once and pressed the green button.

'Yes?'

'It that Serena Smith?'

Resisting the temptation to reply, 'So whose mobile did you ring, dumbo?' Seri simply said, 'Yes,' again.

'I take it you have a key for this cottage, Miss Smith?'

'Yes.' Seri's blood seemed to have turned to ice. She stood in the warm spring morning with the sun flooding through her window and shivered.

'Can you get up here quickly, with it? We don't want to break in if we don't have to.'

'Go ahead and break in!' Seri shrieked down the phone. 'It's my cottage, I give you permission! Don't waste any more time! It'll take me at least an hour to get there!' She pressed the off button hard and ran for her car.

Driving recklessly up the M2 – it was no occasion to go by the infinitely more beautiful, but much slower, Antrim Coast Road – Seri sobbed out prayers.

'Let him be okay, God. Let him be okay!'

A few of the paparazzi were still hanging round the cottage when Seri's soft-top Mini Cooper stormed up the winding track and screeched to a halt by the front gate, careless of who she forced to scatter out of her way. Overhead, she could see a helicopter high up in the pale blue sky, hovering dark and ominous like a thundercloud.

Bursting out of the car, she shouted, 'What's going on?'

Sergeant Macpherson came over to her. 'Miss Smith?'

'Me.'

'I'm very sorry to have to tell you this –' he began.

Seri's face crumpled and the tears poured from her huge brown eyes. 'What?'

Macpherson's red, fatherly face was creased with sympathy. 'I'm really sorry,' he repeated. 'We broke in as per your instructions. Mr Fitzgerald was unconscious. We had the police doctor with us just in case. Mr Fitzgerald is being removed to the Royal Victoria Hospital in Belfast. The helicopter has just taken off. The paramedics are doing everything they can for him.'

Seri raised her eyes. Hovering high above the cottage, gleaming silver now against the pale blue early morning sky, she saw the helicopter again like some huge bird of prey. It terrified her. Fitz was inside that monster. What was happening to him?

'Where are they taking him? Oh, yes, you said – the Royal. I must get there – I must see him.'

'He'll be taken straight into intensive care, I think, Miss. Or maybe the operating theatre?' Macpherson frowned in perplexity, his medical knowledge failing him at this sort of detail. 'You won't be allowed to see him for a while, Miss.'

'I'll see him.' Seri ground her beautiful white, even teeth. 'No one's going to stop me.' She turned back to the car, and her glance fell on Cindy Baron, Stan Dougan, Hazley Paston of the local *North Antrim Times*. And the crowd behind them.

'And as for you,' she said slowly, anger giving a dangerous power to her strong voice, 'if anything happens to Fitz, I'll take you to the highest court in the land and I'll ruin you forever, you animals.'

Then she swept open the car door, jumped in, slamming it shut in Cindy's face, and drove off in a cloud of dust, heading for Belfast by the fastest route, and for Fitz in the *Royal Victoria Hospital*.

'Wow!' murmured Robbie Mallet from the rear of the crowd, 'that's some powerful woman!'

'Oh, shut up!' howled Cindy, who in spite of her hounding of Fitz over the past week had suddenly been moved to tears by Seri's outburst. 'What do you care? You're inhuman!'

'Hey!' Robbie Mallet was used to taking abuse. He'd have felt a failure if no one had responded like that to his comments. 'Calm down, sweetie. How about seeing if the pubs are open yet in this backward neck of the woods? I might even buy you lunch in an hour or two.'

And Cindy, in spite of feeling rather ashamed, was sufficiently flattered by the attentions of the media star to let him lead her off to his car, a red Porsche which was suffering, to Mallet's annoyance, from scratches on its gleaming paint gouged out by the brambles which had trailed across the path last night as he drove up to Fitz's retreat in the darkness.

Chapter Six

<u>Monday</u>

As she waited for Angel, Mary Branagh ran through again in her head the events of the last three hours. First the nearly hyster-ical call from Seri.

Seri, normally so like her name, Serena, so calm and peaceful, had sounded out of control, miserable, despairing.

'Mary? Oh thank God! Mary, I don't know what to do!'

'Seri, what's wrong?'

'Oh, Mary, it's Fitz! He's in the Royal, in Intensive Care! Mary, they say he took an overdose, but I know he couldn't have! Mary, what can I do? Oh, Mary, pray for him – for both of us!'

'Done,' said Mary crisply, before the reality caught up on her. 'Fitz? An overdose? He can't have!'

There was no sound but Serena's weeping down the phone. Mary had seldom felt so helpless.

'Seri. Listen. It's going to be okay. I'll pray, and so will the rest of the community. It'll be all right.'

'Mary, you don't believe it, do you? He couldn't have done it, could he? We were so happy. And he'd given up all that stuff – he was being strong, with God's help. I can't believe it!'

Mary said nothing. In a flash her mind had gone back to the time, years ago now, when she herself had almost died from an overdose.* She'd been a wild child then, flaking out on drugs as a regular thing, not caring what it led to. That was before she'd had the most important experience of her life, when God had spoken to her and shown her his love. But surely Fitz was already past that stage. As Seri had said, he had given up dope months ago. Why should he go back to it? But she knew that people sometimes did.

'Seri,' she said as calmly as possible, 'sit down, relax, read a psalm, and let God help you. I'll come round as soon as possible.'

---

* see *Belfast Girls*

Then she had hurriedly messaged the members of the Christian community, the *Community of the Cross*, who lived with her in the big house on the Antrim Road, and asked them to pray.

It didn't take her long to reach the Royal, and to find Seri.

They sat in the open air, outside the main building, and the story came tumbling out.

'The paparazzi – they surrounded him, pushed him, drove him to distraction. If he took stuff, it's down to them. But I still don't believe he did.'

Mary felt Seri's pain. For herself, she was deep in horror. How could people treat other people like this? For the sake of a story – for the sake of the money that went with it – they seemed to be prepared to drive the famous 'celebs' over the edge with-out compunction. Princess Di swam into Mary's thoughts. And there were so many others. Pushed to the brink by the seekers after publicity. Or, rather, for the sake of a good story which would take its writer to the top.

And yet, had Fitz really been pushed into taking an over-dose by these vultures? Mary still found it hard to believe. She hadn't known Fitz for as long as Seri had known him. But in the two months since he'd been coming to the community meetings, she thought she'd got to know him pretty well. Fitz wasn't a wimp or a weakling. He had an inner strength which had taken him to the top in the harsh, dangerous world of music, against hard-hitting opponents, and which would keep him going against all odds.

Sitting with her arm round Seri outside the Royal Victoria Hospital, Mary made up her mind. Yes, she would pray, and continue to pray. But maybe something practical could be done as well?

It was then that Mary decided to catch up with her friend Angeline Murphy at the BBC.

Angel came through the door of *Clements* and stood for a moment, looking cool and poised, as her eyes searched for Mary. Then she moved forward and slid coolly into the seat beside her friend.

'Sorry for the delay, Mary, pet,' Angel apologised. She noticed with horror as she sat down that there were tears in Mary's eyes. She put her arm round Mary's shoulder and hugged her briefly. 'Now, darlin', tell me all.'

Even as she spoke, Angel reflected how strange it seemed that she, who had run to Mary in despair on the breakup of her horrendous marriage[*], and had relied on her friend's strength, should now be enacting the role of the strong one, the one who was helping Mary.

---

[*] see *Angel in Flight*

Mary pulled herself together with a visible effort. 'I'm not really sure why I should be dragging you into this, Angel. Seri thought, because you're in the media – I'd have asked John, but he's over in London on a training session, right now.'

'I know.' Mary's brother John Branagh was one of the up and coming stars on the local news programme, currently being groomed for an even more central role. Mary had been delighted that John's spell in London was to coincide with the arrangement that his beautiful wife Sheila Doherty, the fashion model, should take part in an important dress show there. 'So, Seri? Should I know her?'

'Sorry, I'm telling this all wrong. Serena Smith. The singer. You might not have heard of her yet, but she's going places. This new song that Fitz wrote with her – like, wow. She and Fitz are an item. So this has devastated her.'

'I'm sure.'

'So, Seri's been coming along to our community meetings for a good while. You know, the thing is no one has to be a member of the community to come to the regular evening meetings, get a bit of peace, let the Lord sort out their lives as they sit with the candles lit and just soak in His presence – so that's what Seri's been doing for a while. Then a few months ago she brought Fitz along and introduced him. A lovely guy. Everyone loves him.'

'Right.'

'No, really.'

'Okay – hard to believe, with his reputation.'

'The media again.' Mary's voice sounded hard, unlike her. Angel stared at her in astonishment. Mary blushed.

'Sorry, Angel. I know there are exceptions. You. For goodness sake, my own brother! But so many of them just want to rake the dirt. Okay, Fitz wasn't so great for a few years there – but never as bad as they said. They made out that he was a real pain, up to everything, punching out people in nightclubs –'

'Yeah, I read about that – so you're telling me there's another side to that story?'

'Fitz punched the guy, sure! The footballer, Ivan George. But only because he was next door to raping the girl he was dancing with – a sixteen year old innocent who'd gone along to the place with George because she thought it was exciting and romantic. Did she get a shock! Fitz saw what was going on, and waded in – and good for him, I say!'

'Fair enough.'

'And, okay, he's been involved in drugs. But recently he's stopped all that.'

'Good.'

Angel tried to keep the scepticism out of her voice.

'One of the first things he did, when he started coming along, was ask for help to get off the drugs. Not that he was all that far gone, mind you. If he'd been really as bad as the press said, we'd have recommended him to a rehab place – somewhere like Betel, in England. But he wasn't as far down the line as that. In a pretty short time, he was well free of it. We all prayed for him, of course.'

'The best thing.'

'And before very long, he was really free. I swear to you, Angel. We get a lot of this sort of stuff coming through. I can tell, by now, if someone's genuine or just letting on. Fitz was the real thing. A guy who'd come off the stuff and wasn't going back.'

'So why would he have something with him – enough to take an overdose?'

'Well, that's it.' Mary looked defiantly at her friend. 'Seri doesn't believe he did, and neither do I. We think someone switched his sleeping pills for something lethal.'

'But, Mary.' Angel stared at her friend in horror.

'What?'

'Are you seriously suggesting that this is a case of murder – or, let's hope, attempted murder?

Chapter Seven

Monday

Mary drained the last dregs of her by now very cold coffee and looked at her friend.

'Angel, I realise you're finding this hard to believe. But there are really only two options. Either Fitz was fooling us all when we thought he was really free from drugs – or else someone else spiked his drink or substituted something for the harmless sleeping pill his doctor had prescribed for specially bad nights. I know Fitz hardly ever took those pills. He didn't want to rely even on something like that – but it's certainly possible that the vicious mob outside pushed him into taking something to shut them out.

'Seri says he rang her in a bad state. She did what she could to calm him down. But then the phone cut off. The reception up there in the Glens of Antrim isn't great. If he couldn't keep in contact with Seri, he might have felt he needed something to send him to sleep. But that's the limit. Neither Seri nor I believe he would have taken anything more.'

Angel nodded reluctantly. She believed in Mary. Mary was really wise. Angel had experienced Mary's wisdom in her own life when she'd run to Mary for help. She didn't think Mary would accept some-one's ideas if they were rubbish, and give a rosy but untrue picture of them, no matter how famous and important that person might be. Angel was prepared to accept Mary's view of Frankie Fitzgerald, Fitz. She knew that if Mary had been meeting Fitz regularly for several months, she would have got to know him. She wasn't the sort of person to be easily fooled.

'So, Mary, what do you and Seri expect me to do?' she asked.

Mary drew a deep breath. 'First of all, I want you to meet up with Seri and hear all this at first hand from her,' she said. 'And then we want to get together with the rest of *Raving*, and do a bit of brainstorming. I really believe we can come up with some ideas about how to deal with this – about how to find the people responsible for the thing that's happened to Fitz. I don't see why we couldn't do it!'

'So, Mary, you think these people, whoever they are, are guilty of attempted murder at the least?'

'I'm sorry to have to say it, Angel, but yes, I really do. And I also feel that the media persecution that's been driving him to desperation for weeks now has had something to do with it.'

'But, Mary, either Fitz was driven by the paparazzi to overdose, whether accidentally or on purpose, or else someone tried to kill him. You can't have it both ways.'

'Oh, I know, you're right,' Mary admitted. 'But Angel, I just feel there's more to it than that. I want to get the truth. And if possible I'd like to stop this sort of thing happening to anyone else.'

'Okay, Mary. I'll meet up with Seri, if that's what you want,' Angel agreed. 'And you can arrange something with the other members of *Raving* if you think it'll help. I really don't know what you think I can do. But I'll certainly do my best for you. After all, it was you who helped me to get my life back together when I really needed help. So it's the least I can do.'

'Great. I'll get back to you later.'

Mary pushed back her chair and stood up. She and Angel made their way out onto the sunlit street where the Arabian Nights fantasy of the City Hall loomed before them and in the light breeze the trees happily flirted the new short skirts of green leaves they'd got for spring.

Mary suddenly threw her arms round her friend.

'And, Angel,' she said into her ear, 'you really are an Angel!'

As she ran up the steps into the BBC building in Ormeau Avenue, Angel heard her mobile ring. She stood just inside the revolving doors at the entrance to the Reception area and listened to the call. It was Nat Deane.

'Angel?'

'Nat.'

'Just wondered. Heard any more about Fitz?'

'Last I know, he's still on life support in intensive care,' Angel told him. 'They don't know yet how things will work out.'

She could hear the choke in Nat's voice.

'It's so horrific. Fitz was such a good guy. Everyone who got to know him thought he was a real star – not just a rock star. I can't believe he went back on drugs. I talked to him a lot about that while I was painting him, Angel. He'd turned his life around. Been going to some Christian community – tried to get me to come along, but it's not my style, right? But I can't believe he wasn't serious about the whole thing.'

'Yes, I think you're right,' Angel said slowly. She was thinking.

'I just wish there was something I could do to help. Even something to prove Fitz wasn't back on drugs,' Nat went on. 'I'm devastated by the whole set up, Angel. There must be something more going on.'

'You really think that, Nat?'

'I really do. If only I could help prove it!'

'Well,' said Angel. 'If you definitely mean that –' She paused.

Nat said nothing. Angel was aware that he was trying to hold back his tears.

'I think there might be something you could help with, Nat,' she said finally. 'Maybe I'll ring you back later when I'm clearer about it myself – okay?'

Chapter Eight

Monday

Johnson Carson, lead guitar in *Raving*, stormed up the M1 motorway towards Belfast in his bright green Mercedes convertible, his newly bleached hair flying in the wind, his twenties style scarlet silk cravat tied loosely round his beautifully tanned neck. As he drove, he sang along to the earphones plugged into his MP3 player and found that once again he was singing along to *Snowball*. He could hear his mobile ringing in the background.

Jonty was responsible enough not to answer while driving on the motorway. A few minutes later he heard his ring tone for calls switch off, to be followed a moment later by the ringtone for messages. It wasn't until he reached his destination, and pulled into the car park of the *Diamond*, Belfast's most recent upmarket hotel, that he checked his messages. It was Seri.

As he read the message, Jonty's face grew still. The colour drained from his cheeks. His throat choked up. It was minutes before he could believe the dreadful news.

'Fitz! I can't believe it!' he gasped to himself, as he felt the tears begin to form in his ice grey eyes.

A second later he was punching Seri's number furiously into his mobile, waiting on tenterhooks for her reply.

'Yes?'

'Seri? It can't be true? Fitz was off the drugs. Even the paparazzi couldn't have pushed him to this!'

'That's what I think too, Jonty. Can we get together to talk about what we can do? Or are you tied up?'

'No way!' spluttered Jonty furiously. 'Tell me where and when and I'll be there.'

It meant cancelling an interview with Jeff Wilson of *Serious Music*, and later, probably, a hot date with a lovely redhead whom he'd met last night. But if it was for Fitz, no problem.

When Fitz had first met him, Jonty had been playing for a third rate band, mostly doing covers in pubs and clubs, for buttons. Fitz had recognised Jonty's amazing skill on the guitar and had invited him to join the new band, Raving, that Fitz was setting up. Jonty owed Fitz a lot. He would never forget it. If this was payback time, that was fine with Jonty.

'Okay,' came Seri's voice. 'Let's make it my apartment, around eight. I want to hang round the hospital for as long as possible, before we meet. Okay?'

'Okay.'

Marilyn Moscow, the female drummer for *Raving*, was lunching with the star reporter on the *Daily Word*, Lucas Somerset, when Seri's call came through. Unhappy that this important interview seemed to be going off the rails, Mar was idly forking up Scallops Jacques, with her fork in her left hand, and waving her right hand in the air to show off her drummer's muscles.

Why, she asked herself, had the interview degenerated from an in-depth about how it felt to be one of the few girl drummers to reach the heights in the music scene, into a scurrilous investigation into her (purely professional) relationship with Fitz?

Okay, everyone wanted to talk about Fitz, she knew that, but surely this interview, which she'd angled for for weeks, was meant to focus on her, Marilyn Moscow, the top girl drummer in the country? Marilyn felt that, much as she loved Fitz, this was a bit too much.

'Drummers need muscles,' she said. 'I'm sure you know that, Luke. I have them, right? I work out every morning, toning up my muscles so's to be able to keep bashing away for three hours or so at every gig. Without the rhythm of the drums – the beat, right – the band just wouldn't sound the same. And when I strip off my T-shirt halfway through, the crowd just goes wild – you've seen them.'

Marilyn Moscow (real name Susan Doyle) was an outstandingly pretty girl with bright red hair and blue, blue eyes, and an amazing figure – in spite of her strong muscly arms. Lucas Somerset, in spite of his profess-ional need to pick up all the dirt, found himself wanting more and more to focus on Mar.

Then her mobile rang.

Somerset was annoyed. Mar should have switched off before the inter-view started. Everyone did. An interview with Lucas Somerset was important.

And if she'd forgotten to switch off beforehand, for heaven's sake she should have switched off now. She certainly shouldn't have answered it. But as he watched her face growing whiter by the second, he realised that whatever the news was, it was more important than any interview.

Like Jonty, Mar found what Seri was telling her about Fitz not only impossible to take in, but also unbelievably upsetting. She didn't have the words to answer Seri. All she could say was, 'No. No.'

And when Seri spoke to her about taking action, and suggested the meeting at her apartment that night, Mar just managed to breath out, 'Okay, Seri. I'll be there.'

Raving's keyboard players, Pete and Ziggy Carmichael, known as the Diabolical Twins, were playing squash in the QUB sports complex when Ziggy's phone rang.

First class on the keyboard, Pete and Ziggy had been playing duets since childhood, when their mother had insisted on piano lessons for both her boys. She had been hugely disappointed at first when instead of becoming classical pianists the twins had thrown over their more formal careers for the opportunity to play with *Raving* and had gone on to add a unique sound to the band and to help to hoist it to the top.

Unlike the other band members, Pete took a serious interest in world affairs and listened regularly to the news, which he then passed on to his brother regardless of Ziggy's lack of response.

Nevertheless he'd managed to miss that morning's news bulletins. He'd sensibly turned off his mobile before the game. So it was Ziggy who picked up his phone and heard Seri's voice, hoarse with unhappiness and sounding so unlike herself that Ziggy at first wouldn't have been sure who was talking if the caller ID hadn't told him.

'What? What?'

Ziggy sat down suddenly on the floor of the squash court, his racket falling from his strangely limp hand.

Pete, uttering an exclamation of disgust, seized Ziggy's phone. 'Ziggy just collapsed,' he told the caller, not stopping to check who it was. 'If it's something important you better call back later. Unless you want to give me a message.'

'Pete – Pete, it's Seri. Wait!'

Pete stopped himself in time from ringing off.

'Seri? What is it?'

'Oh, Pete, haven't you heard yet?'

And Pete listened in horror as Seri once more relayed the dreadful news about Fitz.

And like Jonty and Mar, Pete turned pale as he listened, although unlike Ziggy he managed to stay on his feet.

'Okay. Tonight, at your place? Right, Seri. We'll be there,' he said, before cutting off and handing the phone back to Ziggy.

'Game over, right bro?' he said. 'Better go and eat something before you pass out. Me too, for that matter.'

Although he didn't normally show his feelings as easily as his twin brother, Pete knew that something of major importance, something crushing, had disrupted his life. Fitz had to recover. He had to. And how could it be true that he'd taken an overdose? Pete didn't believe it.

He just wondered how any of them could prove that it wasn't true.

Chapter Nine

Monday

Seri had been at the Royal Victoria Hospital, in the Falls Road in Belfast, all day. Northern Ireland's top hospital, famous for the amazing advances made by its surgeons during the Troubles and the life saving operations carried out by them day after day, the Royal was the safest place for Fitz to be right now.

Seri knew that. As the day crawled on, she kept telling herself that he couldn't be in more expert hands. And that he was in the Lord's hands, which was even better.

Nevertheless every time she was allowed back to his bedside she shivered uncontrollably with fear, and found herself unable to stop praying. He looked so white, so vulnerable. Not the strong, independent Fitz she had known. He had to recover, he had to.

'Please, God,' she prayed, 'don't let Frankie die. I love him so much.'

At intervals she stumbled down to the hospital restaurant and drank endless cups of coffee. Sometimes she ordered a sandwich with it. But it stayed, a crumbled mess, on her plate, as she found that she couldn't eat even a bite.

She sat by Fitz's bedside, her mind numb, as the watch on her wrist gradually moved on to seven o'clock.

A staff nurse rustled in, her starched blue uniform sounding out at every step.

'Sorry, love,' she said. Her voice was more sympathetic than the sound of her uniform dress might have suggested. 'There's a limited time for visitors here – you know that. I'll give you five more minutes – mind you, that's going past the limit – to get used to the separation. Then you'll have to leave, for now.'

Seri panicked. 'Please, I can't bear to be away if anything happens.'

The staff nurse looked distressed. 'You can come back, pet. The hospital rules say only one visitor, for one hour at a time. And then a break. But you can come back for the next slot. And we'll let you know at once if anything changes.'

Seri stood up and wiped her beautiful dark brown eyes with her knuckles. 'It's okay. I don't want to break the rules or make a fuss. I'm just so grateful that you're looking after him. When can I come back?'

She leaned over Fitz's high bed, bristling with life support instruments, drips, monitors, all the baggage.

'Please don't die, sweetheart,' she whispered to him. 'You're so strong, use your strength for this, my darling. You matter so much to me – and to so many other people. Don't die, Frankie. I love you, I love you. God bless you, my darling.'

Her tears dropped helplessly on his pale face. She wiped them off with her hand. Then she kissed his flaccid, colourless lips. It was time to go.

Crying softly to herself, Seri left the small side room where everything she cared for most in earthly terms was fighting for survival.

Out in the corridor, she glanced at her watch.

It was nearly eight o'clock. She'd told people to be at her apartment for eight. Time to move.

Seri's apartment was on the higher reaches of the River Lagan, near *Cutter's Wharf*. With a beautiful view over the upstream river, it was somewhere to dream of, but at the same time the price was lower than the city centre apartments further downstream. Seri had decorated it with crimson velvet cushions and curtains against sand coloured leather couches and easy chairs, and walls painted cream. As her friends crowded in that evening, Seri found herself once more in tears as she realised how much they all cared for Fitz.

Seri tried hard not to weep as she offered and poured out drinks and directed her friends to the cheeses, dips, savoury biscuits and grapes she'd grabbed from the fridge and set out hurriedly on the side table.

Mary drew Seri to one side.

'Seri, this is Angel Murphy. I wanted you two to meet before this evening, but it hasn't worked out like that. Angel was at work, for one thing. And I know you needed to spend as much time as possible with Fitz, Seri.'

'Thanks for coming, Angel,' Seri stammered, looking in awe at the beautiful girl Mary was introducing.

Angel smiled.

'No problem, Seri. I totally want to help.'

'Now,' said Mary briskly, 'nearly everyone's here. Seri needs to get back to Fitz very shortly. Let's get moving.'

But just at that moment, there was a racket at the door, and as Seri moved to open it, the twins, Pete and Ziggy, burst in.

'Hi, guys. Sorry we're late. Just tell us what you want us to do.'

Mary said, 'No problem, Twins. Listen, this is Angel Murphy. You've seen her on TV. She has a bit of experience with this sort of thing – tracked down a villain in Crete last year. And of course she knows about the media. So I've roped her in to help us.'

Angel smiled her bewitching smile at the roomful of people. 'Sure, that's what we're here to talk about, darlin's. I think – let's hope you all agree with me? – that Fitz didn't try to top himself. Somebody else switched his sleeping pills for something more lethal, perhaps. Or spiked his drink. And the paparazzi pushed him over the edge. He'd wouldn't have taken the pills at all if it hadn't been for them. So we want to work on that. Find out who could have switched the pills, or whatever. And find out who – if anyone – was responsible for the paparazzi going to such extremes.'

Angel paused and looked around at them.

'What do you all think? Can we do anything? Have you any ideas about what we can do to help?'

Just then the door bell of Seri's apartment rang.

'That might be Nathaniel Deane,' Angel said coolly. 'You probably all know that he spent a long time with Fitz recently, painting his portrait. He thinks Fitz is great. I told him about this meeting. He's sure Fitz wouldn't have killed himself on purpose. And I think he might have a lot to offer, in a helpful way, to our discussion. Can you let him in, Seri?'

'Okay.'

Seri went to the door and opened it.

Outside stood Nat, his long dark curly hair hanging round his shoulders, his beautiful face creased with pain.

'Come in, Nat,' Seri said. 'I'm Fitz's girl friend, Seri. Thanks for coming. Angel says she thinks you can help us. I do hope you can.'

Over Seri's shoulder Marilyn Moscow's face shone with excitement as she gazed dumbfounded at Nathaniel Deane.

She didn't know when she'd seen a more beautiful man than this one.

Chapter Ten

Monday

'Okay, guys, said Angel briskly. 'Everyone's here. Let's brainstorm a bit. What do we think happened? And what can each of us do?'

There was a moment's silence. Then Mar, the girl drummer of *Raving*, spoke. 'I agree – in fact I'm positive – that Fitz didn't try to top himself on purpose. He just wouldn't have. So I think there must have been someone behind it all. Someone who pushed the media guys into laying siege to him, and who was responsible for spiking his drink or his pills.

'So we need to look into the people who were hounding him, the paparazzi. We all have some contacts with the media. I say we should go first of all to the people we know, poke around, get suggestions from them and follow up the ideas they come up with. Right? And I'll start with the guy who was interviewing me today – Lucas Somerset, the *Daily Word* guy.'

'Good idea, Mar,' Mary Branagh said. 'Start where we have an opening and go from there.'

'Okay,' Angel agreed. 'We should write down the names of the people we think could be helpful.'

'But what are we trying to find out?' Jonty Carson asked. His bleached blonde hair, normally swept smoothly back from his tanned face, was unusually dishevelled from the many times he had run his fingers through it that day – those long, sensitive fingers which gave him the reach which made him one of the greatest lead guitarists for years. His finely boned face reflected the pain he still felt. 'I mean, I had to cancel an interview with Jeff Wilson, the guy from *Serious Music*, this evening – I can easily set it up again, and get him talking. But do we seriously think any of these press guys messed with Fitz's tablets or what?'

'Maybe not,' said Ziggy Carmichael slowly. His intelligent eyes gleamed. 'We know very little right now. The idea would be to find out as much as we can about last night – who was there, what they saw – and work out the possibilities from that, when we've got enough info to begin thinking. We can't come up with the right answers when we have nothing to work on, okay?'

'Fair enough,' his twin brother Pete agreed. Pete was no fool, but he had always acknowledged that Ziggy had a spark of something more, an intuition, an occasional touch of genius which took him to the heart of things while Pete was still working through the facts. 'Let's get on with writing down the names. I don't mind having a go at Simon Fletcher. He's an old mate of ours. He works freelance for the *Telegraph*.'

'Si wouldn't have been there – there's no way he'd have been pestering Fitz,' Ziggy protested.

'Right, Bro. But like you just said, maybe he'll have a good idea who would have been there at the cottage.'

'Okay,' Ziggy nodded.

Nat Deane had been watching Angel. This was a new angle on her, and a fascinating one. The efficient organiser, the girl who held down a high-powered media job and made things work. He leaned forward to get a clearer view of her face.

And as he watched Angel, Mar watched him. And saw the desire in his eyes.

Seri said, 'I have media friends, too. Martin Craig, for instance. The music critic on *Forward*. I could maybe get time to talk to him some time soon. But I – ' Her voice broke and she tried to choke back the tears which kept coming in spite of all her efforts. 'I need to get back to the Royal, before long. They said they'd let me back in to Fitz around half nine. I – I need to be with him.'

'Of course you do, honey,' Mary said warmly. 'We all know being with Fitz is your priority right now. No one wants you to do anything else. It's the rest of us who are making plans, right, guys?' There was a unanimous murmur of ascent from around the room. 'I'll talk to my brother John – John Branagh, in the BBC Newsroom, that is. He's over in London, but he could probably suggest the most likely people to be involved, the ones who've mainly been chasing Fitz.'

'Great, Mary,' Angel said briskly. 'And I'll plug in to the grapevine at the BBC here and see what I can stir up from its murky depths.'

'Didn't know grapevines grew in murky depths, Angel,' Pete chipped in.

'Whatever. You might be surprised, boy!'

Pete grinned.

'Nat,' Angel said, 'what about you? Any suggestions?'

'Can't say I have all that many media contacts, apart from this here Angel Murphy girl,' Nat drawled, smiling at Angel in a way which sent a shiver down Mar's spine. 'But I know a few Art critics. I could see if any of them have picked up some useful gossip, right?'

'Good thinking, Batman.' Angel grinned at him. 'So if anyone comes up with something useful, message me. I'll give you my number now, before we wind up. And you'd better give me yours, in case I want to get us together again – probably need to when you've all talked to your first contacts.'

Mobiles were produced and numbers exchanged. Mar was pleased to get Nat's number as well as Mary's and Angel's. The band members and Seri already had each other's, naturally. She wondered how easy it would be to leave with him tonight. Depended on what Angel's plans were, she supposed.

'So, Seri, we need to let you go now,' Angel was saying briskly. 'May not seem as if we've done much tonight, guys, but I think we've made a good start. Let's be in touch as soon as you have anything.'

'It's been good to be together,' Jonty Carson said abruptly. 'Like, I guess we all need each other right now, as much as anything. Well, I know it's been good for me. Let's not all split too soon. Okay, Seri, we'll get out of here, but hey, why not everyone come round to mine now and go on talking, maybe jam a bit if we feel up to it?'

'Good idea, Jonty,' came a chorus. The band members and Mary began to leave.

'Seri, can I just keep you for a few words, darlin'?' Angel said. 'Nat, see you soon – thanks for coming.'

Nat's face fell. 'Okay,' he said. It was clear that he'd hoped to spend the rest of the evening with Angel.

'Why not join us, Nat, if you aren't tied up?' Mar said quickly.

'Yeah, sure,' Jonty agreed.

'Why not? Thanks, guys,' Nat said. He didn't sound too enthusiastic. More just polite.

Mar's face brightened. So, Nat wasn't just going to disappear.

It wasn't that Mar didn't care about Fitz. She was still devastated. But undoubtedly Nat Deane was the most beautiful man she'd seen for a long time.

As soon as the others had gone, Angel began to ask Seri about the cottage and the events of last night. But she soon saw that Seri was too upset to talk at any length. So when she had got clear directions and the key, Angel reluctantly decided she would have to leave it for now.

'So, it's okay with you if I go up there now and take a look, before any traces have been spoilt, Seri?'

'Sure, go ahead, Angel. Maybe you'll find something.' Seri hesitated. 'And, Angel – I don't know if I've thanked you properly. I really do appreciate what you're doing.'

'Get away with you! Sure, I want to do it – Fitz is a great guy! Now, be away off to the hospital. And keep believing that there'll be good news there, soon, darlin' girl.'

And Angel gave Seri a swift hug, as they both left the apartment.

Chapter Eleven

Monday

It was still early, not much later than nine o'clock.

Angel's car, a tiny Seat M11, was parked near Seri's apartment. As she strolled over towards it, mulling over in her mind what exactly she should do next, the early spring sky was still light enough to show the tiny blue and yellow flowers shining in the grass verges of the car park.

The cottage was at least an hour's drive away. It would be dark by the time she arrived there. Good. That meant that no one would see her – she hoped.

Angel drove fast as a regular thing, but kept to the speed limits. Tonight she was tempted to forget about them, but decided against it. The sea, shining in the distance as she drove across country, gleamed rose red rather than silver in the light of the dying sun. The small blue, white and yellow flowers in the hedges and banks, the huge bunches of cow parsley which rioted along the verges of the country lanes, as she left the main roads behind her, were reflected purple and orange and pink and beautiful.

Nevertheless it was still only a quarter past ten when the little blue Seat M11 drew up beside Seri's cottage – Fitz's intended 'shelter.' The front door was crudely fastened shut, a board hammered over it, That must be because the police had broken in there.

Perhaps she should park out of sight, not here on the road.

Cautiously she manoeuvred the car along a track on the left side of the cottage, along the hedge. Turning left again, she pulled up behind the enclosed back garden. A gate in the fence proved to be unlocked. Angel undid the bolt which held it shut, reaching easily over the low top of the gate to do it.

Even in the growing darkness she could see the trampling of many feet which had left their mark on the flowerbeds and the previously smooth green lawn. She could smell the scent of the bruised grass ming-ling with the still vibrant perfume of the poor crushed roses and carnations wafting towards her through the warm night air. It must have been through this back garden that the paparazzi had got so close to Fitz. He had told Seri that they had sounded like wolves on his doorstep.

Anger burned deep in Angel, but she reined it back. Anger wasn't going to help her just now. She had a job to do which wouldn't be made any easier if she lost control of her emotions.

She'd brought a pair of rubber gloves with her from her own kitchen, previously reserved for washing up. Wisdom had told her that it would be better to leave no traces of her presence, no fingerprints, in Seri's cottage. She slipped them on now, hesitated, then went back and wiped the back gate and the bolt where her ungloved hands had touched them.

Seri's keys were in her pocket. Angel sorted out the key to the back door and inserted it. For a moment nothing happened. Then she remembered that there were two locks and quickly found the second key.

The alarm system was just inside the door, Seri had told her, a head high box on the right as you came in. She'd given Angel the code. As soon as the door swung open, Angel dived forward and punched in the numbers before the alarm could ring in Cushendall police station. They would be very much on the alert there, she supposed, for any sound from the cottage, after this morning's events.

When the alarm was safely turned off, Angel quietly pulled the door shut behind her, found the master switch which controlled the elect-ricity and switched it on, and began her search.

The cottage, although so small, had a spacious room which took up most of the downstairs. She thought a wall between kitchen and front room had probably been taken out to create the larger space. The room stretched from the window above the kitchen sink and worktops to the wider front windows looking out to the small but pretty front garden.

The kitchen area, Angel noted, had all mod cons – microwave, electric kettle, toaster, dishwasher. In the area to the front of the room a fireplace on the right showed the remains of a turf fire, radiators were discreetly positioned along three walls, and a very up market audio system almost covered the wall to the left. A huge soft armchair near the fire had clearly been pushed back by the paramedics that morning, making room for themselves to examine Fitz, then to carry him out to the waiting helicopter.

The crucial question was, had the police then carried out a thorough search of the cottage? Angel had questioned Seri at length, and was reasonably satisfied that they hadn't.

'They just wanted to get him to hospital as quickly as possible,' Seri explained. Her voice quivered and she fought to keep back the tears as her memory transported her back to those moments of horror. 'They sealed up the front door, and then they headed back to the police station, I suppose to make their report, once the helicopter had taken off. I wasn't in time to go with Fitz – the helicopter was already on its way when I got there. So as soon as the police had sealed up the door, I drove as fast as I could after them and then on directly to Belfast, to the Royal.'

'And you don't know if they came back later to search?'

'I don't see how they could have done. I had the keys. They broke the lock the first time – I told them to go ahead – but they sealed it up before they left. I don't think they'd have broken in a second time.'

'Yes.' Angel thought about it. 'I suppose they were assuming it was attempted suicide or accident. They would wait to see if Fitz recovered before treating it seriously, before even considering murder. They made sure the cottage was fastened up. They could get the keys from you and come back if they needed to. If Fitz ...' she had hesitated, trying to put it as gently as possible – 'if Fitz didn't get over it.'

Seri's gulp had made Angel realise it was time to stop the questions. But that was okay. Angel thought she had heard enough. It seemed safe to act on the belief that no one had searched the cottage before her.

Adjusting the rubber gloves she'd brought with her, Angel began to look round.

On the worktop to one side of the kitchen area she saw a bottle of Bushmills whiskey. It had been opened, and a small amount poured from it. Moving on, Angel noticed a greetings card propped against a mug on the next shelf. It was from a well known MLA – a Member of the Legislative Assembly, the local equivalent to an MP. 'To the wonderful Fitz, from your friend and one of your greatest fans,' she read. 'Keep on boosting Belfast!' And then the famous signature. Richard Bell, known province wide as Dinger Bell. He'd signed himself Dinger, with his full name beneath.

Angel moved back to study the bottle. As far as she could tell without measuring, only two singles had been poured from it. A glass with a little left in the bottom sat beside the bottle on the same worktop.

So at least Fitz hadn't been overdoing the booze. That confirmed some of what she'd heard from his friends earlier tonight.

Angel's eye drifted round the kitchen area. If Fitz had taken something, whether with the deliberate desire for death or not, surely there had to be some sign of it here? Unless the police had removed it without Seri noticing?

But Angel didn't think so. Seri had been sure. She had convinced Angel that the police hadn't touched anything without Seri noticing.

So there must be a bottle – or packet, or something – if Angel looked hard enough.

Her glance swung momentarily upwards.

Against the wall were a number of high line cupboards with glass doors. They would contain plates, other crockery, possibly tinned food.

Angel reached up one long arm and swung the door of the nearest wall cupboard open.

On the lower shelf, facing directly towards her as she gazed inside the open door, was a small plastic bottle containing pills.

Chapter Twelve

Monday

Angel took the bottle over to the nearest light, a lamp on a low coffee table not far from the turf fire. The label stuck to the bottle said, 'Twenty 10 gm, one to be taken at night if required,' and the name of the tablet, *Temazepam.*

Angel had heard the name before. It was a mild sleeping pill, of the sort doctors prescribed when it seemed necessary to give something. Not really dangerous. You'd have to take an enormous amount before it had any serious effect. The label said there should be twenty tablets here.

Angel unscrewed the child friendly top and tipped out the tablets onto the coffee table. Then she counted them carefully. And again. And a third time.

There were nineteen.

At most, Fitz had taken one sleeping pill last night.

There was no way one tablet of *Temazepam* could have had such a serious effect on him.

Angel replaced the bottle on the cupboard shelf. If the police ever needed it for evidence it would be important that it should be there for them to find. She continued her search quietly and efficiently, but there was nothing of importance. A note from Seri explaining where to switch on the electric and the water and hoping he had a nice restful time.

No other personal letters. But why should there be? Fitz had only just arrived at the cottage, and wasn't planning to stay for long. There would be no build up of personal paperwork. Only the few things he'd brought with him, mainly clothes and music.

She'd been here long enough. It was time to go, before anyone noticed her.

A slight sound alerted her. She looked up abruptly and glanced round. She heard the sound again. It came from outside the cottage.

Through the back window she could see what might be a face. The face of someone watching her.

With slow, careful movements, concealing the fact that she'd noticed anything, Angel looked away. Could she slip out quietly enough, come round behind the intruder and catch them? Angel thought she probably could. She was certainly going to try.

Angel moved to the back door and opened it. Then she switched off the electricity, reset the alarm, punching in the code, and slipped outside, pulling the door shut behind her. The Yale lock caught immediately. The second lock needed to be fastened by her key. She turned the key and stood listening for a moment by the door, hidden by the walls of the small porch.

Then she moved quickly. Out of the porch. Speeding along beside the back wall towards the window where she'd seen the face.

No one there. Whoever it was must have run for it while Angel was locking up.

She stood very still, listening. The intruder couldn't have gone far. She should be able to hear him if he was still moving.

What was that rustling sound she could hear among the trees behind the cottage? It didn't sound human.

Probably an animal, she thought.

Angel, a city girl by birth and upbringing, wasn't sure what the options were. A fox? A badger? Or what?

Somehow it sounded like something much larger. She was glad there were no lions or tigers in Ireland. No bears either, since the Middle Ages. Or wolves. Not real ones, anyway.

She moved quietly towards the back gate of the cottage and slipped through it out into the night.

There it was again. A crackling, rustling noise, as if someone who wasn't used to it and hadn't mastered the technique was trying to move through the trees and bushes without making a sound. And failing miserably. The intruder.

But who was he, and what was he doing there? Why had he been watching her through the window?

Maybe it was a poacher? Or a nature lover, someone out watching the creatures of the night about their business? But in that case, Angel thought, they would be making a lot less noise. They'd be used to moving quietly so as not to disturb the animals they were after, whether as victims or as objects of interest.

No, this was something else.

As she came nearer to whoever it was, Angel was careful to place her feet on ground free from broken twigs and to avoid brushing against tree trunks or bushes. She didn't want to alert this character before she had some idea of who he or she was and what they were doing there. She had come to the conclusion that it was one of the paparazzi, returning to follow up the Fitz story. But she could be quite wrong about this.

She slipped behind a thick, sturdy tree and peering round it realised that she was within a few yards of the intruder.

A voice, clearly a man's voice, abruptly cursed aloud as there was a sound of tripping. Angel heard a heavy body crashing through the undergrowth and landing with a thump on the ground. Time for action.

She sprang forward and before the intruder had realised she was even there she was kneeling on his sprawled out body, twisting one arm painfully behind his back.

'Don't try to get up!' she commanded him harshly. 'Just tell me who you are and why you're creeping around out here?'

The man squirmed helplessly beneath Angel's weight and tried in vain to free his arm. Face down as he was in the forest mud he found himself unable to move or to escape.

'Let me go!' he groaned. 'What's it got to do with you?'

'Tell me your name!'

'Okay, okay – I'm Billy Nelson. Local newspaper, the *North Antrim Post*, okay? Let me up! I'm doing no harm!'

'Not so fast,' Angel said coolly. 'Have you any identification?'

'Sure, my driving licence is in my jacket pocket.'

Angel fished for the licence, keeping a hard grip on the man's arm with her other hand. By the struggling moonlight she could just make it out. Billy Nelson. Okay.

'And just what do you think you're doing here, Billy? Haven't you and your mates done enough damage already?'

Angel relaxed her grip on Nelson's arm, with the intention of letting him get to his feet. She began to slip the driving licence back into the pocket of his bomber jacket. But she had released her grip too soon.

Before she had replaced the licence, Billy Nelson had moved. With a wild squirm, the newspaper man staggered to his feet, found his balance, and rushed off into the trees, regardless of the branches whipping his face and the creepers catching at his legs to trip him.

Leaving Angel dumbfounded, the licence still in her hand.

Chapter Thirteen

<u>Monday</u>

Angel, with an annoyed shrug, admitted to herself that she hadn't been functioning at the top of her form. However, she would correct that now.

Springing to her feet, she propelled her agile body through the woods after the fleeing reporter. Dodging the whipping branches, forcing her slender legs powerfully over and around the clinging creepers, she followed the crashing sounds of Nelson's escape.

She had nearly caught up with him. Another moment would do it.

Then directly ahead of her, she heard the crashing sound of something falling hard, the wild yells of Billy Nelson, the thud of his large body hitting the ground. Then a desolate wail which sent shivers up Angel's spine.

'Cindy! Cindy!'

The voice was Billy Nelson's, almost unrecognisable with the pain and grief which flooded through it.

Angel with a final bound reached him.

Billy was kneeling on the ground, his head bowed, his hands helplessly stroking the face of someone who lay before him – someone who had lain in his path of escape and must have been the cause of his blundering fall. Someone called Cindy.

Angel pulled out her torch and shone it on the girl.

She was dead. Angel had no doubt of it from the moment she saw her.

Still, she went through the motions, kneeling down beside Billy, putting the grief stricken man gently aside and feeling for the girl's pulse.

'I'm sorry, Billy,' she said softly. 'I'm afraid she's gone.'

Billy burst into uncontrollable floods of tears. Angel laid a hand on his shoulder and lightly patted it, offering what sympathy she could.

Presently Billy Nelson regained control of himself, and Angel felt she could venture on a few questions.

'You know her, Billy?'

Billy nodded.

'Who is she?'

'Cindy Baron. She's my girlfriend.' Billy hadn't taken in the need for the past tense in referring to Cindy Baron, as yet.

'Did you know she was here?'

Billy nodded again. With an effort he found his voice.

'She asked me to drive her up here. She had an idea for a scoop. Something about Fitz, right? About what happened.'

He choked again as misery overtook him.

'It's okay, Billy. Take your time.'

'Okay?' Billy's voice flared suddenly. 'No, it's not okay! That murdering skunk killed her! How can that be okay? I'll get him, so I will! I'll give him what he deserves and more!' His voice failed him again.

Angel looked at Cindy Baron. She had been stabbed. Blood had spurted from beneath her heart, pooled around her where she lay face up on the mossy undergrowth. Her pretty, foxy face showed white in the sparse moonlight. Angel could feel Billy's pain. He had loved Cindy. Now this.

'We'll get him, Billy. I promise you.'

Something else white was caught for a moment in a flicker of the moonlight. A piece of paper half out of Cindy's pocket. Angel, unnoticed by Billy Nelson, put out one hand and unobtrusively slipped the paper on out of Cindy's pocket and into her own.

She stood up.

At the same moment they both heard it. The engine of a motorbike revving up, back in the lane. They stood, looking at each other for a second, then Billy gasped out, 'That's him!' and began to run. Angel followed him. They crashed through the trees and reached the lane by the cottage in a very few minutes. But the motorbike, if that was what it was, had gone.

Billy swore loudly. 'Missed the slimeball! We'll never find him now!'

Angel put a comforting hand on his arm. 'Yes, we will, Billy. And if we don't, the cops will. Time we brought them in on this. Murder isn't something you can keep to yourself. We need to phone this in. But before that, I want to talk to you. There's a good bar down the road in Cushendall. Are you up to going there and talking? A drink might help you. And when you've told me what you know, we can decide what to do, okay?'

Billy nodded again. 'Okay.'

'On second thoughts,' Angel said, 'maybe we'd better go along the coast a bit, somewhere a bit farther away. We don't want to be noticed here on the spot. I know we need to tell the police about Cindy, but I'd rather do it in a way that doesn't bring either you or me into it, right, Billy?'

Billy Nelson nodded miserably. 'Right.'

'You have a car, Billy?'

'Yeah.'

'Right, you can take that, and I'll drive mine. We don't want to leave either of them around here to be seen. And, Billy, I'm on your side. I want to find the villain who killed Cindy, just as much as you do. So don't drive off and leave me before we've talked, okay? And just in case you were thinking of it, remember I still have your licence. You don't want me showing that to the cops, do you, boy?'

Billy knew he didn't.

'I'm not going anywhere,' he said. 'You lead the way, and I'll follow.'

As soon as she was inside her car, Angel took the opportunity to examine the paper she had found half out of Cindy Baron's pocket. It was a brief note.

'Cindy – running late. But I'll be there. Don't go away. Wait in the woods. I'll call you on the mobile when I get there.'

The signature was simply 'R.M.'

Angel put it carefully back in her pocket to look at again later. She wondered if Billy Nelson would know who R.M. was.

They pulled up at the *Londonderry Arms* in Carnlough, further along the Antrim Coast Road in the Belfast direction. Angel knew it well, knew that it had several small, secluded rooms attached to the main bar.

As usual, the place was hiving. Light and colour and chattering voices filled the air. Angel put in an order at the busy bar and waited. She was glad to see that the member of staff who took her order wasn't someone she knew. She'd hoped the bar manager, Sandy, a good friend of hers, wouldn't be on duty on a week night. If he'd been there, she'd been confident that she could have trusted him to respond helpfully to her request, and say nothing about her presence there. But it was better not to have to ask.

She lifted the drinks and steered Billy Nelson ahead of her round a corner and through a couple of doors.

Then she slid onto a bench opposite Billy in a booth in one of the side rooms, knowing that they were out of sight and hearing of anyone else there. Now they were in a better light, she could see that Billy was a man in his mid thirties, with a thin red face and sandy hair. And at the moment, an expression of blank misery.

'Now, Billy,' she said, setting down a whiskey before the devastated man, and pulling a glass of red wine over towards herself, 'let's begin.'

'Begin how?' Billy Nelson asked hopelessly. 'She's dead. There's nothing we can do.' He buried his head in his hands, ignoring the whiskey glass on the table in front of him.

'Oh, yes, there is!' Angel said briskly. 'For a start, we can find out who killed her. And why. And then we can get him locked away where he can't harm anyone else. And I think you know who it was, Billy – am I right?'

'Oh, yes,' Billy answered. He lifted his face from his hands for a moment. 'Yes, I know.'

Angel drew in a breath of barely concealed satisfaction.

'I thought you did, Billy,' she said.

Chapter Fourteen

Monday

Billy Nelson lifted the whiskey glass and sat looking at it without drinking for a moment. The firelight from the huge turf fire at the near end of the room twinkled off the glass in lively reflections.

'So, now, Billy,' Angel said. She twirled the stem of her half empty wine glass and set it down carefully. She smiled at Billy Nelson encouragingly. 'Tell me about it.'

'What is there to tell?' Billy Nelson said hopelessly. He took a quick slug of whiskey. 'I loved Cindy. I thought she loved me. We've been going together for ages, I thought we were getting married soon as we could sort it out, then this guy came along and she fell for him like a ton of bricks. I don't know why, he had nothing.'

'This guy?'

'Robbie Mallet.'

'The *Who's on Top* guy?' Angel may not have sounded as surprised as she felt. She certainly hoped she didn't.

'That's right. Big name, huh? He made up to Cindy and got hold of her. Okay, I guess she thought he'd help her with her career. Likely! A real pain, and looks like a horse, right?'

'Definitely.'

'So Cindy was, like, flattered, see? So she went out with him a time or two. But it didn't mean anything – she'd have come back to me, I know she would. Then today – he took her for a drink after the helicopter went off.'

'The helicopter that came for Fitz?'

'Yeah.'

They were silent for a moment.

'So?' Angel prompted at last.

'Well, he was boasting to her, she said. It turned her right off. Said he'd ruined Fitz – said he could do that sort of thing dead easy. Cindy thought he sounded like a horror. She hated him.' Billy paused and snuffled.

'So she texted me. Didn't say too much. You don't in a text, right? But she thought she could find out what'd happened to Fitz. Get the story. Wanted to come up here tonight. Asked me to drive her.'

'So you did.'

'She'd set it up to meet with this Mallet. Said she'd ask him stuff, pretend she still thought he was great. Then she thought she'd get a lot out of him, get her scoop, get him arrested, okay? But she wanted me there for back-up. Didn't feel all that safe with him on her own.'

'I can see that,' Angel said. She was wondering how Cindy Baron, suspecting what she did, could have been so stupid. So 'R.M.' was almost certainly Robbie Mallet, then.

'If he'd used a gun I'd have heard him. I didn't think of a knife,' Nelson said desperately.

'But if he'd used a gun you'd still have been too late,' Angel reminded him.

'You're right.'

Billy took another pull at his whiskey. Bushmills. Angel had made sure when she ordered it. It reminded Angel of the bottle Fitz had had at the cottage. A bell rang in her head. But she couldn't think why or what it meant.

'I should never have let her meet him alone. They met at the pub in Cushendall, then they went for a walk up into the wood and I followed them. I thought she was safe enough – I didn't reckon she knew all that much. So why should he be worried about her? Tell you the truth, I thought her biggest risk was if he came on too heavy, and if he'd tried anything like that all she had to do was scream and I'd have been on him like a shot. But she must have worked out more than she told me. And she must have let him see she knew more than he reckoned was safe.'

'I think so, Billy,' Angel said gently. 'So now we need to work out what Cindy knew.'

'Yeah.'

'So what exactly did she tell you? What had Mallet said to her? More detail, if you have it.'

'I don't know.' Billy's head drooped despairingly. 'I'd have to think. Give me a chance, why don't you?'

'Okay.'

'And who are you, anyway?' Billy suddenly blazed up. 'What's it got to do with you? You aren't a cop, are you? Show me your warrant card if you are?'

'No, Billy, I'm not a cop,' Angel smiled. 'My name's Angeline Murphy. Angel to my friends – devil to my enemies. I'm a friend of a friend of Fitz. We're trying to find out what happened to him.'

'Angel Murphy. I've heard of you.'

'Well, that's always nice to know,' Angel said.

'Something on TV, aren't you?'

'Yeah, sort of.'

'Okay.' Billy struggled to his feet. 'I'll believe you. You and me are on the same side. So I'll try to remember what all Cindy said. And I'll let you know. Give me your number.'

They exchanged numbers.

'Now I must ring in the cops,' Angel said briskly. 'You drive on, Billy, and get offside. Don't want anyone to link you up with this.'

'I never thought of that.'

'Get yourself an alibi – call a couple of friends and go somewhere public with them, somewhere where they know you, if possible,' Angel advised him. 'And try to keep your feelings under cover. It won't help Cindy if you get suspected.'

'Right. I'll get some mates to meet me at our local.'

'Good. And stay there as long as you can.'

They left the *Londonderry Arms*, and Angel watched Nelson drive off in the direction of Ballymena in his battered Polo.

Then she considered her own position thoughtfully.

She didn't think it would help Cindy for anyone to know she and Nelson had been the first to find her. On the other hand, if the police were going to find any useful clues to the murderer, the sooner they were on the job the better. An anonymous call from a public phone some distance away would be the best thing.

She drove on down the coast road towards Larne, found a public call box which wasn't currently vandalised, and rang the Cushendall police station, whose number she had got from Seri earlier in case she wanted to talk to them.

She pitched her voice much higher than its normal soft mellow tone to make it unrecognisable and squeaked, 'There's a body in the woods near Cushendall!' Then she put the phone down quickly.

Even modern technology would find it hard to trace such a brief call.

Chapter Fifteen

Monday

It was as she left the phone box that Angel's own mobile rang. She opened it and saw that the call was from Josh Smith. He must be back from the States.

She spoke as she hurried back to her car.

'Josh? Great to hear from you. Give me a minute.'

Settled comfortably in the driving seat, she put the phone on Hands Free and took off for a parking space a bit further from the phone box she'd just used – just in case.

'Josh? How're you doing, babe?'

'All the better for hearing your voice, Angel.'

Angel pulled into a car park at a suitable distance.

'Are you back over here, Josh?'

'Sort of. I'm in London.'

'And are you planning to make it to Belfast?'

'Well, that's the thing.' Josh's warm voice sounded unhappy. 'If I do, it won't be for a while. The current job is going to be very full-time for a week or two at least, I'd guess.'

'Oh.' Angel didn't try to keep the disappointment out of her voice. Josh Smith, whom she'd met last year while on holiday in Crete, worked for Interpol. Shortly after their first meeting, Josh had been whisked back to his headquarters in Washington, and since then their only contact had been by phone and Internet.

'Any chance you can get over to London?'

'I don't know, Josh. I'm tied down here by contract.'

'Couldn't you arrange to meet some actor or writer or something over here, who's planning to come to Belfast shortly, and record an interview for future use? Wouldn't the boss men think that was great forward planning?'

'Well. I suppose I could arrange to borrow a cameraman and other facilities from BBC London, why not? I'd have to find the right subject and get them to agree. It wouldn't be tomorrow.'

'Even in a few days – better than waiting until I'm free to get to Belfast.'

'Yeah. I'll see what I can set up. Leave it with me.'

Angel smiled happily. The idea of meeting up with Josh Smith so soon was a very pleasant one. 'But, hey, Josh, talk to me, baby. What's been happening in your life?'

It was a long time later that Josh and Angel reluctantly finished their call. Angel came back out of a day dream to notice that she was sitting in a rather cold car which had lost its heat over the last hour, in a car park still rather too near the phone which she'd used to report Cindy Baron's death. She'd advised Billy Nelson to get offside. Time she did the same herself.

An hour later she drew up in her personal parking slot at her Lagan bank apartment. It was getting late. She went in, switched on the percolator, and headed for the shower. Ten minutes after that, clean and warm and wrapped in a huge bath sheet, she poured herself a hot mug of decaf, and snuggled down in one of the huge armchairs in her living room to complete the warming up process.

There were people she needed to phone. Seri, for one. Mary for another. But probably most important of all, Billy Nelson. Had he sorted out his alibi? Was he back home yet? And had he thought of any more details about Cindy Baron's conversation with Robbie Mallet?

She punched in Nelson's number.

The phone rang. At last someone answered.

'Hi.'

The voice was so weak that Angel could hardly hear it. She frowned at the phone. Was it a bad connection? Should she cut off and try again? She could hardly recognise the voice – but something told her it was Billy Nelson's.

'Billy?' she asked urgently.

'Angel? Is that you, Angel?' The voice sounded momentarily stronger.

'Billy? Is something wrong?'

'He came here, Angel. He told me ... told me ...' Then came a groaning sound.

Silence.

'Billy!' Angel said sharply. 'Billy, are you okay?'

She heard a thud, as if something or someone had fallen. The phone cut off, and there was nothing more to hear.

Chapter Sixteen

Monday night/Tuesday

The first thing to do was to ring the police and ambulance services and get Billy some help as soon as possible. There was no way she could get to him in under an hour – probably more. So she needed these people to take up the slack.

And as soon as that was sorted, she needed to get moving.

For the second time that evening, Angel rang the police. But this time there was no need for disguise. She had nothing to conceal.

'Ballymena Police Station?' she said into her mobile. 'This is Angeline Murphy. Urgent call. I want to report a probable burglary, and what sounded like an attack. I've just come off the phone with my friend Billy Nelson, and it sounded as if he'd collapsed in the middle of the conversation – as if someone had hit him. He'd just said, 'He came here ...' I don't know what he meant.' She gave the address, crisply and accurately, and answered a few, as it seemed, unnecessary questions.

'I'm just heading up there myself to see what I can do,' she finished. 'I expect you, and I hope a doctor and/or ambulance, will be there long before me. See you shortly!'

Angel pressed the off switch, threw on some clothes, grabbed her hand-bag and keys, and left.

Billy Nelson's address was a flat on the outskirts of Ballymena. The cheaper area. Billy, on his journalist's salary, couldn't afford anything better.

Angel drove at her usual fast, but legal, pace. No point in being pulled over for speeding. In three quarters of an hour she was pulling up in front of the block of flats in the housing estate where Nelson had told her he lived.

One of the inmates of the block opened the front door promptly and foolishly when she buzzed.

Billy's flat was four floors up. She was too late, she knew. There wouldn't be anyone still there, hanging about. Get in quick and get out quick, taking anything telltale – that would have been the plan. And while there, hit any troublemakers, like Billy Nelson, hard enough to deal with him. She seriously doubted if the police, doctor, or ambulance would have got there much sooner than herself. Almost certainly not in time to catch whoever had broken in.

It seemed that Billy had come round for long enough to answer his mobile. Then collapsed again. When he talked to her he hadn't sounded as if he was okay and unharmed. The collapse hadn't been the result of a first blow. Billy had sounded groggy, like a man who'd already been attacked. Angel didn't have much doubt about that. Billy had been hit and had recovered briefly, just enough to answer his phone and talk to her. But what then?

Angel wasn't sure what she'd find. Would Billy have survived? Or not?

'Hello?' she called, as she climbed the bare concrete stairs. The scruffy, dirty looking lift had proved to be out of order, as she found out when she'd pressed the buttons a few times with no response. So what was new, in cheap flats like these?

There was no answer.

Surely the police or someone should have arrived by now?

But Angel knew from things she'd been told that often the police response was a lot slower than it might be. She kicked herself for not simply phoning 999. It had seemed obvious that the nearest police station, a few minutes away, would be the best bet.

The door of Billy Nelson's flat was closed. Angel rang the bell for some minutes without getting an answer.

She wasn't going to stand there ringing all night.

Hoking in her handbag, she brought out a couple of picklocks which a friend had shown her how to use recently, when she'd shared some of her recent experiences in Crete with him. He'd pointed her to the right place on the Internet to buy a set, and when they arrived, he'd spent some time training her in their use.

'If you're ever in that sort of situation again, girl, these'll help you,' Big Hughie had told her. He'd winked in an appealing manner. 'But don't be letting on I showed you how to use them, now, if anyone catches you with them! Okay?'

She'd met Hughie when she'd been researching a BBC programme about the number of break-ins there had been recently, before her promotion to *Belfast Shout Out!*, and had found him a lovable sort of guy, in spite of his record.

Big in every sense of the word, with a round freckled face, a shaved head, and a lot of muscles, Hughie never robbed the poor – he'd gone exclusively for the better off. And he'd specialised in the sort of objects anyone could do without – DVD players were his favourite. Angel had enjoyed meeting him and interviewing him, with his back to the camera and a lot of blur, of course.

Chapter 16

She'd tried out the picklocks on her own door several times, and was confident of making them work. And sure enough, a few moments later she had the front door of Billy's flat open.

The light was on in the hall and in what was probably the living room.

'Billy! Are you there?' she called as she moved forward cautiously.

She was answered only by a groan.

Chapter Seventeen

Monday night/Tuesday morning

Angel moved forward swiftly. Light shone out from the flat's living room as she pushed its door further open.

The tiny hallway of the flat was carpeted in a neutral colour and had walls painted to match. Either Billy or the landlord had some style, Angel thought.

There were four doors leading off the hall. Probably living room and kitchen on the right hand side as you came in. Bedroom and bathroom on the left. With possibly other connecting doors between each set of rooms.

Angel knew she needed to be careful. The groan she had heard might or might not have been from Billy Nelson. For surely he should have been taken away in the ambulance long since, if he was still alive? If it wasn't Billy, it might be an attempt to lure her in, and to deal with her in turn.

No sense in blundering in, straight into the light, and being grabbed by Billy's attacker.

She slipped quietly through the door. Her hand felt at once for the light switch, and turned it off immediately. She had taken just enough time to get a mental snapshot of the room. Medium sized, cosy, central heating, and soft chairs facing towards a huge TV on a wall bracket. A coffee table placed for ease of use between the two armchairs. And no one else there. At least no one living.

But someone on the floor.

In the sudden pitch black darkness, Angel heard another groan, and moved towards it in silence.

She had a thin torch in her hand which would throw out a minute sliver of light. Time to switch it on, Angel thought.

The minuscule beam of light shone across the floor and lit up the figure lying sprawled face down in the centre of the room, one arm outstretched towards the coffee table.

A dark stream of something was flowing from his head, forming a small pool on the cream coloured carpet. Angel had little doubt that it was blood.

But it was still flowing, and that was good news. Whoever it was, he was still alive.

Angel moved silently across the room, her torch now switched off, until her foot touched something solid and warm.

She turned on her torch again and lit up his thin red face. Billy. As she had expected.

Kneeling down beside him, Angel felt his neck with her fingers for a pulse.

Yes, there was a regular beat, strong enough to remove all doubt of his survival. Angel was more relieved than she had realised she would be. Okay, he'd seemed a nice guy. And two corpses discovered in one night might be too much for anyone.

'Billy. It's me, Angel. Can you speak?'

A groan was the only answer.

'Have the police been here? Or a doctor?'

Silly question, she knew as she asked it. For why would they have left Billy lying on the floor like this?

Clearly the call she had made to the police hadn't been taken seriously enough. Either they'd believed it was a hoax, or they were coming, but not with any sort of urgent speed. Angel felt anger well up inside her.

She held out her torch closer to his face and body and examined Billy Nelson thoroughly by its tiny light. She could see enough to be sure that nothing too serious had happened to him.

His head was bleeding from a blow above his left ear. Feeling the area with one hand, Angel was sure the skull hadn't been damaged. No bones were broken. He'd have a sizeable bruise, probably a black eye as well, for a week or so. Apart from that he'd be fine. She'd take him to the A&E in a few minutes, so that a doctor could confirm this view.

There was only one question left to answer.

Was anyone still here?

It seemed unlikely. But Angel wasn't taking any risks. She stood up, switching off the minute beam of her torch as she did so. The brightness thrown by it had been small enough as it was. The amount of light which it cast had done no more than shed an infinitesimal glow on its surroundings. When it was gone, the darkness seemed absolute.

Moving on soundless feet Angel crossed the room. She'd seen a door on the far side – kitchen, bedroom, bathroom? One of these, no doubt.

The door was closed. Taking out a scarf from her bag, Angel wrapped it round her hand and took hold of the door handle. With all the essential vigilance needed, she pressed down on it and pushed carefully. The door moved.

Chapter 17

Angel put her eye to the crack and looked into the obscurity. If her nerves had not been of ice, she would have jumped, even screamed.

For looking back at her was another eye, gleaming brightly, only a few inches away.

Chapter Eighteen

Monday night/Tuesday

It was no time to hesitate. Angel gathered herself together and shoved the door hard open with her full strength.

Someone screamed and went crashing back. With a leap Angel was through the door and on top of him. She pinned the wriggling body to the floor with her legs, grabbed the wrists, and had control.

Something was wrong. This was no bulky man or even woman. Small, skinny, not very strong. And the voice. High pitched shrieks, someone saying, 'Hey! Leave off, you're killing me!' in a voice several tones higher than she'd expected.

Her opponent was a child.

Angel changed her grip on the wrists to make it one handed, releasing her right hand to find and switch on her torch. She shone it on the apprehensive face of her captive.

Huge, shining eyes. A trembling mouth, trying hard to be brave. Fair hair flopping over a very sweet face. A face which certainly belonged to someone very young. Twelve, Angel thought, at a guess. A boy, probably, going by the body.

She stood up carefully, dragging him to his feet as she did so.

'Okay. Who are you, and why were you spying on me?'

'I wasn't spying!' The voice quivered with anger. 'I was looking to see who you were, and what you were doing to my dad!'

'Dad?' Angel couldn't for the life of her prevent the amazement from showing in her response. 'Are you telling me that Billy's your dad?'

But, yes, it was possible. Billy would have had to be a very young father – but why not?

'Yeah. He and my Mum split up. Years ago, when I was just a kid.' (What did he think he was now? Angel wondered.) 'I come and stay with him every other weekend. And sometimes for a week, during school holidays, like now. When I'm not with my mum.'

'I see. And you were here tonight? When the break in happened?'

'Break in?'

'When these guys – or guy – attacked Billy – your dad?'

'I don't think there was any break in. Dad had to go out. Urgent news-paper business, he said. It happens.' The boy shrugged.

'He knows when stuff like that comes up I'll be okay. I'm not a baby any more. So after a bit I went to bed with my iPad. Then before I knew it I was asleep. I get the bedroom when I'm here. It's on the other side of the hall, okay? Dad sleeps on the sofa – it's a pull out bed when you want it to be – really cool!

'So I didn't hear much to start with. I sort of heard him coming back home. In my dreams, like. He looked in and took the iPad off me and set it over. Then he said, 'Night night, Will,' and I just about managed to say, 'Night night, Dad,' back. I must have clocked right out.

'First thing I heard was just the doorbell ringing, and Dad going to answer it. Then Dad's voice – I couldn't hear what he was actually saying, or at least I couldn't make much sense out of it – and the guy who'd rung the bell, and Dad, in the hall together.

'I was just snuggling down to sleep again when I heard a noise. Some-thing that worried me. I sat up in bed. I didn't know what was happening, but it didn't sound good. A sort of crash, like? So I got myself up – not straight away, see? – I think I went back to sleep for a while, I don't know how long, but maybe quite awhile, or maybe only a few minutes.

I was dreaming, and in my dreams I was sort of worried, see? Dreams about someone killing Dad, or something. And so I kept on worrying about what was happening. So I woke up enough to think about it. And I sort of staggered out into the hall, still more or less half asleep, right? I didn't know if anything bad was happening – but I couldn't help worrying that maybe it was. So then I thought it might be better if I went into the kitchen and looked in from there.'

'You did good, pet,' Angel said encouragingly. 'By the way, what's your name?'

'Will. I'm called William after my dad, but Billy is very uncool, isn't it? I'm Will.'

'Good. Hi, Will.'

'Hi.'

'I'm Angel.'

'Hi, Angel.'

They smiled at each other, suddenly friends.

'So, Will?'

66

Okay.' Will took a deep breath. 'So, I looked in from the kitchen and I saw this huge, dark figure. It was hard to see him properly. He had some sort of mask over his face. His girlfriend's tights, I guess.' Will grinned weakly. Angel was glad to see him able to make a joke, however feeble.

'Yeah.'

'So, I didn't realise just what was going on, until he started in and hit Dad over the head. You'll think I was a real wimp.'

Will gulped, and Angel hastened to relieve his anxieties.

'No way, Will. He must have been very scary – and twice your size.'

Will pulled himself together. 'I think the crash I heard must have been when he pushed his way in. Dad musta been going to shut the door in his face. Well, hey, you wouldn't let a man in a mask into your house, right? And he musta knocked Dad across the hall into the front room, into the coffee table, and sent it flying. Anyway, I could see it lying on its back on the floor, and Dad staggering round. Like, he was a really big guy, or Dad could have handled him, you bet.

'So I pulled the kitchen door open. And went to come out. And I said, 'Hey!' but that's all I remember. I have a sort of mental picture of the guy in the mask going for me, but maybe I'm imagining it. Anyway, next thing I knew I was lying on the floor here.

'And when I managed to get up, and looked through the door, there was someone with Dad, I didn't know what they were doing. Okay, I know now it was you, just looking to see what was wrong. But I didn't know that then. And before I could make up my mind to butt in, you pushed the door open and knocked me over – and that's it!'

Angel could sense the guilt in the boy's heart. He believed he had let his father down, it was clear. But what could a child of his age have done against an adult who didn't hesitate to attack both his father and himself?

'Will, you've done your best, and I think you've done good,' Angel said gently. 'Now, stop worrying about it. The main thing now is to get your dad to a doctor. Do you want to come – or would you rather go back to bed? That's probably what you should do.'

'No. I'm coming.'

Will's mouth was grim.

'Okay, darlin'. So I'm going to ring for an ambulance to take us to the local A&E, right? Better than trying to find it myself – they'll know where it is. And your Dad needs proper medical attention. I don't want to drag him out to the car. He'd be better in a wheelchair or a stretcher until he recovers properly.'

'Okay, Angel. And thanks.' Will's lip quivered.

'He'll be okay, Will. I know a bit about this stuff,' Angel said. 'There's nothing seriously wrong.'

'Yeah.' Will did his best to smile.

Angel took out her mobile. 'Do you have a telephone directory somewhere?'

She reckoned a job of work to do would help Will to calm down a bit.

'Sure. In Dad's desk.'

Angel watched the boy as he searched the desk where his dad had his computer. He was a very pretty child. No doubt he'd be annoyed at the adjective. What boy wanted to be described as pretty? But it was certainly the best description of him. Billy was so far from being 'pretty' himself that Angel guessed Will's mum must be a very good looking lady.

'Got it, Angel,' the boy announced triumphantly.

'Okay, read it out to me.'

Angel punched the number into her mobile.

Chapter Nineteen

Monday night/Tuesday

The wait in the A&E was so long that Will, in spite of his worries, fell asleep after the first hour. Angel found herself looking down at his sleeping head, pillowed against her arm, with some sort of protective concern. The child should be in bed. It was the small hours of the morning. Getting to be the bigger hours, in fact.

Billy still lay, unconscious, on the trolley where he had been put when the ambulance men slid him carefully from the stretcher.

The A&E was bleak and dismal. It seemed as if their turn for the doctor would never come.

A girl approached them. She had a clipboard in one hand and a stethoscope round her neck. Her fair hair was caught back in a ponytail.

'I'm Dr. Kennedy,' she announced briskly. 'You're with this patient?'

'Yes.'

'Wife? Girlfriend?'

'No. I'm just a friend. I called in and found him like this. But this is his son, Will.'

They had already given all the details to the reception clerk, but Angel realised that repetition was the name of the game. She tried for Will's sake not too let it annoy her too much.

'Billy will have to stay here overnight,' Dr. Kennedy said. 'We can find him a bed shortly. Leave your contact details and we'll ring you when he can go home – probably tomorrow.'

'But – ' Angel began, then cut herself off. She'd taken this on, she would clearly need to follow it through. 'Okay,' she said. She would ask Will tomorrow if Billy had other family. He wasn't that old. He probably had parents or brothers and sisters who should be informed. To say nothing of Will's mother, Billy's ex-wife.

She took Will back to the flat, saw him to bed, and arranged herself on the 'cool' pull out sofa bed in the front room. No way was she going to leave Will alone tonight. Tomorrow she'd get him back to his mother. But there might be a few answers to questions he could give her before he left.

She wondered how the rest of the team were getting on. There just hadn't been a spare moment for her to contact them all evening. It was a bit late now.

Mar floated round the small dance space in Club 13 in the arms of Nathaniel Deane. It was one of the last tunes, a slow, romantic one.

> '*Heaven, I'm in Heaven,*
> *And the cares that hang around me through the week,*
> *Seem to vanish like a gambler's lucky streak,*
> *When we're out together dancing cheek to cheek.*'

Retro, but none the worse for that. Mar was feeling in need of romance.

Nat Deane was certainly the most attractive man she'd seen for a long time.

She realised clearly that Nat was fascinated by Angel Murphy. If there was one thing Mar was good at, apart from drumming, it was picking up on people's emotions, on their feeling for other people, especially those of the opposite sex. Nat was mad about Angel, right. No question.

But it hadn't been so very hard for Mar to get together with him.

They'd congregated at Jonty Carson's flat, drunk beer, chatted, talked about their plans. About who they would talk to, how they would follow it up, what they hoped to find out. Then one by one they'd drifted off.

Mar had no car, but Nat had one he'd hired for the duration of his Belfast visit. She'd asked him for a lift – as simple as that. Then, as they drove, she'd said, 'Do you know what, Nat? I don't think I could sleep if I just go straight home now.'

'So? Is there something you'd like to do instead?'

She was pretty sure he hadn't meant anything by what he'd said. It was just a straight question.

'I don't know. Would you like to go somewhere and dance for a while? Not if you don't want to.'

'Sounds good to me, Mar. I don't much feel like sleeping, myself.' Nat smiled at her in an unhappy way. He seemed in need of support. Of help. Mar realised for the first time how upset he was about Fitz. It seemed to bring them closer together.

'I can't just forget about Fitz and go to bed,' she said honestly. Other motives were temporarily forgotten. 'Fitz is one of my closest friends. I love him to bits – just as a friend, mind you.'

'Me, too,' Nat said. Mar thought, looking round at him discreetly, that she could hear a break in his voice. She watched his hand as it clutched the steering wheel. She thought, irrelevantly, how strong that hand looked, with the watch fastened round its muscular wrist.

Fitz had so many friends. And they all cared about him. How many friends had she, Mar wondered?

'There's a nice place not long opened. Here in Belfast. *Club 13*,' Mar said. 'Maybe we could go there for a bit. Not so much drown, as dance away, our sorrows. What do you think?'

'Lead me to it.'

Mar reached over and took Nat's hand. She couldn't help smiling involuntarily as he squeezed it in return.

Half an hour later, as they circled the dance floor to the slow retro music of '*Let's face the Music and Dance*', followed by '*Cheek to Cheek*', she thought that this might not be getting them any further towards finding who or what had happened to Fitz, but it was certainly helping her to deal with it all. A thought struck her.

'Nat,' she said into his ear, 'do you think we could both go and check out my friend Lucas Somerset from the *Daily Word* tomorrow? I think we could tackle him better together. And then we could follow up anyone he thinks worth talking to?'

'Yeah, why not, Mar? My own contacts are probably pretty useless. Art critics and such – they wouldn't know about the sort of people who were hounding Fitz. But your guy Lucas Somerset might know a lot. Okay, let's do it. I'll pick you up tomorrow morning.'

But the night wasn't over yet, Mar thought. Maybe Nat wouldn't need to pick her up. Maybe if he left her home soon, he'd still be there tomorrow? Angel or not?

Chapter Twenty

Monday night/Tuesday

Jonty Carson wandered aimlessly round his very upmarket apartment in the city centre, near, of course, the river Lagan. That was where all the upmarket apartments were. He picked up a small, expensive artefact by a local sculptor. A dolmen. Three stones, two upright and one set across the top, made of granite. What they called a Portal Grave. A relic of Ireland's stone age. There were still some about. Up at the Giant's Ring, just outside Belfast, for instance. Jonty set it down again and wandered on.

He stood in front of the Monet which he'd finally afforded last year, and as always looked at it in amazement. He'd always wanted one. Ever since he'd visited the National Gallery in London as a teenager and had fallen in love with the Monets there, in the Impressionist room.

Water lilies floating in a lake, ablaze with light and colour and beauty. Monet had been obsessed with them. He'd painted them, in varying perspectives, hundreds of times.

Jonty loved his painting. He always tested new girl friends by their reaction to it. Did they even notice it? Did they ignore it? Or did they say something silly?

Many a girl had been rejected by Jonty because of their reaction to the Monet.

Jonty wanted a companion. But in spite of the many opportunities on offer, so far no one had been the woman he wanted to share his life with.

He had been close to Fitz. As a friend. He'd been grateful to Fitz for inviting him to be part of the band. To be lead guitar. It had changed his life around. Given him the chance to do the thing he'd been sure he was meant to do. Jonty laughed as he remembered the first band he'd been part of. A gospel rock group. It had done well. But soaring ambition had forced him on. He wanted to make a million – to be famous.

Okay, he wasn't quite there yet. The band was one of the frontrunners in the *New Music Awards*. If they won that, they'd be established right at the top. If Fitz was okay –

Jonty shuddered. He didn't just want Fitz to survive so that *Raving* could keep climbing high and he could be rich and famous. That wasn't what it was about. He wanted Fitz to go on living because he loved Fitz. He didn't want Fitz to die.

He didn't want to be alone tonight. To think about Fitz.

He had invited the guys back, partly out of an instinctive hospitality, but more out of a need for company tonight.

And it had been great while they stayed.

But one by one they'd left, muttering excuses. He supposed they mostly wanted a bit of time to themselves.

Apart from Mar, that was.

Jonty had no illusions about Mar.

She was great, he loved her. But, hey, she needed a man – or men– in her life.

For a short while, when she first joined the band, he had been that man. No regrets. It had been a whirl. She had so much to offer.

But before long he'd noticed, with no difficulty, that there was a new man in the offing. Then another.

Mar needed to feel loved, needed to be admired.

One man's admiration was never enough for her. Like a chocolate or a strawberry, right? One was never enough.

Probably some problem stemming over from her childhood or youth. Some scars. He'd never tried to find out. He'd simply dumped her when the third new man had been well established. No regrets on either side.

'I think we've gone the distance, Mar, okay?' Jonty'd said. 'It's been great, but we're both ready to move on, am I right?'

And Mar had smiled sweetly, and murmured, 'Jonty, you know I love you. But Clem is my special one – at least, I think so right now. But we'll still be friends, won't we? For the sake of the band?'

And they had been.

Well, time he did something about this business of looking into what had happened to Fitz. Jonty had promised to contact Jeff Wilson, from *Serious Music*. He'd been booked to meet up with Jeff earlier on that evening, for an interview, but he'd cancelled. He just hadn't felt up to it. And it had been far more important to get together with the rest and think out what they could do for Fitz.

He lifted his mobile and got Jeff's home number. He would set something up as soon as possible. Maybe even tonight – it wasn't so late yet.

But the number wasn't answering. Presently a message came.

'Hi, you're through to Jeff Wilson. I'm not available to take your call right now, but please leave a message after the tone, and your number, and I'll get back to you.'

Jonty shrugged. Like many people, he didn't like leaving messages. People either didn't check them, or ignored them. Instead he texted Jeff rapidly.

'Hi, Jeff, ring me. Jonty Carson. Let's get together. If you're free – now, even.'

Then there was nothing to do but wait until Jeff replied.

Jonty began to wander round the empty room again. There was nothing that would fill up his time well enough. Music, normally the first, automatic choice, wouldn't work for him tonight. There were too many memories of Fitz tied up with it.

Everyone had headed off much sooner than he'd expected or hoped. He'd have liked the company for a bit longer. But they'd drifted off. Okay.

He was conscious of a feeling that he'd have been pleased if Mary Branagh had stayed.

There was something about her. He'd never met her before tonight. But he'd been struck straightaway. What was it that made her seem special?

Pretty, yes. Fair hair, blue eyes. Traditional fairy princess looks, okay?

But a lot more.

Mary had something. Strength, individuality. She made her own decisions, he thought. She knew she wanted to live her life. She wasn't going to let the world push her around – was that it?

He remembered hearing that she'd been seriously into drugs as a youngster. Had nearly died from an overdose.

It didn't seem likely, looking at her now. At the calm, beautiful peace which flowed through her.

But, hey, she was into all that religious stuff, wasn't she? Not for him!

Her remembered his teens, when he'd been really enthusiastic about God. He'd gone out every Saturday with his friends from the church youth group, giving out tracts, outside the City Hall. It was funny to think of it now. All that was far behind him.

But he was conscious of a lingering regret that Mary Branagh hadn't stayed.

Chapter Twenty-one

Monday night/Tuesday

Mary went home to the *Community of the Cross*, the big, dilapidated old house on the Antrim Road with the spreading gardens and the solid, green-painted front door, where she lived as a member of the mixed Catholic and Protestant community.

As she expected, she found that most of the other community members had gone on to bed. They all had demanding jobs and would, moreover, be getting up early to join in daily prayers before taking their turn to make breakfast. Mary herself was a teacher, and needed to be well rested and bright and alert to deal with her classes every day. But before she went to bed, there was some-thing she intended to do.

This was a good time to use the communal computer, when no one else was around. Mary sat down at the keyboard. This was no laptop, but a friend's rather out-of-date PC, handed on to the community when the friend got a new laptop. No one there minded. It worked, Internet connection included. That was what mattered.

Mary signed in – each of the members had their own private account – and connected to the Internet.

A few minutes later, she was talking to her brother on Skype.

Mary's brother John Branagh, up and coming star of BBC Ulster's Newsroom, was, as she had told the others, over in London just now. He was working alongside a well known BBC News anchorman, doing on job training for a similar post on the local news programme when he came back. But although he was offside just at the moment, Mary had boundless confidence in John's knowledge of the Northern Ireland media scene. And especially of its grapevine. It was, after all, part of his job to know these things.

'Hi, John.'

'Hi, kid.'

'How're you doin'?'

'Great!'

'And Sheila?'

Mary listened for some minutes while John talked enthusiastically about his wife, beautiful fashion model Sheila Doherty, and then about his current job. Finally she managed to switch the conversation to her own topics. Not that she wasn't interested in John and Sheila's lives. Of course she was. But it wasn't for that that she'd sat up late to ring him.

'So, kid, what's been happening in your own life?' John asked at last, and Mary jumped in without hesitation.

'John, some awful stuff! Have you heard about Fitz?'

John had, of course. 'But I didn't think you knew him, Mary, love?'

Mary explained. She went into great detail. When she'd been talking for five minutes or so, John knew everything she knew herself.

'So, bro', what do you think? What's the fruit on the grapevine? Who would have been behind this media frenzy?'

There was a pause. Mary waited, watching John's handsome face showing up on the camera, white skinned and dark haired, one straight lock falling over his forehead, while he thought about it. She remembered the days, long gone, when he had wanted above all else to train for the priesthood. He'd dropped that in the end, realising that although he still believed, he wasn't cut out for celibacy. Mary wondered if he ever regretted it. But, no. For God had given him Sheila, and Mary knew how happy John and Sheila were together.

'Okay, Mary. I don't know for sure. But a mate of mine, Dougie Mitchell, from the *Sunday Wire*, emailed me a couple of days ago to say there was some stuff being stirred up about Fitz. A heap of the guys were talking about going up to Cushendall, to the cottage he was staying at. The story was, something would be happening there. Some suggestion that Fitz was back on drugs again. Anything might happen.'

'And do you know who was doing the stirring, John? Or who was mainly doing it?' Mary spoke breathlessly. It looked as if she was about to get some real information.

'I don't know for sure, Mary,' John replied slowly. 'But I heard more about it after that, from more than one source. The idea seems to be that it was that guy Robbie Mallet. The panellist from *Who's on Top.*'

'Wow!'

'But, Mary.' John suddenly looked serious. 'Don't get yourself in trouble, kid. Think about it. Maybe the rumour was true. Maybe Fitz was back on drugs like they were saying. Maybe this idea that there was somebody working behind the scenes is rubbish? Don't get involved in something that can only hurt you, kid.'

'No way, Bro.' Mary spoke confidently. 'I know Fitz. He's been coming here for more than two months now. I don't believe he was back on drugs. If he'd been tempted to do that, I know he'd have asked for help. Fitz is too strong a guy to go down the drain like that without trying, see?'

'Okay, Mary. I'll take your word for it. All the best with the detective work, kid. But look out for this Robbie Mallet guy.' John spoke seriously. 'He's a bad lot – I'm warning you!'

Chapter Twenty-Two

Monday night/Tuesday

Pete and Ziggy Carmichael, *Raving*'s Diabolical Twins, whose joint keyboard playing added so much to the individual sound of the band, had gone straight to the Red Horse Bar without even needing to discuss it.

It wasn't that either of them felt much like drinking.

But that was where they could be pretty sure of finding their mate Si, six out of seven nights a week, on a good average.

They pushed in through the swing doors and the sound of loud music and many voices hit them in the face. The bar was warm, crowded, noisy and full of life. A typical Belfast bar on a busy night.

This was what Si – Simon Fletcher – loved about it.

Simon was a successful journalist and contributor to Northern Ireland's most popular newspaper, the *Belfast Telegraph*, as well as to half a dozen others. Northern Ireland representative for *The New Paper*, one of the English biggies right now. A popular panel member on local TV political shows. And a well-established radio presenter.

Pete and Ziggy had known him since their schooldays. They had jammed with him in his Dad's garage at a time when Si thought he was going to be the greatest rock drummer of these times – until the complaints of the neighbours grew too steady and persevering to be ignored any longer.

They had gone for long walks and shared their views of life with each other. Later, they had played squash together until Si decided it didn't fit into his image as a hard drinking reporter. And they had remained regular drinking buddies ever since.

The twins didn't have far to look to find Simon. A tall, lanky figure, pale in the face and with an almost colourless lock of hair hanging over one eye, and thick rimmed glasses, was propping up the far corner of the bar, chatting with half a dozen different people at once, including a very pretty dark-haired girl, and the barman, Joey.

'Si! How'ya doing, mate!'

Pete surged forward, cutting Simon off from his surrounding audience and throwing one arm round the thin shoulders.

'C'm'ere till we get talkin'!'

Si, smiling, allowed himself to be drawn away from the bar to the only quiet corner of the room.

'Guys, great t'see yous! So, how's things?'

Then he saw Pete's face fall. Ziggy had been out of sight behind his more boisterous brother. Now Simon saw Ziggy's face too, and he caught himself up.

'Hey – I know, guys. It's Fitz, right? I guess yous are both pretty upset.'

'Right.'

'Look, Si.' For once it was Ziggy who took the lead. 'We need you to help us. Can we go somewhere a bit quieter where we can hear ourselves think?'

'No problem, mates.' Si set down his half full glass – an unheard of action – and followed his friends out of the Red Horse.

Pete drove the red Corsa to the outskirts of town and parked near Shaw's Bridge, in sight of the upper Lagan. The night was quiet. Tall weeds and grasses waved along the banks, just within sight. Trees drooped their leafy branches towards the water. When Ziggy opened the windows the Lagan smell, sweet and individual, drifted in.

There was a full moon. Against the dark navy blue sky, it shone, bright and full of romance, beckoning. The faint blur of the lights of Belfast gleamed in the background like sunset or sunrise. The stars lit up the dark sky with their clean, clear magic. Pete recognised the Plough and the North Star, the Pole Star. That was about his limit. Some day he would look into it in more depth, he thought idly, learn the other constell-ations, be able to identify them.

Meanwhile.

'Sorry if we're spoiling your evening, Si.'

'No problem, Pete. I know Fitz matters to you both.'

'Yeah.'

'So – what did yous want from me?'

Again it was Ziggy who took the lead.

'Si, Pete and me – and none of the band – we don't believe Fitz was still on drugs. So how could he have OD'd?'

'Okay.'

'So what we think is, either the paparazzi – well, sorry, I know you don't like that name, it's like talking to a cop about pigs, right? –'

'Right.'

'Well, let's just say some elements of the media – maybe they drove him to extremes and he ended up taking too much. But where did he get it from? It was months since he'd have had anything around. So maybe someone else deliberately spiked his painkillers.'

'Or his booze?' suggested Simon. They could see that he was getting interested. His pressman's nose was twitching with interest. If this wasn't a good story, he didn't know when he'd ever heard one.

'So,' Pete took over, his logical mind wanting to keep the conversation on track. 'Some of us – the band and a few other friends – are trying to find out just what went on that night at the cottage. We thought, if anyone was on top of current events in NI, it was you, old Si.'

'Ah.'

Simon looked down. He was clearly thinking.

'Like,' Ziggy rushed in, 'do you know from the grapevine who was in the crowd last night at Fitz's cottage? And why were they there? Is there any background that would help us sort out who was behind it? These things don't just happen by accident – we all know that. Someone, or more than one person, worked it up, right, Si? You're the expert.'

'Fellows, fellows, give me a chance!' Si, relaxing in the back seat of the twins' red Corsa, shook his long colourless lock of hair back from his forehead, pushed his thick rimmed glasses further up on his nose, and grinned at the excited faces of Pete and Ziggy as they gazed at him over the backs of the front seats. 'Let me think!'

'No, you're right, guys,' he said presently. 'It didn't just happen. That crowd was there because it had been orchestrated. And I can tell you exactly who did it. Robbie Mallet!'

Chapter Twenty-Three

Monday night/Tuesday

'Robbie Mallet?'

Pete and Ziggy spoke as if with one voice.

'The *Who's On Top* guy? The one who cuts all the contestants to pieces?'

'Yeah, that one.'

'I hate him!' Ziggy said quietly. 'A girl I know, a lovely girl with a fabulous voice – he cut her to ribbons – made her cry in front of millions. Made jokes and got the audience laughing at her. What are people like?'

'I know. But that's why people watch these shows. They're like the crowd in Ancient Rome at the Coliseum watching the lions and the Christians. Getting a thrill out of it. Doesn't say much for the human race, does it?' Simon smiled wryly.

'So, you think he was behind the crowd who picketed Fitz in Cushendall, in the cottage?'

'I know it.' Simon breathed in deeply. 'Listen. Robbie Mallet came over here a few days ago. He spent his time going round all the main papers, talking to their music and news people. Hey, he even talked to me!

'And what he was saying was that Fitz was back on the drugs, that he was staying in this place in the Glens of Antrim to be able to trip without people knowing about it, and that there was a great story to be had if anyone would take the trouble to get up there and talk to him.

'When he said that stuff to me, I laughed in his face and said no thanks. But he was trying to put it over that this was just between him and me, that if I came up there with him, we could break the story between us – I could do the local stuff and he'd bring in the English papers – between us we could be really big. I bet he said that to all the guys.'

'As the saying goes,' Pete put in.

'Right. I heard from more than one of my mates that he'd said much the same to them, individually, okay? So you can take it that he was doing the same thing all over.'

Pete was convinced. But Ziggy wasn't so sure.

'But, Si, mate, what could this Mallet guy have against Fitz? Why would he be setting up a hate campaign against him?'

'Ziggy, who knows how guys like Mallet operate – what goes on inside their heads? I guess he does this stuff – like the things he says on *Who's On Top?* – partly for kicks and partly because it gets him noticed, gets him well paid. A story about Fitz would get him a lot of dosh and would give him the sort of publicity he wants, get him lots more TV spots, and so lots more money, see?'

'Yeah. It's a sad old world, Si.'

'Listen, let's go round to mine, jam a bit, have a few beers, okay?' Simon had obviously had enough of the misery. 'It's yonks since I seen yous guys. Come on, let's get this show on the road!'

'Right.' Pete turned the key and headed the Corsa for Simon's familiar flat.

Simon lived in the area of Belfast popularly known as the Holy Land because the streets had names like Jerusalem Street, Palestine Street, Carmel Street, and so on. The Holy Land was mostly a student area these days, and cheap but not particularly beautiful flats were the norm.

Simon, while making a reasonable amount by his journalism, had never moved from this place. He'd bought it on leaving university, as soon as he could afford anything.

They piled in. The twins knew their way round the flat nearly as well as Simon himself. They headed for the scruffy kitchen, grabbed a beer each from the fridge, and settled in the tiny living room to make music to their heart's content.

It was only after several hours that Simon stopped blathering his drum kit and said. 'Here's a thought, guys.'

The twins put down Simon's guitars, which they'd borrowed (no keyboards being available). And listened.

'I heard some stuff on the grapevine about Robbie Mallet after he turned up here. I reckon it might be important.' Simon stopped and frowned to himself.

'Well, what, then?' asked Pete presently, when there seemed no sign of Simon continuing.

'Look. I'll have to think about this, Pete,' Simon said. 'I was told some stuff in confidence. I promised not to repeat it. I don't think I can break my word. But, tell you what, tomorrow I'll get hold of the –' Simon hesitated and then obviously substituted a word for his original choice – 'the person who told me. See if it's okay for me to share it with you guys in the circumstances – Fitz and all that. I guess I'll get the go ahead.'

'Tell us now!' Ziggy demanded, and Pete, while less aggressive about it, added his voice to his twin's.

'This is important, Si. I think you have to tell us.'

But Simon was adamant.

'Tomorrow, guys. I'll check it out, and let you know tomorrow.'

Suddenly he let out an enormous yawn.

Pete and Ziggy found themselves yawning, too.

'Okay, Si,' Pete said. 'Time for beddy-byes, I guess. We'll wait to hear from you tomorrow with bated breath.'

And on this note of laughter they parted.

Chapter Twenty-Four

Monday night/Tuesday

Nat hadn't stayed long with Mar, to her disappointment. He'd accepted a coffee, sat beside her on her huge soft sofa with one arm stretched carelessly along the back so that it was also round Mar's shoulders, and talked about Angel Murphy. While Mar tried to be a good listener.

'I've known her for a long time, Mar,' he said. 'Since we were both at school. Then she went on to Queen's and I went to the Slade.'

Mar knew that Queen's was the local university, of course. She hadn't gone there herself – or to any Uni, come to that. She'd had to start earning, in McDonald's, as soon as she left school at sixteen. Her parents had simply expected it. Okay, they'd been hard up. They needed her contribution. But she hadn't stayed with them for long after that, anyway.

Mar's home life was something she'd tried hard to forget, to put behind her. The constant rows, the loud angry voices which had terrified her as a child and which still upset her badly as a young teenager. Not some-thing she ever talked about. There was no one close enough. No one she'd trust with the truth about her life. Not with all the men she'd loved and slept with for a short while. She'd known, instinctively, that none of them cared enough, there were none of them she could really trust.

'So?' she asked, just to keep Nat there and talking.

'I suppose I've been in love with her almost since I first saw her,' Nat said. 'The traditional love at first sight stuff. We were teenagers. I wrote poetry for her. Never showed it to anyone else. I used to tell her I'd leap into the sky and pick her a handful of wild stars if she wanted me to. She liked that – but she laughed, see? She never took me seriously. She told me I ought to use my creativity.

'Okay, she was right. Her saying that was one of the main things that encouraged me to go for it. This was before I started painting. I thought about poetry, writing, things like that, at first. But then I moved on to the visual arts. I started at Art College. Then Angel went off round the world, building up her business career, and ended up in a disastrous marriage.

'When I met up with her again not long ago, she'd got free of that, thank God. I don't know the ins and outs of it, but I know she walked out on the bastard. And later the guy was killed by some villains he'd got mixed up with. So Angel was on her own again.

'But she'd changed. She's more beautiful than ever, no doubt about it. But the whole business has left its mark on her. She's wary of a new relationship. Oh, there's some guy in America, but I don't think it amounts to anything, or ever will.'

'Or you hope it won't,' Mar interposed. She wished he'd talk about something else.

Nat laughed. 'Okay – I hope it won't. Clever little thing, aren't you Mar? And very pretty.'

He set down his empty coffee cup, bent over and kissed Mar's lips softly. For a moment Mar thought things were taking off. But then Nat drew back, gently.

'Better be going now. Thanks for a great time.'

'Stay if you like.'

'Maybe not. Better not.'

And, surging to his feet, Nat went.

Mar was sad, disappointed, angry. She didn't know which feeling was strongest. She lifted Nat's coffee cup and hurled it against the nearest cream coloured wall.

Stupid. She'd have to clear it up, now.

It took ten minutes to wash down the mark on the wall – thank goodness the cup had been empty – and to sweep up the broken pieces and bin them.

'Broken pieces – like my life,' Mar told herself melodramatically, and noted that it would be a good line for a song. Then she laughed.

Time to do something positive. She was supposed to be working with the guys to find out what had gone on with Fitz last night. She'd arranged with Nat that he would come with her to talk with her most useful contact, Lucas Somerset. She'd try to set it up for tomorrow morning, if the guy was available.

She reached for her mobile and texted Lucas Somerset, who covered Arts and Music for the *Daily Word*. If it suited Lucas, she'd look forward to meeting him with Nat as soon as possible.

She thought about the situation with Fitz. Who could possibly have anything against him? Everybody liked Fitz – he was a really nice guy. Why should someone have taken against him? Why should anyone want to harm him? She didn't know. But maybe Lucas Somerset would have some idea.

Seri sat by Fitz's bed for as long as the staff nurse allowed her to. She looked at his face, pale and expressionless, and wondered what was happening in his mind, if anything. Was he dreaming? Or was everything a blank?

She prayed, and held Fitz's hand, and wondered how she could go on living if Fitz never recovered.

Presently the staff nurse came in and suggested that she should go along to the waiting room.

'I'll bring you a cup of tea,' the nurse said kindly. The badge pinned to the front of her uniform told Seri that the nurse's name was Eileen MacDougal. 'You need a bit of peace. And the doctor wants to look at Mr Fitzgerald again, okay?'

Seri understood that Nurse MacDougal was telling her, as kindly as possible, to get out of the way.

'Can I come back when the doctor's finished, nurse?'

'Sure you can,' replied Nurse Eileen. 'No restrictions, pet.' She beamed encouragingly at the beautiful girl so full of grief for her boyfriend. Eileen MacDougal hadn't really taken in who Fitz was. To her, he was just a youngster who was hovering at death's door. But she understood grief when she saw it. It was her daily portion here in the Intensive Care Unit at the Royal. No one who came here was free of it.

Seri smiled with difficulty.

Then she remembered what Angel had asked her to do.

'And Nurse – Eileen – could I possibly have a few words with the doctor when he's finished seeing Fitz? I won't keep him long – I'd just like to know –'

Her voice broke off as she struggled to hold back the tears.

'Sure you can, pet. The doctor always wants to keep the family and friends up to date with what's happening. I know you aren't, like, family, but you're his girlfriend, aren't you? We count that as family, these days. I'll tell him.'

Seri remembered what Angel had said before they separated.

'We need to know more about what Fitz actually took, Seri. I know this hurts to talk about. That's why I didn't want to bring it up in front of the others. But if we don't have that sort of info, we're working blind. And you're the only one the medical staff will speak to, right? Ask for as much info as they'll give you. I don't know how much they'll know at this stage. But it'll be more than we know right now, so anything will be helpful.'

Seri had promised to ask.

She sat in the comfortable sofa in the waiting room and sipped the hot tea Staff Nurse Eileen MacDougal had brought her. It was curiously comforting. After what seemed an eternity, but which her watch told her was half an hour, Eileen came back.

'If you'd like to come with me, Doctor will speak to you, Serena.'

Seri smiled inwardly at being called Serena. No one but her mother had called her that for the last ten years. Maybe Eileen MacDougal wasn't usually called Eileen, either?

The Staff Nurse led her quickly to the room where the nurses rested between duties.

'This is Serena Smith, Doctor Quinn,' she announced primly. ' Do have a seat, Serena.'

Seri sat opposite the doctor. He was a young man maybe two or three years older than Seri. He looked tired. His sandy hair hung lankly over his forehead. His stethoscope was draped round his neck. He wore a white coat, still clean but crumpled from hours of wear.

Dr Quinn propped himself against the desk where forms were filled in, clearly not intending to sit down and relax and give Seri more than a few minutes.

'Mr Fitzgerald is doing well, Miss Smith,' he announced briefly. 'I fully expect him to recover. We were in time to give him the right treatment – to empty out the contents of his stomach. It may take him a while to recover consciousness and be able to leave hospital. But we won't rush him.'

'That's really good news, doctor.' Seri breathed a sigh of relief. 'But what I wanted to ask you was if you know what caused his collapse? What had he taken? I wouldn't ask, but it's really important, actually.'

Dr Quinn looked at Seri. He saw a sweet, beautiful face, full of yearning. Her huge dark eyes looked into his. He tried not to get too involved in the troubles of his patients and their family, their friends. He'd developed a thicker skin than he'd had as a youngster. But this was somehow different. He looked back into Seri's eyes, and he felt her pain.

Perhaps if Dr Quinn had been ten years older, he'd have found it easier to resist, to follow his training and to tell Seri little or nothing. But something about Seri Smith moved him absurdly. He found himself telling her everything he knew about the causes of Fitz's coma.

Chapter Twenty-Five

Tuesday

Angel slept for four hours and woke at eight o'clock. She could hear some-one moving round in the kitchen of Billy Nelson's apartment.

'Will! Is that you?' she called.

A tousled fair head poked itself round the door.

'You awake, Angel? Fancy a cup of coffee?'

'Will, you're an angel yourself!'

The boy withdrew, grinning, and a few minutes later emerged again, carrying a steaming cup carefully in one hand and a piece of toast in the other.

'This is what I get for Dad when I'm staying with him,' he explained. 'I'm pretty good at making it, he says.'

The coffee smelt wonderful. The toast was brown and crisp and thickly buttered.

Angel said, 'You can add my vote to that, Will,' and was rewarded by a quick smile.

'I'll just get my own,' the boy said. 'That is – I usually eat in here with Dad – is that okay?'

'Sure it is, darlin'.'

Will came back in with his own coffee and toast, and sat gingerly down on the edge of the sofa bed.

'Angel. Have you thought any more about what happened to Dad? I mean, like, who did it and why? And what we can do to prove it?'

'Yes. I've thought about it, Will. I want to start by asking you some questions, right?'

'No probs.'

'Will, you told me you heard your Dad say something to this guy. Some-thing you didn't quite hear – or didn't understand. Can you remember what it was?'

'Yeah. I've been thinking about it, Angel, and it's come back to me.'

'Okay. Good.'

'Dad said, "Worried about Christine, are you? " And then the guy said something I couldn't make out, and then Dad said something else, and all I could make out of that was, "Hammerhead?" At least,' Will explained carefully, 'I'm pretty sure that was what it was.'

Hammerhead? The hammerhead snake was what Angel thought of immediately. A nickname, clearly. A nickname for someone called Mallet? But who was Christine?

'Will, that's really helpful. I'll have to give it a bit of thought myself, but I should think it's a pretty good clue.'

The boy's huge innocent eyes shone. 'So, do you think it'll help you to track down this attacker who put Dad in hospital?'

'I wouldn't be surprised, Will. And you definitely didn't see the guy's face? You wouldn't recognise him?'

'No, sorry, Angel, like I said, I didn't see him properly because of the mask.'

'Okay, no problem. Now, moving on, what are we going to do with you today?'

'Sure, I'll be okay here, Angel. I'm not a kid. Dad will be home from the hospital later today, they said, didn't they? I need to stay here for him, be here when he arrives.'

'Sure, that sounds fine, Will. But I think I'd better let your Mum know the situation.'

'No! She'll want me to come home!' Will's eyes were filled with distress.

'Maybe. Maybe not. But she has a right to know you'll be on your own all day.'

'No, please, Angel. She knows that already. Like I told you, Dad works – he's often not here when I am. As long as he comes later today, it's no different from any other time!'

Angel had her doubts. But she compromised. 'Okay, Will, I'll leave it for now. But I'll ring you this afternoon, just to check. And if your Dad isn't home, that'll be it – you'll have to ring your Mum.'

Clearly Will wasn't happy about this. But Angel was firm, and in the end he accepted it as the strange way grown ups thought.

'So now,' Angel said cheerfully, 'I have to get in to my own work, boyo! Speak to you later.'

She gave Will an enthusiastic hug, and went, leaving him standing at the door waving to her. Not without a certain amount of worry. And doubt. Was she doing the right thing? But Will wasn't really a child. He was over the legal age for being at home on his own. And surely there was no question of 'Hammerhead' coming back?

Chapter Twenty-Six

<u>Tuesday</u>

Lucas Somerset got back to Mar early the next morning.

'Hi, Mar. You wanted to speak to me?'

'Yeah. Like, it's about Fitz. You heard what happened?'

'Oh. Yeah, right. I heard. Dreadful.'

'Some of us – the band, and some of Fitz's other friends – are trying to find out what happened. Who set up the paparazzi frenzy. Can we meet up?'

'Sure we can, Mar. I'd be glad to help – if I can, that is.'

'Great! It'll me be and my friend Nat Deane.'

'The painter? Wow! Love to meet him!'

'And can we make it the *Riverside*, where we had lunch yesterday? Does that suit you? As soon as you can make it?'

'No problem. Say around eleven?'

Mar rang Nat, and at eleven o'clock that morning they pulled up at the *Riverside Bar*, a new place on Lanyon Quay near the River Lagan.

Nat found a parking space and they went in. Lucas Somerset was sitting at the bar waiting for them.

'Hi, guys!' he greeted them. 'Mind if we sit outside? I'm dying for a feg!'

Mar had forgotten that Somerset was a smoker. It was a lovely morning, the sunny spell was lasting, and the tables outside overlooking the river would be perfect for sitting at while they had a drink, if only it had been later in the day, or with the heat at mid summer level instead of spring. It amazed her what smokers were prepared to put up with for the sake of a cigarette, rather than give them up.

Smiling resignedly, she pulled her denim jacket more closely round her and they followed Lucas Somerset outside.

'This is Nathaniel Deane, Luke. Nat.'

'Hi. Love your work, Nat!' Somerset shook Nat's hand enthusiastically, and began to talk about his paintings. He clearly knew a lot about them, and had strong views about his favourites. Mar reflected that she would have to take hold of the conversation at some point and steer it in the right direction if they were to find out anything.

When they were settled at a pleasant wooden table with benches, partly sheltered by a fence and some flowering bushes from the breeze blowing from the river, and a waiter had taken their order – lager, for Luke and Nat, coffee for Mar, who felt it might help to keep out the cold – Somerset lit a cigarette and leaned forward across the table.

He seemed, Mar thought, more relaxed than when he'd been interviewing her yesterday. But then, that had been business. This wasn't. And she was glad to see that he was ready to change the subject himself. 'So, something about Fitz, is it? Dreadful thing. Fitz is a such nice guy.'

Mar plunged straight in. 'Luke, some of us are sure there was something else going on there. Fitz didn't OD himself. There's somebody behind it all. We thought we'd maybe start by seeing if we could find out who set him up for that paparazzi trouble. Have you heard any talk?'

Somerset grinned. 'Sure, the place has been buzzing with talk for days. "Fitz is going up to Cushendall – if you head up there you'll get a quare good story – make sure you don't miss it!" That sort of stuff.'

'And have you any idea who it started from?'

'Sure, that's easy too. It was Robbie Mallet, so it was. Yer man from *Who's On Top?* He's been running round stirring it since he came over last Thursday. He lives in London normally. Has a place over there. But he hops over here occasionally if anything big comes up. He got hold of me on Friday evening and started bending my ear about it, trying to get me to join in. But I've no interest in that sort of thing. I write about the music, not about the guys' private lives, see?'

'Unlike most,' said Mar drily. 'Luke, that's really helpful. Anything else you can add?'

'Sorry, Mar. That's my limit. Like I said, I wasn't interested. I cut him off as soon as I could. But if you're looking for who started the gang warfare, Robbie Mallet is definitely the man.'

'And do you know where we would find him? Where's he staying, like?'

'Ah, well, as to that, I heard he'd gone back to London already. The business with Fitz meant his story was wrecked – blown up in his face. Okay, there's another story, but it's not Mallet's type of thing. Fitz has the sympathy vote right now, see? Not Mallet's game at all.

'In a week or so, when Fitz recovers, as we all hope he will, well, then, Mallet will jump right back in and start spreading a lot of dirt about him. But nobody's ready to listen to anything like that while Fitz is still in Intensive Care.'

'Yeah,' said Nat soberly. 'And that's why it's important for us to make sure the truth comes out before Mallet starts in.'

Somerset nodded agreement. Then he smiled at Mar as he stubbed out the butt of his cigarette and lit another one. 'Hey, while I have you here, Mar, when do you want to finish off that interview?'

Mar was surprised. She'd imagined that because she'd cut the interview short yesterday, Somerset would have been too annoyed with her to want to bother again. It was good to know that he was still keen.

She said so, and Somerset laughed.

'Hey, Mar, I totally understand that you didn't feel able to go on with it yesterday. The news about Fitz really knocked you back, didn't it? It's okay, girl – I like it when people are human. Give me a ring when you feel up to it, right?'

'That'd be great, Luke. See, just now, I'm sorta tied up – the whole band is, and some of Fitz's other friends – trying to find out what happened. We know Fitz didn't take any stuff himself. We need to come up with the facts, and take the black mark off him.'

'Yeah. Good for you, guys. All the best with it. Now, how's about another pint? And this time we'll drink to Fitz!'

Chapter Twenty-Seven

<u>Tuesday</u>

Angel saw the headlines when she had left Will and was on her way into work.

Local Girl Reporter Stabbed to Death in the Woods!
What Happened to Cindy Baron?

So the police had followed up on her phone call and found Cindy's body. That was good. She bought a copy of the paper and scanned the report, looking for any information she didn't already have.

Cindy Baron was twenty-four – younger than Angel had realised. Her parents lived in Portstewart and were said to be 'devastated'. No wonder, thought Angel grimly.

There were details of her journalistic training and the papers she'd worked on. Her promotion to *'Hi'* magazine had been a triumph – her parents said they'd been, 'So proud of her.'

Nothing to explain why she'd been in the woods above Cushendall by herself – or rather, by herself except for the person who'd murdered her. No mention of a date with Robbie Mallet. No explanation, either, of how she'd got there. Since she'd come in Billy Nelson's old Polo, and Billy had driven it away, there was nothing to help the police to work out the answer to that.

Angel wondered if there were any telltale car tracks. There had been several cars around – Billy's, her own, and the murderer's chosen form of transport. But none of them had left the road, as far as she knew. There had been that sound of something which could have been a motorbike engine. That was probably the murderer. But again, it hadn't been in the woods. Probably hidden in a field somewhere along the lane.

The weather had been dry lately. The lane, and even the tracks in the wood, would have shown no marks.

On the whole, Angel was thankful for that. It was a pity that there would be little or no trace of the murderer's car or, more probably, motorbike. But it was just as well that there would, equally, be no trace of herself or Billy.

She took the paper out of her bag which she'd picked up lying half out of Cindy's pocket, and read it again. Stupid of the killer, whoever he was – and she could only think it was Robbie Mallet – not to have made sure he'd taken it with him. But the whole thing was stupid.

'Cindy – running late. But I'll be there. Don't go away. Wait in the woods. I'll call you on the mobile when I get there.'

And it was signed 'R.M.'

'R.M.' could be a lot of people. But added to what Billy Nelson had said, it was pretty certainly Robbie Mallet.

She'd look up the Internet News when she got into work. But it was unlikely that it would have anything more to tell her.

It was late enough by the time Angel got to her desk. Fortunately no one was looking for her. During the day her mobile buzzed continually with text messages. She took time out during a coffee break to reply. A joint text to the whole gang.

'Let's get together tonight, okay? At yours, Seri?'

The confirmations came rolling in. Everyone was set to be there.

Angel rang Will during the afternoon as she'd promised. Billy was still in hospital. They were planning to keep him there for one more night. Will agreed that he should phone his mother and go home to her. It was a weight off Angel's mind.

Then it was time to record the interview with Nathaniel Deane. As she had expected, it went extremely well. Angel was very pleased with it. And so was her boss, Minerva Daley, when she saw the initial footage.

'That'll cut into a great interview, Angel,' she said. 'You're starting to shape up well, girl.'

Angel couldn't help feeling pleased. It wasn't often that Minerva praised anyone.

'The guys are going along to get some cut-in shots of Nat and the actual exhibition tomorrow afternoon, Minerva,' she said. 'That should add everything we need.'

'Good girl,' Minerva said, and Angel realised that, cool as she usually was, she'd flushed with pleasure. For a brief time she'd almost forgotten the horror of what had happened to Fitz.

Snatching a quiet bite to eat in her apartment before heading to Seri's, she read through the various text messages from Fitz's friends.

Mar. 'Looks like the best bet is a guy called Mallet.'

The twins. 'Si guesses Mallet.'

Mary. 'John thinks Mallet would be the main man.'

Jonty. 'Jeff says try Robbie Mallet.'

It was what you might call a consensus, Angel thought. Add to that Billy's words as reported by Will about someone called 'Hammerhead' (Mallet?) and his earlier story about Mallet and Cindy, and it seemed pretty definite. The next step was to track down Robbie Mallet and talk to him.

'Yeah, and beat him up!' said Ziggy, throwing his usual gentle pacifism to the winds. They were sitting drinking coffee in Seri's apartment and pooling their research and discoveries.

'Whoa!' said Mary.

'Well, we can decide what exactly we want to do about him when we're sure about what he did,' Angel said.

'We're sure now,' Ziggy muttered rebelliously, but he responded to Pete's hand on his arm patting and soothing him into quietness, like a nervy horse responding to his jockey.

'It seems clear enough that Mallet engineered the media attack,' Angel said. 'But we still don't know what happened to put Fitz into a coma, do we?' She turned to Seri. 'You were hoping to find out more from the doctors today, Seri. Any joy?'

Seri smiled wryly. 'Joy may not be the exact word, Angel. But, yes, they gave me some more info. They think, from the symptoms and from blood tests and stuff like that, that Fitz swallowed a huge amount of some prescribed drug. They haven't finished testing to find exactly which one, but it's likely chloral hydrate. There's no way Fitz would have had anything like that with him. All he had were his sleeping tablets. And he hardly ever uses those now.'

'And only one of them had been used,' Angel interjected. 'The number on the bottle was twenty, and there were nineteen left. So it can't have been that.'

'So we don't believe that Fitz was driven to take an overdose of something,' Jonty spelt it out. 'First, he wouldn't have. Second, he wouldn't have had prescription drugs with him. If he'd had anything it would have been a street drug. H, or weed, or something like E.'

'Right,' put in Nat eagerly. 'So someone gave him this prescription stuff.'

'But how?' asked Mar. She was sitting close to Nat, leaning against him, Angel noticed fleetingly, with a flash of annoyance. But hey, she told herself, don't be a dog in the manger! You don't want Nat, yourself – so no need to be possessive about him.

'Spiked his drink, I should think,' suggested Pete.

'There was a bottle of Bushmills, opened,' Angel remembered. 'Someone could maybe have slipped into the cottage earlier that day, when Fitz was out for a walk, d'you think?'

'He told me he'd taken a walk through the woods,' Seri put in, 'about lunchtime, not long after he got there. He went on and on about the peace and the beauty.' She laughed with a faint note of hysteria in the sound.

Mary put her arm round Seri comfortingly. 'So, it seems to me,' she said, 'that there are two things to do. First, track down this guy Robbie Mallet. And second, get the whiskey tested to see if we've guessed right. Then we can work out our next steps, okay?'

'There was one thing,' Mar said. She removed her hand, which had been resting casually on Nat's knee, sat up and leaned forward. 'When Nat and I were talking to Lucas Somerset, he mentioned that Robbie Mallet was normally in London. He has a place there. He was over here on a flying visit, like. Just following up on Fitz. Luke thought he was away back by now.'

'Yeah, Si told us much the same,' Ziggy nodded.

'Okay, somebody has to track him down in London. As it happens –' Angel grinned at them, ' – just as it happens, I'm due to head off there myself in a day or two. Or maybe even sooner.'

Chapter Twenty-Eight

Wednesday

It was the next day before Simon Fletcher finally got back to the twins, as he'd promised to do.

Ziggy was about to ring his chemist friend, Tommy Harrison, to ask him if he could be available to do some quick analysis for them, when his mobile tinkled just before he'd begun to punch in Tommy's number.

Instead, he pressed the green button.

'Hullo?'

'Hi, Zig. It's Si here.'

'Yeah.' Ziggy didn't bother to point out that his phone had already told him who the caller was.

'I said I'd get back to you about this Robbie Mallet guy.'

'Yeah.' Yesterday, you said, Ziggy thought.

'Look, sorry I wasn't quicker about it. I had to get hold of my friend, and then I had to talk her into it.'

Her, Ziggy noted.

'Look, this doesn't work on the phone. Can we get together?'

'Sure.'

'So, *Clements* in Botanic Avenue in half an hour?'

'Okay.'

Ziggy turned to Pete.

'Si seems to have some info for us.'

Half an hour later, the Diabolical Twins were seated in the Botanic Avenue branch of *Clements*, at a table with a view out of the window, with cappuccinos in front of them, and their eyes fixed on the door.

The place was hiving, students and lecturers loaded down with files and books passing up and down the Avenue, and people of all sorts crowding the long narrow room of the café. The smell of coffee filled the air and the noise of excited chatter was everywhere. It was a place where you saw everybody. Pete had already spoken to one of his former lecturers, and two girls had approached the twins asking them to sign copies of *Raving*'s latest CD.

Finally Si arrived, slouching along Botanic Avenue in his usual careless way, his pale no-coloured hair falling over his forehead and his dark rimmed glasses falling down over his nose. The twins weren't too surprised to find that he was late. That was Si's way.

'Hi, guys,' he greeted them, collapsing into a seat at their table, facing them. 'Good to see yous.'

A waiter bustled up and took Si's order for a shot of Expresso, black, and Si smiled at Pete and Ziggy.

'Glad you could make it,' he mumbled.

'So, stop wasting time, Si,' Pete ordered. 'Tell us your story.'

'In a minute,' Si protested. 'Let's wait until the waiter gives me my coffee. I can't do a thing without coffee in the morning.'

Pete, who knew perfectly well that this was a pure affectation, was ready to clock Simon one, but managed to restrain himself. They waited in silence until Simon's black Expresso arrived. The journalist lifted his cup, drained at least half its contents in one go, and breathed a sigh of relief.

'Now I'm human again,' he remarked. 'Okay, guys, I'll give you the story.' He leaned back, cradling his coffee cup in both hands, and began.

'I told you that a friend of mine had told me something about Robbie Mallet in confidence, didn't I?'

The twins, unwilling to sidetrack him by commenting, nodded.

'So, I won't tell you her name, but she's a singer, and she's up to take part in *Who's on Top?* next season. So, not unnaturally, she was concerned about what Robbie Mallet would say about her. She wasn't worried about the other three judges, see? She knew they'd be fair enough. Okay, their views would be super subjective – personal – right, but she could live with that. But she also knew that Mallet would say whatever came into his head, regardless. And almost certainly nasty stuff.

'So, she'd heard on the grapevine that Mallet wasn't above taking a handout to make his comments a bit more friendly. And – get this – she hadn't any money to bribe him, but she'd also heard that he wasn't averse to taking payment in kind, from the more attractive girl competitors. In other words, if a girl was willing to sleep with him, he'd give her a good mark up. So what's new, eh? The casting couch, or what?

'So my friend wangled an introduction to him. Got herself invited to a party where she knew Mallet was expected, and made up to him until he didn't know if he was on his head or his heels, and succeeded in going home with him at the end of the evening and getting into bed with him. Horrific, or what? Don't know how she could! And, mind you, she's a nice girl, actually.

'Anyway, Lisa – whoops! Forget that name, guys! – my friend has been sleeping with Mallet for several weeks now, and still hasn't caught the mange. And what I wanted to tell you guys is this. A week ago or so, just before Mallet came over here, he got up after they'd had sex to answer his mobile. He went over to the door, but you know how people are when they're on their phones. They just seem to shout their heads off regardless of who's listening. Still, I suppose he thought Lisa was asleep – zonked out after his marvellous performance, or something. But she was wide awake and heard every word. And she told me what he'd said.'

'So, she was over here?'

'Naw! But we keep in touch on *Facebook*, right?'

'Oh.'

'So, you want to hear what Mallet was saying?'

'Of course we do, you eedjit! Get on with it!' Pete roared.

'Then don't keep interrupting.'

Pete and Ziggy bit their lips, unwilling to cause any more delays.

'Apparently he was talking to some guy who he thought a lot of. Or at least someone he didn't want to upset. Lisa said he was sounding really polite and stuff. And he said, 'You're the boss, okay?' several times. And she heard him mention Fitz's name, which made her sit up and take notice because she's a top fan of *Raving* and she thinks Fitz is super special.

'And then she heard Mallet say something like, 'No problem, boss, I can get a big crowd of the paparazzi together easy enough. Up near Cushendall, you say this cottage of Fitz's is? Right! I'll see to it. We'll drive poor old Fitz round the bend before we're done, you bet. And you might think of doubling up that sum of money you promised me, boss, how's about it?'

'So Lisa couldn't believe her ears, but she was pretty sure she'd been listening to some plot against Fitz. Only she didn't think it could be that serious, because the media all love Fitz and she didn't think Mallet could do him any real harm.

'But just then Mallet switched off his phone and came back over to the bed, and Lisa spread out her arms and made sure she looked as if she was out for the count, and he never knew she'd heard a thing. Only she had, and she told me all about it by *Facebook* message.'

The twins could say nothing for a moment. All their ideas were proved true. And besides that, it turned out that Mallet was working for some man he called his boss.

'So, when I told Lisa about what had happened to Fitz, she was so angry you wouldn't believe it,' Si continued. 'And she told me I could certainly pass the info on to you guys, and she really hoped you could prove what had been going on and clean up Fitz's reputation.'

'Well.' Pete spoke slowly. 'Tell Lisa how much we appreciate her letting you tell us all this, Si.'

'Done.'

'And tell her that we don't know for sure if we can prove what Mallet and his boss have been up to, but we'll certainly do our best.'

As soon as they'd left the café and Simon, the twins looked at each other, then Pete opened his mobile. 'First thing to do – you agree, bro'? Message Angel and let her know that Mallet isn't working on his own. He has someone he calls his boss calling the shots.'

Chapter Twenty-Nine

Wednesday

As Angel stepped on board the late afternoon shuttle plane at *George Best Belfast City Airpor*t she was smiling happily to herself. In less than two hours she would be seeing Josh Smith again. They were meeting for dinner at Angel's hotel, the *Sinclair*. The BBC travel branch had booked her into the hotel, and onto the flight, without too much difficulty.

It had taken a bit of skill to manoeuvre her boss at the BBC, Minerva Daley, into allowing her to go over so soon. The fact that Minerva had been so pleased with Angel's interview with Nathaniel Deane had helped quite a lot. And the excuse of an interview with one of the really big names, Sir Marshall O'Neill, a recently created theatrical knight, born and bred in Northern Ireland and now famous across the world, had been readily accepted, once Minerva realised it was definitely going to happen.

The hard work had been getting through to Sir Marty's agent and cajoling him into agreeing that this interview would be great advance publicity for his client's forthcoming appearance in *Macbeth* at Belfast's *Grand Opera House*. Sir Marty was everyone's darling in his home town, but he hadn't graced Belfast with his presence for some time. The interview, Angel urged his agent, would remind his audience how normal and down to earth the great man was, and would be a brilliant ticket seller.

So tomorrow Angel was to interview him, borrowing a cameraman from the BBC London studio. An exciting occasion in itself for Angel, who had never before met Sir Marty.

But her main feeling of happiness came from the idea of seeing Josh Smith again. When she'd first come across the young American in Athens, and then in Crete, last year, they had hit it off straightaway. Angel had found that she could talk to Josh about herself in a way she couldn't even talk to Mary. And together they had run into danger and out of it again, working as a team, each contributing to the final result and the end of the villain they had been up against.

After her disastrous marriage, Angel had been sure she would never again trust any man enough to fall in love with him. But sometimes she felt as if Josh Smith was making her change her mind about that.

The one hour flight was smooth and easy. Then, of course, there was the further hour spent getting out of Gatwick airport into the centre of London, and to her hotel, the *Sinclair*.

Angel registered, hurried up to her room, showered and changed in twenty minutes flat. She took the remaining ten minutes to fix her hair and make-up. Then she made her way, not rushing too much, down to the Shaftesbury Bar on the ground floor of the hotel, where she and Josh were to meet.

She had packed her newest dress for the occasion, a smooth creamy white satin gown which clung to her slim body with stunning effect. The neckline was low cut and folds of satin swooped round at both sides to fasten, halter style, at the back of her neck. A gold belt emphasised her waist and hips. Checking the effect before she left her room, Angel knew she looked good.

Josh Smith's reaction when he saw her confirmed this.

'Wow, wow and triple wow!' he said, standing up from his seat at the bar and coming forward to take Angel's hands in both his. 'Angel, I'd forgotten how lovely you are, gorgeous girl.'

He bent down slightly to kiss her cheek. Only slightly, because Angel was almost as tall as he was.

'Josh, darlin', great to see you again. Skype just isn't the same.' Angel allowed herself to be led to the bar, seated, and given a drink.

'I've booked a table for us at *Carlo's*,' Josh said. 'We've just time for one drink, then we'll hop into a taxi and be there in five.'

'*Carlo's?*'

'Yeah, it's the latest sensation. Fusion food. See all the celebs. Don't you Irish keep up with anything?'

Angel kicked him lightly on the nearest shin. 'Another crack like that, boyo, and it won't be just a light touch from my foot you'll be feeling, okay?' She sat half sideways on her bar stool and swung the tip of her foot threateningly in Josh's direction. He pulled back his leg hastily and swung his own stool away from her.

'Whoa, whoa, girl!'

They laughed at each other, and both felt the mounting excitement as they looked forward to the evening ahead.

Angel sipped the vodka martini Josh had known to order for her, and decided that, much as she wanted to talk over the whole Fitz affair with Josh, it would be a crime to spoil this evening together. Time enough for trouble tomorrow.

Carlo's was all Josh had promised and more. The ambience was European, a mixture of many countries, with French copies of Renoir paintings on the walls, Spanish bullfight posters, Greek prints of the

Parthenon and copies of famous Greek statues scattered around. The crowd contained many famous faces which Angel recognised with interest.

'Wow, is that Sir Tony? And Sonia Kelly?' she murmured to Josh as the headwaiter led them across the room.

'You bet! And there's the Minister of Housing, Graham Downshire, over there,' Josh murmured back.

But when they were sitting across from each other at a table in one corner of *Carlo's*, starters finished and the main course of duck in cherry sauce before them, Angel found her problems bubbling up in her mind again, and the desire to confide in Josh right now became overwhelming. Josh noticed it too.

'Might as well tell me about it, honey,' he said. 'No point in pretending you aren't worrying away at it like a dog with a bone.'

'And here's me thinking I was doing a class act as light hearted, not a care in the world!'

'I know you better than you think, honey.'

'Okay, Josh,' Angel decided suddenly. 'I didn't want to spoil this evening, but maybe it's spoiling things even more for me to be keeping my thoughts secret from you. And I bet you can help.'

It took longer that she'd expected to fill Josh in on all the details. They had moved to the bar area with their liqueurs by the time she'd brought him up to date.

'So you see,' she finished, sipping contentedly at her Cointreau, 'it's pretty clear this guy Robbie Mallet was behind the media persecution. But was he the only one involved, or were there others using him, or working with him? And did someone spike Fitz's drink? And if so, who?'

Josh looked thoughtful for a few minutes. Then he grinned. 'Tell me, Angel, did you and this gang of yours never consider going to the police with what you've got so far?'

Angel looked astonished.

'Oh. Right. Yes, I get you, Josh. It would be the obvious thing to do, okay. But I suppose now we've started, now we've got our teeth into the business, we sorta want to finish it ourselves.'

'But if someone poisoned Fitz's bottle of Bushmills whiskey, the police are going to need to get hold of that bottle at the crime scene, and test it themselves. If it isn't there, it's not evidence, see? You need to start them on that track before someone pinches it – hides it.'

Angel gazed at him, her mouth open. Josh stared back, silent for a moment.

'You didn't? Tell me you didn't? You and your gang didn't take it away?'

'None of us thought about it that way,' Angel confessed. 'About evidence, I mean. Not tampering with evidence if it's to stand up in court. Though now you mention it, I knew that perfectly well, and I'm sure we all did.'

'So what did you arrange?' Josh spoke grimly.

'Nat and Mar – that's Marilyn, from the band, right? – last night, when we were talking about future moves at Seri's flat, they offered to go up and get hold of the bottle so we could get a chemist friend of Ziggy's to test it.'

'Then, honey, you'd better get on your phone right away and tell them not to go near it, let along remove it.'

'Well, yes, but – what time is it, Josh?'

'Coming up to ten.'

Angel spoke sadly. 'Then I'm afraid it's too late. They must have been and gone by now. They'll be on their way to Ziggy's chemist friend I should think. Oh, Josh – what a fool I am!'

Chapter Thirty

Wednesday

Nat and Mar, armed with Seri's key, arrived at the cottage just before nine o'clock. They had timed their journey so that it would be dark by the time they got there.

'Better not go up during the day,' Nat had said last night. 'There might be police on the watch or even nosy neighbours.'

'The nearest neighbours are a mile or two away in Cushendall village,' Seri told him.

'Whatever. Maybe some of them will be around, having a look at the cottage after what happened. But they won't hang about after dark.

'Besides,' Nat said firmly, 'I need to put in an appearance at the Gallery – my exhibition opens day after tomorrow, guys. Thursday. There's still some stuff I need to check. Even though I spent this morning and most of this afternoon at the Gallery, after I left the BBC, sorting out where to hang each painting, I'll need to be there finalising things – and dealing with these cameramen from the BBC, right, Angel? – most of tomorrow as well. But I'll be okay to go tomorrow evening, Wednesday, right, Mar?'

'Right.' Mar smiled happily. She still thought Nat was the most beautiful man she'd ever seen, even though she didn't seem to be getting much further with him.

They drove up in Nat's hired car, stopping off for a quick bite en route at a small pub on the outskirts of Carrickfergus. They sat outside in the soft evening air with the last of the Spring sun warming them just enough.

'I thought we'd go by the coast road – the scenic route, as they call it,' Nat explained. 'There's no rush, is there? And it must be yonks since I drove up this way. One of the most beautiful places in the world, I used to believe.'

'Fine with me.'

Mar sat back and relaxed dreamily, swirling her white wine in its long stemmed glass. Nat, since he was driving, was drinking spring water, but Mar didn't see why that should render her teetotal for the evening. The sea lapped softly against the long stretch of promenade which lay directly across the road from their table. The magic of the night trailed its perfumed tendrils around her, drawing her deeper and deeper into its clinging embrace. She felt helpless, trapped by emotion, not even wanting to escape.

'So Fitz still hasn't come out of his coma,' Nat remarked presently. 'He's still in Intensive Care. Doesn't that mean we don't know yet if he'll recover? Or recover fully, even?'

Mar shivered suddenly. The evening air seemed less warm. Or was it just the reminder of the danger Fitz was still in? It wasn't that she didn't care about Fitz, she assured herself. She loved him, she really did, she so much wanted him to be back to himself. But she didn't seem able to help it – Nat's presence so close beside her was a serious distraction.

They drove on up the beautiful Antrim Coast Road, the sea on their right hand side, the low craggy hills on their left. The breeze from the sea had freshened and the sun, lingering on like the last guests reluctant to leave the party, sent a handful of sparkles scattering across the rippling surface of the water.

As they drove past Carnlough and drew nearer to Cushendall Mar watched the colours changing. The sun was a brilliant orange now which tinted the sky across its width in broad bands of pink and yellow and gold. Gradually it sank beneath the distant horizon, and dusk crept around the car and the countryside.

As they drove up the steep, winding side lane which would eventually take them to Seri's cottage, darkness finally descended. They drew up at the gate and when the car's headlights disappeared they sat looking round them at utter blackness.

'Okay, Nat, got your torch?'

'Sure, I'd be a fool not to have it, Mar!'

'And I've got mine, too.'

The beams of their two torches cut a frail path to the gate and on along the short driveway to the cottage door. It was still sealed up as the police had left it.

'Okay, we'll need to go round the back,' Nat realised. They moved away from the front of the cottage and made their way round to the back. Moving cautiously to avoid unnecessary noises or stumbling, they went forward through the broken down rose bushes and across the trampled grass, and came finally to the cottage porch.

Now that they were here, Mar found herself unaccountably nervous.

'We aren't breaking the law, or anything.' She spoke to reassure herself more than Nat. 'Seri owns the cottage and she gave us her key and knows we're going in.'

A sudden loud creak from somewhere behind the little building interrupted her. Mar jumped uncontrollably and clutched Nat's arm.

'What was that?'

Nat, a city boy by upbringing, was no more familiar with country sounds and animals than Mar, but he did his best to be reassuring in turn.

'Probably a fox or something in the wood. It won't trouble us if we don't trouble it.'

Mar wasn't particularly soothed. 'I really, really don't want to have to deal with a fox, Nat.'

'You won't have to. Come on, let's get on in.'

'And suppose,' Mar went on worrying, 'suppose it's not an animal? Suppose it's Robbie Mallet? Suppose he's thought about the whiskey, himself? Suppose he's come here like us to get hold of the bottle and take it away and dump it, so's no one can test it? Come to think of it, he must be pretty dumb if he hasn't thought of that.'

'Thought he was supposed to be in London? Isn't that why Angel's gone there?'

'Yeah – but that was just a guess. He could be still here.'

Nat said nothing. Instead, he took Seri's key from his pocket and inserted it in the lock. With Mar still chattering distractedly he opened the door. Clinging to his arm, Mar followed him in. Nat punched in the code to turn off the security system.

The cottage was in darkness, the electricity switched off again at the mains as Angel had left it.

'We go into the kitchen area and find the mains switch first,' Nat said. 'You stay here, Mar. No sense in both of us stumbling round in the pitch black. Pity there's no moon yet.'

Mar stood just inside the cottage door. She swung her torch casually round from side to side, wanting to see more of this cottage she'd heard so much about. Two gleaming eyes caught the torchlight and glared at her across the room. They were hard and ferocious and their height suggested that they belonged to someone very tall and probably very dangerous.

Mar screamed. The scream would have been louder if she had been able to take in sufficient breath.

As it was, it was loud enough to bring Nat rushing back to her, bumping into anything in his path as he came and hacking his shin painfully on the metal corner of a wrought iron table which usually lived in the garden.

Crash went the table.

Crash went the piles of books and headphones which Fitz had used the table for.

Nat muttered something which he hoped Mar didn't hear.

'What is it? Are you okay?'

'The eyes! The eyes!' Mar sobbed. The wavering beam of her torch still picked out the gleaming eyes across the room. Strangely enough, they hadn't moved since the torch first shone on them.

A moment later Nat burst out laughing.

With the help of his own torch, he could see that the eyes belonged to an enormous white teddy bear propped up on a shelf high up against the wall. Mar saw it at the same second.

'Hey, Fitz told me some fan sent him a bear just the other day – he was dead pleased. He said he never had one when he was a kid, so this would make up for it. This must be it. He musta brought it here with him. He was going to call it Yogi.'

'So.' Nat rubbed his exceptionally painful shin ruefully. 'Nothing to worry about, then. That'll teach me to rush about in the dark in a strange place.'

'Sorry, Nat.' Mar, still shaken, now also felt stupid and guilty.

'Hey, it's okay, babe.' Nat's voce was enormously gentle and comforting, coming to her with a sense of safety out of the dark room. He came closer and put one arm round her shoulders. Mar was aware of his presence, of the strength and warmth coming from him. She lifted her face towards him and her mouth met his.

It was a long, satisfying kiss. It might have gone on much longer if a wild shriek from outside the cottage hadn't torn them abruptly apart.

'Oh, what is it?'

Nat pulled himself together. 'An owl, at a guess. Mar – Mar, maybe we'd better leave it at that right now. Okay, kid?'

'Okay.' If Mar had been shaken before, she was much more shaken now. Her legs trembled beneath her, and she leaned against the wall by her side, fighting to recover control. She badly wanted to sit down, and would have staggered to the nearest chair if she'd been able to see one.

'I'll get this electric switched on, okay?'

Nat headed back towards the kitchen area. It seemed forever to Mar, but it was really only a few minutes before the cottage was suddenly flooded with light.

'Gotcha!' said Nat's voice. He sounded very pleased with himself.

Mar blinked in the sudden brightness, and looked round, trying to focus.

'Okay,' she said. 'Angel told us that the whiskey was on one of the worktops in the kitchen at the rear of the one big room. Do you see it yet?'

'No. But I haven't really looked yet. Come and help.'

Mar moved quickly towards Nat where he stood looking round the kitchen worktops.

They both looked. And looked some more.

They moved things aside. A toaster, an electric kettle, a stand hung with mugs. Coffee and sugar containers.

They opened cupboard doors and took out everything inside to make sure they had missed nothing.

Then they did it all over again.

But however long or thoroughly they searched, in the end they had to admit it.

The bottle of Bushmills whiskey which Fitz had drunk from was no longer there.

Chapter Thirty-One

Wednesday

Nat and Mar looked at each other.

'Wait a minute!' Nat said suddenly. 'Those sounds in the woods. We thought they were animal noises. But, maybe –?'

'You mean it could have been Mallet?'

'Yeah.'

'And if we're quick enough, we could still catch him?'

'Let's try, anyway!'

'Out the back,' Mar suggested. 'The woods are that direction – that's where the sounds came from.'

A moment later they were tumbling out of the back door of the cottage, torches waving wildly round them as they dived out of the ruined back garden and into the woods.

'There's the moon just coming out!' panted Mar.

'Yeah – just as well. Otherwise these small torches wouldn't help much.'

They hurried on, pushing their way through the thickets, pausing every now and then to listen for the telltale sounds of someone else nearby. The moon grew brighter and brighter as it climbed the sky, and it wasn't hard to see the obstacles in their way.

There were no real paths, but a number of faint tracks criss-crossed each other, leading in various directions, and Nat, followed closely by Mar, who had no intention of losing him, made their way as fast as possible along the easiest of them.

'Wait a moment, Mar,' Nat said presently. 'I'm not sure this is getting us anywhere. We're making too much noise. Mallet – if he's anywhere about – is bound to hear us and keep out of our way. We need to take it much slower – and much more quietly, right?'

'Right.'

They slowed down to a cautious creep, and tried, with their unfortunate lack of familiarity with woods and the countryside, to keep the noise of their progress to a minimum.

And that was how they were able, shortly later, to hear someone groaning.

Or that was what it sounded like.

They looked at each other, a question on each face. Then Nat took the lead.

'Come on. It's coming from over there to the left of this track. Let's find out what – or who – it is.'

Mar followed him. They left the faint track, if it could be called that, which they had been following, and plunged through the bushes towards the groans.

There was a small clearing just ahead of them. The groans grew louder as they reached it. They began to make out a huddled bundle crouched on the grass beneath a bramble bush, its head bowed and its hands clutching one ankle.

'Hi there.' Nat shone his torch on the stranger's face as he spoke.

Their first thought was that it was a girl – quite a young girl, with a blotched, tear-stained face which peered up at them along the torch beam. Her mouth was open as if to scream.

'It's all right,' Mar said hastily, coming forward and shining her own torch on her face and on Nat's to let the stranger see them. 'We aren't going to hurt you.'

The youngster spoke, and simultaneously they realised their mistake. 'I'm not frightened of you. You just gave me a shock, that's all. And I can't get away because of my leg.'

The voice, gruff but occasionally cracking up into a higher range, was that of a boy whose voice had recently broken.

'Who are you?' Nat asked.

'My name's Will Nelson.'

'Wait. I know that name. Aren't you Billy Nelson's son?'

A pleased smile broke over Will's face. 'Hey, do you know my Dad?'

'No,' said Nat. 'But who we do know is Angel. Angel Murphy. She told us about you.'

They watched as Will's face lit up, then suddenly grew very worried.

'Please don't tell her you found me here!'

'Why on earth not –' Mar began, then realised why. 'You promised Angel you'd phone your Mum if your Dad wasn't coming home straight-away,' she said accusingly. 'Didn't you do it? You were supposed to go home to her, not hang around by yourself!'

'I did phone her.' Will sounded indignant. 'But I knew it might be hard to get her. She was going off for a few days with her boyfriend, Sean McLernon, while I was with Dad. She warned me there might not be good reception. It's a holiday cottage they've rented in the Mournes. I did try, really. I just couldn't get her. So I got to thinking about what Angel said, and about how the guy who hurt my Dad was mixed up with what happened to Fitz, so I thought I'd come up here myself and see if I could find out any more.'

'Great! So now we have a kid as part of the team!'

Will flushed indignantly at Mar's words. 'I may be a kid, but I bet I've found out more than you guys,' he snarled. 'If only I hadn't tripped and hurt my ankle, I'd have been able to follow him.'

'Follow him? Follow who?' asked Nat.

Will's face fell. 'That's the problem,' he confessed. 'I saw him slipping out of the back of the cottage, but I didn't see him clearly enough to recognise.'

'But would you know him again?' Mar asked urgently.

'No. No way. Sorry, guys.'

'That must have been who we heard in the woods,' Nat said.

'I suppose so. I thought he'd be long gone by now. But maybe it wasn't as long ago as I thought, that I saw him. I've been sitting here on the ground for what seems like hours, wondering what I'd do. Not being able to move. Wondering if anyone would ever find me. My mobile's out of credit, too, so I couldn't even ring for help. Boy, am I glad to see you guys!' As he remembered the nightmare, tears threatened the boy again, but he kept himself under control, biting his lip to keep it from quivering.

'Right. Cool it, kid. Too bad you didn't see this guy properly. But it can't be helped.' Nat spoke firmly. 'What we need to do now is get you away from here. Find somewhere where we can see what we're doing, and get a look at that ankle. Probably take you to the nearest A & E to get it sorted. And while we're waiting for the doctor to see you, you'll have plenty of time to fill us in on the detail, right, Will?'

'Right.'

Mar and Nat crossed their wrists and gripped each other's hands firmly, to provide a secure seat for Will. Kneeling down on the rough ground among the weeds and scanty grasses, they slid their linked arms carefully under the boy.

'Put your arms round our necks, Will,' Nat instructed him. 'Make sure you've got a good grip. That's the way. Now, we're going to stand up, so don't do anything daft. We can't afford to have you rocking the boat.'

They stood up slowly, taking the boy's weight between them. Mar staggered slightly, but managed to keep her feet and adjust to the burden. Will sat back gratefully in the improvised seat made by their linked arms, wrists and hands, his own arms each round one of their necks.

The first problem was to get out of the woods, struggling through briars and creepers, low brushwood and bushes.

Will's face was very close to theirs. Mar knew when a thorny bramble branch swept across their faces that it hit Will too. She marvelled at the courage of the boy. He was already suffering from his hurt leg. She knew that when she herself was in pain, an additional smarting from some extra cause was likely to be the last straw. But Will remained silent, only stiffening occasionally at a particularly fierce blow.

Then after what seemed an eternity they were back on the path, and the journey became slightly easier. They backtracked their way along the faint track to the edge of the woods. From there it was a short distance to the lane where Nat had parked his car.

They deposited Will on the back seat, and arranged him so that he was half lying on it, his injured leg stretched out along it and safely supported.

Then they breathed collective sighs of relief.

'Okay,' Nat said briskly. 'Now for the nearest A&E.'

Chapter Thirty-Two

<u>Wednesday</u>

At almost exactly the time when Nat and Mar were arriving at the cottage near Cushendall, Mary Branagh was lighting the candles in the meeting room at the community on the Antrim Road.

'There!' she said to Jonty Carson, as she saw the flame leaping up on the last candle, and blew the taper out. 'Doesn't that look great?'

Jonty nodded. He had succumbed to the instinct which had drawn him to contact Mary again, and had rung her earlier that day.

Mary, just back from the school where she taught, had seemed pleased to hear his voice.

'Jonty! Hi!'

'Mary, I don't want to be a pain,' said the famous pop star hurriedly, 'but I just thought it would be nice to get together for a drink or something, or a chat, this evening, right? Or a meal, if you're free?'

'Aw, that would be lovely, Jonty,' Mary responded warmly, 'but I have to be here tonight for the evening prayer time. We take it in turns to be there. I don't know – maybe you'd like to come along? Eight o'clock. Then we could go wherever you liked afterwards?'

Jonty hesitated. It was a long time since he'd been to anything like that. Then he made up his mind. 'Sure thing, Mary. Give me the address again, and I'll see you there.'

So now he was sitting in the small room used for meetings, with a dozen or so other people, watching Mary light the candles. He wondered what it was about this girl that he found so attractive. Sure, she was good-looking, and a type – fair curly hair, blue eyes – that he himself had always admired.

But there were piles of girls out there equally pretty. He came across them all the time, crowding round him after gigs and wanting to meet him. He'd been scared of them as much as anything else. Strange people who knew nothing about him except that he was in a band whose music they liked. And who were ready to jump into whatever he wanted on that basis alone. Weirdos. Not the sort of people he wanted to connect with.

Mary suddenly smiled at him across the room and he felt his heart jump.

'I think we'll make a start now, right, everyone?' she said to the room at large. 'If anyone else arrives they can slip in quietly.'

There were chairs, soft chairs and harder ones brought in from the dining room, arranged in a loose circle round the walls. In the middle of the room was a low table where the candles were arranged beside a book which Jonty thought must be a Bible or a Prayer Book. Mary sat down not far from the table.

People who were still standing found a seat and for some minutes there was silence. The curtains were drawn, and the candles alone gave a soft, flickering light. Jonty saw that his neighbours had closed their eyes, and hastily copied them.

Mary picked up the book and began to read one of the psalms:

'I will sing of thy steadfast love, O Lord, forever ...'

Jonty found that he remembered the words from his teenage years when meetings like this had been part of his life.

A sense of peace descended on the room. Jonty, his eyes still closed, was content to soak it in, to allow himself to be still and relaxed. Presently he realised that the reading from the psalm was finished and that Mary was praying.

'Lighten our darkness, we beseech thee, O Lord; and by thy great mercy defend us from all perils and dangers of this night; for the love of thy only Son, our Saviour, Jesus Christ.'

Others joined in with their own prayers, some in the formal words written many centuries ago by men and women whose needs were the same as those of today, and some in whatever words came to them.

To Jonty's amazement – he'd forgotten that Fitz was known to these people – he heard a man seated not far away say, 'Lord, we pray for our dear brother Frankie – Fitz – who is still in Intensive Care tonight in the Royal. Pour out your healing power on him in your great love.'

Jonty found himself saying, 'Amen,' with the others. 'Heal Fitz, dear father,' he prayed aloud brokenly. 'Don't take him yet.'

Then the praying finished with the Lord's Prayer, spoken in unison by everyone present – including Jonty.

As the people left quietly, Jonty remained sitting with his head down.

He heard Mary come back from seeing the others out. Only a handful of people, a mixture of Catholic and Protestant, actually lived in the community. Another twenty or thirty, equally a mixture, came on whichever evenings suited them to join in the community's simple time of worship.

Mary sat down beside Jonty. For a while she said nothing. Then finally she spoke.

'I didn't know you were a believer, Jonty.'

'Well – I didn't think I was, any more,' Jonty said honestly. 'Oh, I was, a long time ago. When I was a teenager. But I drifted until there was nothing left – or I thought there wasn't. Funny how it all came rushing back to me tonight. The need, I suppose. Needing to pray for Fitz. And something else – the atmosphere.'

'I'd call that the presence of God,' Mary said straightforwardly.

'Yes.'

The silence surrounded them again, warm and heavy.

Presently the candles flickered a little more, and first one, then another, went out. Mary laughed and stood up.

'Hey, what about this meal you promised me, boy?'

She went round carefully extinguishing the remaining candles. Then she slipped her hand through Jonty's arm and led him to the door. 'This way out!'

Jonty took her to *The Diamond*, the best hotel at this end of town. He'd rung beforehand to make sure of a table, even though it was a weekday. *The Diamond*'s restaurant was popular and busy. But Jonty was well known to the Maitre d' and a table had been organised for him.

Mary, who normally lived on a shoestring and donated whatever was left of her wages as a teacher to various charities, was enchanted by the beautiful room where they ate, with its tables decked in white linen and laid with sparkling cut glass and shining masses of cutlery.

The impressive Maitre d' swept them over to their table with a bow, pulled out Mary's chair for her, and then lifted the crisp white napkin, folded in the shape of a swan, shook it out dextrously, and spread in across Mary's lap. He followed this up with a wink at Jonty, and handed them two enormous leather backed menus hung with tassels.

'Something to drink, Madam? Sir?' he murmured.

'Mary?' Jonty asked.

'I'll have a glass of red wine, thanks.'

Jonty ordered a bottle, and when the waiter had gone, he said, 'I'm glad you're not teetotal, Mary.'

'Why should I be?' Mary said simply. 'Jesus wasn't!'

Everything came back to that, Jonty noticed, but somehow he found he didn't mind. Mary knew her own mind. Her life was consistent. It had a centre and she was never far from it.

Perhaps, Jonty thought, this was her attraction for him. She was real. She wasn't pretending anything. He liked her more and more.

Chapter Thirty-Three

Wednesday

Angel and Josh strolled together through the bright London streets, making their way back to Angel's hotel, the *Sinclair*. Angel was enjoying the buzz, the people, the lights. But she knew that she needed to move into action before long. She had done the research for her interview that afternoon, as soon as she knew for sure that tomorrow's meeting with Sir Marshall O'Neill, newest theatrical knight and native of Northern Ireland, was definitely agreed with Sir Marty's agent.

The BBC Library had pulled out all the stops to help, producing video clips of Sir Marty in past roles and interviews by the cartload. She had thought out suitable questions, and had spent the flight in revising and adding to them. She was ready for tomorrow. Tonight was her own.

But much as she'd have loved to spend it on the purely personal aspect of her life, giving the time to Josh Smith, she knew she couldn't do that. The team of anxious people back in Belfast were relying on her to move things forward with Robbie Mallet during this flying visit. Angel sighed.

'Josh,' she murmured presently, 'do you have any thoughts about how we might track this guy Mallet down?'

Josh grinned. He'd been expecting something like this. Waiting for it.

'Funnily enough, Angel – ' he began and then stopped teasingly.

'You have? Sure, darlin', you're brilliant!'

'I don't actually know where he lives, myself,' Josh said. 'But I know someone who probably does.'

Angel reached up to kiss his cheek, smiling.

'And if you like, we'll go and meet this someone right now.'

'You bet!'

'He's a journalist himself,' Josh explained, as he took Angel by the elbow to steer her off the Strand into a narrow side street where the lighted-up sign told them they could find *Charlie's Bar*. 'He hangs out in *Charlie's*. He's a good guy. An old pal of mine. And what he doesn't know about the media in London isn't worth knowing, right?'

He pushed open the old style swing doors and they went into *Charlie's*.

The bar itself was also old style inside. A horseshoe shaped counter, backed by a mirror reflecting hundreds of glasses hung high, and optics for every possible type of drink, ran along one side and across the back. The other side was occupied with booths, each with high wooden walls giving privacy and wooden high backed benches on either side of the oak tables.

The lighting was dim enough to give an air of secrecy and romance. On every side were people. People talking, laughing uproariously, drinking and spilling their drinks. There was barely room enough to move among the throng of customers.

Josh pushed a way for himself and Angel across the width of the long room, until they reached a short, plump man with a smiling face and a shaved head. Josh leaned forward and tapped him on one shoulder.

'Jacky, you old rogue. Knew I'd find you here!'

Jacky spun round and gazed at Josh Smith incredulously.

'Josh! It's never you! What the hell are you doing here? I thought you were in the good old U.S. of A! And how the hell are you?' He dumped his drink on the bar, spilling part of it in the process, in order to be able to greet Josh the better by throwing both his arms round Josh's shoulders and giving him a stifling bear's hug.

'What're you drinking, boy?'

Then he noticed Angel, as Josh, freeing himself from Jacky's grip, drew her forward.

'Angel, this is Jacky Witherspoon. Ignore his bad manners, he's an okay guy underneath. Jacky, this is Angeline Murphy.'

'Angel to my friends,' Angel murmured.

'And devil to her enemies,' Josh added, as he had done that first time when they met in Athens last summer.

Jacky took in Angel's beauty and began to stutter. 'Like, s-s-sorry, man. D-d-didn't know you'd anyone with you. S-s-specially someone like this! Boy, you have all the luck, Josh Smith,' he added, recovering himself as he saw that Angel was smiling at him.

'Yeah, I think so, too, Jacky,' Josh said, smiling in turn.

'So, what're you both drinking?'

'No, I'm buying, Jacks. Fair's fair. We want to pick your brains. So we buy the drinks, okay? What is it, Scotch on the rocks as per usual?'

'That'll do me.'

'And, Jacko, any chance of finding a quiet spot in this bedlam?'

'Not a lot, Josh, man. But, hey, someone's leaving, over there. Come on!'

Pushing his way belligerently through the crowd nearest to him, using both his elbows and treading on any number of toes, Jacky reached one of the booths just as the people who'd been sitting there stood up. Josh and Angel, amused but rather shocked by the way the fat journalist was suddenly demonstrating such an aggressive streak, followed in his wake. Jacky dived into the booth in front of a group of drinkers who'd assumed they were next in line for the seats, and Josh and Angel slid thankfully after him.

'I'll keep this,' Jacky Witherspoon said. 'You get yourself back to the bar, my friend.' He winked at Angel. 'I'll keep her warm for you, okay, sweetheart?'

Angel prepared to ward Jacky off politely yet firmly. After all, they needed his help. But there were limits to what she was prepared to do for it. She resigned herself to an annoying quarter of an hour at least before Josh could get back and rescue her. But with this incentive, Josh somehow managed to get to the bar and arrive back with their drinks in an incredibly short time.

He set them down on the table. 'All doubles, to save time,' he announced. 'Scotch, Jacky. Red wine, Angel. And lager for me. So, Jacky,' he went on smoothly as he settled himself at the table, 'can you help us? We're looking for a guy called Robbie Mallet. A fellow journalist of yours. Tell me you know him.'

'Oh, I know him all right – crafty so-and-so. Know him and don't think much of him.'

'How so?'

'Aw, he's the sorta guy gets us media people a bad name. Writes just what he feels like, whatever makes a good story, whether there's a word of truth in it or not. Build someone up as a Celeb one month, for the pleasure of tearing them to pieces the next. And he isn't above taking a hefty backhander from one of his victims to keep their name out of the paper, if he can manage it. I know for a fact he's done that a good few times, see? Makes you want to spit.'

Jacky took a large gulp of his Scotch, apparently to clear the taste of Mallet out of his mouth.

'So, what do you want to know about the creep?'

'Simple, Jacks. Where do we find him?'

'Comes in here sometimes. Pity. Spoils the place to see him in it. Still, we get all sorts in here, have to put up with it.'

'But he's not here tonight?'

'Naw, haven't seen him.'

'So, where else?'

'Well, he has what he calls an apartment – scruffy sort of place – in one of those rundown streets down near Millwall. Wait a tick, I should know the address, I've been there – a while ago, before I caught on the kinda guy he is – I'll write it down for you. But you won't find him in during the day, he's out and about most of the time following up stories. Or recording at the TV studios.'

'But you think he might be there now?'

'Could be. Could very well be.' He took a scruffy red-backed note-book from his pocket and scribbled the address on a page, which he then tore out and handed to Josh.

Josh looked at it dubiously. 'Quite a distance. We'll need a taxi for this one, Angel.' He grinned at the enquiring face of the journalist.

'So, is that it?' Jacky asked them. 'Will this do the job?'

'Jacky, you're a gem. Twenty-four carat diamond, boy. Thanks. I owe you one.'

Jacky's plump face broke into a wide grin, which Josh returned.

Angel stood up as Jacky and Josh continued to grin happily at each other.

'Okay, guys, we'd better move on, then, if we want to catch Mallet tonight.'

'Right.' Josh shook Jacky warmly by the hand, narrowly saved from a further bear hug from his old friend by the width of the table between them. He and Angel made their way out of Charlie's through the happy, noisy crowds.

'Okay, back to the Strand to find a taxi.'

This didn't take them long. In the centre of London finding a taxi was usually an easy task. They piled into the first one to stop at Josh's signal, and Josh gave him the address.

Angel gave a sigh of relief. 'It all seems too easy. What it is to have contacts, darlin'. Now all we have to do is work out what we want to ask this guy when we get him.'

'I though you had all that under control?' Josh teased her. 'Aren't you the professional interviewer, honey?'

'Sure I am. That bit's easy. But I'm just not sure if this Robbie Mallet is working for himself – getting up a good story – or if there's someone in the background. It seems extreme, even for a slimo like Mallet, to poison someone's drink just to get a front page – you think?'

'Yeah, I get you. No, can't see that one happening. There's something else behind it.'

'But does Mallet himself have some other motive? Or is he working for someone else? Your man Jacky said he'd not be above taking a backhander. The way I'm thinking is this. Has he been paid for all this by someone else – someone with a real, big motive?

'The twins thought that was the way of it. Their mate Si gave them a line on that. Pity he didn't have the name, in the end. But it looks like there's someone. Who is it? That's what I want to know. And it'll take some skill to get the name out of Mallet.'

Angel spoke grimly. Difficult or not, that truth was what she was determined to find.

Chapter Thirty-Four

Wednesday

Robbie Mallet's apartment was in a sleazy side street near, as Jacky Wither-spoon had said, Millwall Football Club. Going by the names on the door-bell of the rundown three storey town house, he was living on the highest of the three floors.

'Probably has a few rooms separated off from below by pasteboard walls, with a door he can lock, leading off the common staircase. Someone's renovated the building into apartments without spending too much in the process, judging by the outside,' Josh speculated. 'This must have been a fine house once.'

'Well, it isn't now,' Angel replied briefly. 'Shall we go in?'

She pushed the front door and found that it opened straightaway. It wasn't locked, not even properly shut.

'I expect they leave it open until the last one's in,' Josh said. 'Makes it easier for post, or pizza deliveries.'

'Or even visitors? Or burglars?' suggested Angel.

There was no lift. They went up the uncarpeted stairs until they came to the top floor. Here on a landing they were confronted with a recently painted blue door, with a spy hole and a lock. There was no bell.

'Knock?' Josh asked.

'Go ahead.'

Josh knocked politely on the door. Then after a pause, rather more loudly.

Then he hammered as hard as he could.

'No one in,' said Angel.

Josh looked at her as she stood beside him smiling.

'You don't seem disappointed.'

'Well, I'd like to talk to him. We can wait till he comes back. But mean-while, it would be interesting to have a look round inside.'

Josh, a cop to his fingertips, looked horrified as Angel produced her set of picklocks from her bag.

'Angel, you'll get me thrown out of the force. Interpol will never get over it if one of their's is caught breaking and entering!'

'Who's going to catch you?' Angel was working busily at the lock, but took the time to give him an impudent grin. 'Anyway, I'm doing the breaking and entering, not you, big boy.'

The lock clicked open.

'Ah!'

Angel pushed the door cautiously. It was always possible that Robbie Mallet was there, but simply reluctant to open his door for one reason or another.

No one spoke. There was no movement. Angel pushed a little harder and the door swung open.

Followed by a reluctant Josh Smith, Angel stepped over the threshold.

The first thing she noticed was a chain, hanging down on one side of the door, with its fastening on the opposite side. Robbie Mallet was eager to preserve his privacy. But since it was unfastened, it was 99% certain that he wasn't in right now. Angel looked around.

She was in a minute, box-like rectangular hallway, long and narrow, with four doors opening off it in the usual way of small apartments. Living room, kitchen, bedroom, bathroom, Angel guessed. Rather like the last apartment she'd illegally entered, Billy Nelson's, but with a different shape of hall and possibly a different arrangement of rooms.

She clicked on the nearest light switch and pushed open a door at random. As she'd guessed, it led into a pleasant living room. Much more pleasant than anything they'd seen so far, from outside the flat, would have suggested.

There were several comfortable chairs in black leather, a low coffee table, a TV and DVD set on a custom built stand, and in the far corner, a computer on a small desk with a suitably comfortable computer chair in front of it which could be raised or lowered and which spun round on its supporting leg as required. A filing cabinet stood beside it. The floor was covered in a thick, pale green coloured carpet which blended in well with the beige painted walls and the mixture of black leather chairs.

Angel's eyes brightened at the sight. This was what she wanted.

'You keep watch, Josh, will you?' she asked. 'I'm going to need a few minutes with this laptop. Let's hope Mallet doesn't come back just yet.'

'Let's hope,' murmured Josh resignedly. He moved back to the apartment entrance and stood leaning against the door jamb, hands in pockets, the picture of ease in spite of the fact that discovery would probably get him kicked out of his job.

Angel opened the laptop, and as she'd hoped it lit up immediately and took her straight into Robbie Mallet's account, which he'd left open for convenience. No need to try out passwords, then. Good. Unless some of his files were password protected, that was.

She looked quickly down the list of icons. The computer was an Apple Mac, like her own. Even better. She knew her way around it easily enough.

Email first. Angel moved the cursor on top of the email icon with one finger on the touchpad and clicked once. A list of recent emails came on screen, with a menu to the left showing inbox, etc and further down, folders where past emails were saved. She scanned the current messages quickly, looking for anything which might be important. Nothing rang a bell.

Next, the folders. Names of newspapers and editors for whom Mallet did freelance work. The TV programmes where he'd had a regular spot, pouring scorn on hapless contestants who wanted to make it big in the world of music. A few politicians. She recognised some local names of MLAs from Northern Ireland as well as some MPs from the Westminister Parliament.

Okay. No time to read through these folders now. The pressure of time made it too big a risk. Angel fished in her handbag for her memory stick. She had some of the major research on it for her interview tomorrow with Sir Marshall O'Neill, together with a file of her proposed questions. But there was still some memory left. Enough, she hoped.

Inserting the stick, she saw its menu box come up and moved the cursor to 'copy,' clicked once again and watched as the coloured line moved across the menu box, showing the information copying to her memory stick. 40%. 60%. 85%. Then a sudden rush and it was 100%. Everything in the email folders was now copied.

The other things that might prove useful were Mallet's Word documents. She repeated the process, copying all the Word files.

Then Angel removed the memory stick and tucked it safely back in her bag.

'Josh!' she called softly. 'I want to have a look at the filing cabinet too. Okay?'

Josh was about to answer when his phone began to play its ringtone. 'Just a second, sweetie,' he said. 'This is my boss. I'd better take it.'

He moved away to the other side of the apartment door onto the communal landing, to be out of earshot. Angel shrugged, and went over to the filing cabinet. A moment's work with her picklocks and she had the first drawer open. She was skimming through the alphabetically filed folders when she heard Josh come back in, and his voice, sounding apologetic.

'Sorry, honey. Gotta go. Something important's come up. I'll get you back to the *Sinclair* first. And we'll meet up tomorrow, before you leave, okay?'

'I'll stay on for a minute or two, Josh,' Angel said. 'This is too good a chance to miss. I can ring for a taxi when I'm ready.'

Josh frowned unhappily. 'I don't like it Angel. It's way too risky.'

But Angel was determined.

'You go on, darlin'. I'll be fine. I'm a big girl now, okay?'

Josh shrugged. He knew argument would only be a waste of time. 'Okay. I'll give you a ring later, make sure you're home safe.' A quick kiss, and he was gone, running swiftly down the staircase.

Angel went over and pulled the apartment door shut. For a moment she thought of attaching the chain which hung down with its hook on one side of the opening to its link on the other. But that would tell Mallet straightaway, if he came back before she'd finished, that there was someone in his apartment.

Instead, she closed the living room door, which they had found shut, as she went back in. No point in leaving the open door either, to warn Mallet that someone was inside. The thing would be to finish her search quickly, then wait outside until he arrived.

She continued to shuffle hastily through the open drawer in the filing cabinet. But now she had one ear alert for the sound of anyone approaching the apartment.

There seemed to be little of interest in the files in this drawer. Details of Mallet's insurance. (Car, Home and Contents, Life.) Mortgage statements for the apartment. Information from various estate agents – apparently Mallet was hoping to go upmarket sometime. Perhaps when he'd saved up enough backhanders, Angel thought cynically.

She thrust the folders back into place, pushed the drawer shut, and unlocked the next one.

Copies of articles Mallet had written. Plus the first twenty thousand words or so of a book of memoirs, for want of a better word. Glancing at it Angel saw that it was mostly based on his articles, and consisted of scurrilous attacks on well known personalities, plus similar anecdotes about the people he'd destroyed as a TV panellist. She put the papers back in disgust and was pushing the drawer shut when she heard a noise at the apartment door. A key in the lock.

It could only be the owner. Robbie Mallet. She hadn't been quick enough.

The last thing Angel wanted was to be found inside the flat. Spinning round on her toes, she raked the room for a hiding place. Her eye caught sight of a door in one wall. Sprinting across the room, she had it open in a flash and was inside pulling it shut by the time the footsteps in the hall told her Mallet was about to enter the room.

Her first assumption had been that the door led to one of the other rooms of the flat – bedroom, kitchen, bathroom – any one of these. Once there, and Mallet settled down in his living room, she'd hoped to slip quietly out of the flat and knock on the front door again as if arriving. Instead, she found to her surprise that she was in a large cupboard hung with its owner's clothes. Suits, an overcoat, piles of shirts on a shelf to one side. Mallet obviously used it as a substitute wardrobe. Probably his bedroom was small. It suited him to save space there by using this cup-board.

She took several deep breaths to calm herself down, then stood perfectly still, listening for clues. What was Mallet doing? Did he have any idea that someone had been inside his flat?

She'd had no time to check that everything was in order before diving for the cupboard. The computer looked untouched, she was pretty sure. She'd made certain of that before moving on. The filing cabinet? Yes, she'd shut both drawers. And the files inside were neatly replaced just as they had been. Okay, she hadn't had time to re-lock the second drawer. Problem? Only if Mallet wanted to use it now and started to open it. Even so, he might assume he'd forgotten to lock it himself.

It looked as if she was stuck in this cupboard for a long time. Until, in fact, Robbie Mallet took himself off into another room, and that might not be until he went to bed. Angel wondered if he was a night bird, an owl. Most media people were. Unless, she thought hopefully, he had an early call for the television studios in the morning? Well, all she could do was wait and see.

At the moment he seemed to be drifting aimlessly round the living room. She could hear him whistling tunelessly under his breath, moving about, his footsteps muffled by the thick pale green carpet. She heard the clink of glasses and bottles. He must be getting himself a drink, from the cabinet she'd noticed on the wall on the opposite side of the room from his desk. A nightcap, she hoped.

Then more faint footsteps and a louder noise, a creaking sound made by one of the leather chairs as he sat down. At the computer, she guessed. The noise made by the computer chair as it spun round under his weight was distinctive. She had done the same with her own similar chair often enough to recognise the manoeuvre. Settling down, getting into the most comfortable position.

Angel ran through in her mind everything she'd done on the computer. She knew she'd closed the lid. It should come up in the normal way when Mallet opened it. The icons along the left side of the screen.

Suddenly she gave a gasp of horror. Had she left Word open? Try as she would, she couldn't conjure up any memory of shutting it down. Mallet could hardly help noticing.

He was on his feet again, prowling round the room. Angel stood rigidly, waiting.

She could just make out the footsteps. He was walking softly, trying not to be heard, helped by the thick carpet. She strained her ears.

It sounded as if he was opening a drawer. She could hear a click which must surely be a key turning in a lock. One of the drawers in the filing cabinet? The lowest drawer, at a guess, since she could hear him breathing heavily from not much above floor level. Then he began to move round the room again. She could hear his quiet footsteps.

The footsteps came to a halt directly in front of the cupboard. She could hear the man's indrawn breath as he stood there. With, if she had interpreted the sounds she'd heard correctly, something in his hand. Something he'd taken out when he unlocked the bottom drawer of the filing cabinet.

Angel strained her ears. Directly in front of the cupboard door, there came a faint click. It might be anything. But Angel's guess was that what she heard was the noise of the safety catch on a gun being released.

Time for action.

Angel took a second to haul up the skirt of her creamy satin dress and tuck it securely round her waist. She couldn't afford to be hampered by it.

Waiting, allowing Mallet to have the first move, wasn't an option. She couldn't afford to give him an advantage.

Angel drew a deep breath and with one panther-like movement she thrust open the door hard in Mallet's face and sprang out of the cupboard.

Chapter Thirty-Five

Wednesday

The cupboard door hit Robbie Mallet with cruel force all along a direct line from forehead to chin.

As he staggered back, one of Angel's legs, the left, swung up stiffly and lashed out, kicking high up on the journalist's right arm. The hand holding the gun went numb. He had no time to aim. The gun spun from his hand and hurtled across the room. Angel spun round on her other foot and with the edge of her right hand chopped at Mallet's neck just below the ear.

Robbie Mallet gasped. His knees buckled under him. He slid downwards in a heap, landing on the floor in a strange, folded position, his head bowed forward onto his chest.

Angel didn't pause to watch. Before Mallet hit the ground one flying dive took her to where the gun lay against the foot of the filing cabinet. She seized it in one hand, and whirled round to point it at the man huddled in front of the cupboard.

'Okay, Mallet. Don't move.'

The man on the floor showed no sign of moving. For a second Angel wondered if he was dead. Then a weak groan told her that he had survived so far. Still pointing the gun straight at him, she moved nearer and stood beside him at a safe distance.

From there she could see his face. It was covered in blood, from the door, but she didn't think there was much wrong there that could be serious. The blow to the neck was the thing which might have caused fatal injury, if she had mistimed it. But in that case, Mallet wouldn't be groaning. He'd be dead.

'Look at me, Mallet!' she commanded.

With what was clearly a tremendous effort, Robbie Mallet looked up at her.

'Who are you? What are you doing in my apartment?'

'Angel Murphy.'

Mallet groaned again. The name clearly meant nothing to him.

'What do you want?' he managed to say. 'I haven't much money here. But you can have what I've got.'

Angel laughed. He was taking her for a burglar.

'I'm not interested in your money,' she said scornfully. 'I want to talk to you, Mallet. You have some information I need.'

Robbie Mallet groaned again. Then he managed to get out, 'If it's about that article I'm doing on 'Dog' Nichols ...'

Angel ignored the reference to the shadow politician whose nick-name was a constant plague to him.

'You hounded Fitz until he was desperate,' she said.

Mallet looked up in amazement. 'Me?'

'You.'

'Hey, there was a whole crowd of media guys there!' he protested. 'I just went along to see if there was a story, right?'

'Wrong. You orchestrated it, boy. A clever piece of work.'

Robbie Mallet's mouth twisted into a self-satisfied grin at the implied compliment, even as he continued to deny it. It was a cynical grin which was familiar to millions of viewers of *'Who's On Top?'* 'It wasn't me!'

' Oh, I suppose a big boy did it and ran away?' Angel suggested contemptuously. 'Grow up, Mallet! Even if I didn't know it already, your horrible little grin just now would have told me. But believe me, I've got lots of evidence. Your name is going to be mud shortly, Mallet. Lots of media people out there would be delighted to do a cut and smear on you, boy, after what you've done to others.'

Mallet tried to speak and found his mouth too dry.

'But I know it wasn't just you, Mallet, was it?' Angel continued remorselessly. 'You had someone behind you, right? The big boss man. Someone who paid you to spike Fitz's whiskey. That's the info I want from you, Mallet.' She came closer and glared into Mallet's pale, bloody face. 'Tell me now – or you'll regret it. Or maybe you won't be around to regret it!'

Angel prodded the man's forehead with the gun which she still held firmly in her right hand, and pulled his face up by the hair to stare directly into his eyes.

'I – I can't – I – he'll kill me –'

'But he isn't here, Mallet. And I am. Why do you think I'm pointing this gun at you, creep?'

Mallet's face grew even paler. He stared into Angel's eyes in horror and read there something which frightened him even more.

Then, groaning loudly, his face a mask of terror, he slipped further down and lay stretched flat on the floor.

For a moment Angel was afraid he was dead. Not only would she have been reluctant to scare the man to death, in spite of her threats, but it would have been a disastrous outcome for every other reason. She needed Robbie Mallet alive and talking if she was to discover the name of his big boss. A man she had already been sure existed. And now Mallet's reaction to her questions had made her even surer.

He'd passed out. But he was still breathing. Angel clicked the safety catch back on and tucked the gun into her gold belt, tightening the belt a notch to hold the weapon securely, and went out into the hall. She tried the next door. Yes, it was the kitchen.

She grabbed a glass from one of the wall cupboards, took it over to the sink, and ran the cold tap for a while. When she was sure the water would be cold enough, she filled the glass and returned with it to the front room. Before she went she tried a couple of drawers until she found the one with the clean drying cloths, and took one with her.

Robbie Mallet was still lying where she'd left him, but she was glad to see that a little colour was creeping back into his face.

Kneeling down beside him, Angel propped his head against her knee. 'Wakey, wakey, Mister Mallet. Try this.'

She dipped one corner of the cloth into the glass and flipped water over Mallet's eyes and cheeks. Spluttering, Mallet opened his mouth to protest, and Angel tipped the glass against his lips.

'Drink up, boyo!'

Robbie Mallet choked and coughed, but must have swallowed some of the water. He pulled himself impatiently away from Angel's support and made an effort to sit up.

'Right!' said Angel briskly. 'Now, where were we? Oh, yes. You were going to give me the name of this big boss of yours, right, Mallet?'

'No way!' The look of sheer terror on the journalist's face was enough to tell Angel that this wasn't going to be easy.

'Yeah, you are.'

'I can't! You don't know! He's got connections. He'd kill me – literally, I mean! And he might do a lot more first – or his friends would!'

Angel shrugged. 'Him then, or me now, big boy. But if it's him, you've got a bit of time to get out of the country, see? At least you have a chance, that way.'

'No – no!' Mallet was almost screaming in despair. 'Please! Listen to me! I can't tell you!'

Angel set the glass and the drying cloth down beside her. Then she took the gun carefully out of her belt and pointed it in Mallet's face. She looked hard at him and deliberately clicked the safety catch off again.

'Don't! Don't!' Mallet moaned. But he still showed no sign of giving her the information she needed.

'How will your boss know it was you who gave me his name?' Angel asked reasonably. 'I won't tell him if you don't. All I want from you is the info. I'm not expecting you to testify, stupid.'

Mallet's narrow eyes wavered. For the first time, Angel saw, he was considering speaking.

'Give me time! Let me think about it – time to make some arrangements in case he finds out.'

'No reason why he should find out. You're the only one who could tell him.'

Robbie Mallet looked back at her. She could see the thoughts going round and round in his head.

It was just at that moment that Angel's phone rang.

She couldn't help being slightly relieved, since she intended to stop short of actually carrying out her threat.

'Don't move!' she commanded as she stood up and moved a couple of steps away from the man sitting on the floor. 'I need to answer this. But I can pull this trigger long before you can even get to your feet. And I won't be letting this call distract me, don't worry.'

She kept the gun pointed steadily between Mallet's eyes, fished out her mobile with her left hand and clicked the green button with her thumb.

'Angel?' said Josh's voice. 'Where are you, honey? Not at the *Sinclair*, because that's where I am.'

'Okay, Josh. Stay put and I'll be there as soon as I can get a taxi.'

She rang off. 'Listen carefully, Mallet. I need that name. I'm going to give you until tomorrow at seven p.m. to make up your mind. Come to my hotel. The *Sinclair*. Ask for me at the desk. Angel Murphy. And, Mallet, I have 'connections' too, so I have. And one of them'll be there with me. So don't think you can plan any funny business, boy. Be there, if you want to keep out of serious trouble. Right?'

'Right.' Mallet's lips were trembling. Angel didn't know if he had decided to speak or not, but she was hopeful.

'And if you don't turn up, Mallet – just remember that we know where you live.' Angel kept a straight face, although inwardly she was longing to grin. She'd wanted to say that to someone for years.

But Mallet didn't see the joke. His lips were still quivering. 'I'll be there!' he promised.

'Good.' Angel left it at that, and began to thumb in the number of the taxi service she'd entered in her list of contacts earlier. She gave them Mallet's address, and finished her request by saying, 'As soon as possible!'

Then, still pointing the gun at Mallet, she backed out of the room into the hall of the apartment and hurried down the stairs, to wait for the taxi which would carry her back to the *Sinclair*, and to Josh Smith.

She didn't notice the silent figure in black standing hidden out of sight in the porch of one of the houses just across the street from Robbie Mallet's building.

Chapter Thirty-Six

<u>**Wednesday**</u>

Pete had been waiting for a call from Mar for some time.

'Must be some problem, d'ye think, Zig?' he said. His twin brother Ziggy shrugged. They were leaning against the bar in *The Lion*, where they'd called in for a brief snack and were now putting in time with a pint of Guinness apiece.

'Maybe Mar and Nat just got side-tracked, Pete.'

'What?'

'Well, you could see Mar fancies him, right?'

'But I thought this guy Nat was supposed to be nuts about Angel Murphy?'

'Right. But she's not giving him much encouragement, is she? Tied up with some American, I hear.'

'So you think –? Naw.' Pete might not have as much insight into how people felt or were likely to behave as Ziggy, but one thing he was sure of. 'Both these guys want to help find out who did this stuff to Fitz. They wouldn't mess around instead of getting on with it.' Pete spoke decisively.

Ziggy shrugged again. 'You could be right. I'm wondering if we should give Tommy a ring, tell him it doesn't look like we'll be round with that bottle tonight?'

Pete's phone buzzed.

'Hang on,' he said, and headed outside, closely followed by Ziggy.

'Message from Mar. Just says, "Ring me." '

Pete got the number, heard Mar's voice, and spoke briefly into his mobile. Then he turned to Ziggy.

'The whiskey's gone.'

'What, someone pinched it?'

'Maybe. Or maybe the police collected it.'

Ziggy whistled. 'Could be. They might be more on the ball than we thought.'

'But, mind you, Mar says they found a kid in the woods. The kid Angel was talking about. And he told them someone else was prowling round the cottage earlier. He thinks they were inside and then came out of the back door. So that doesn't sound like the cops, right?' Pete was on his way back to retrieve his unfinished drink as he spoke.

'Wait, man – gotta give Tommy a bell.'

'Fair enough. You do it – I'll go back and keep an eye on the drinks. Dunno why you came after me and left them!'

The practically minded Pete hurried back inside, leaving his twin to ring the chemist friend who had been lined up to analyse the bottle of Bushmills Whiskey when Nat and Mar had retrieved it from the cottage. If the bottle had disappeared, there was no point in keeping Tommy hanging around any longer.

Nat and Mar took Will to the A&E at Antrim Hospital. It seemed the nearest.

The boy's ankle, when at last a doctor was free to examine it and arrange an x-ray, turned out to be sprained rather than broken. When it had been strapped up firmly and Will had been equipped with a crutch and told to come back in six weeks, one problem remained.

What were they going to do with him now?

According to Will, his mother was away and wouldn't be back until the end of the week. And his father was still in hospital, unlikely to be home for another few days. Indeed, still unconscious, as far as Will knew.

'I'd take him if I had anywhere to put him up,' Nat murmured to Mar, out of earshot of the boy, while he was off having the ankle x-rayed. 'But since I'm staying in a hotel while I'm over here, that isn't really on.'

'Maybe they'll keep him in overnight?' Mar suggested.

'No chance. To be kept in these days, you have to be next door to dying, and even then they prefer you to go home to do it.'

Mar sighed. She could see what was coming. 'Okay,' she said before Nat could suggest it. 'He can come home with me. I'll sort something out for him. He can have my room and I'll have the sofa.'

'No need to be a martyr.' Nat spoke more sharply than he intended.

'Oh, don't worry. It's actually a very nice sofa bed. Pulls out into a very comfortable single. I got it for the rare times when I have a girl friend stay over.'

'And if it's a boy friend, he gets to share your room, right?'

'How did you guess?'

'Well, the kid doesn't come into either category, but I don't see why he shouldn't have the sofa bed if it's as comfortable as that.'

'Fair enough. And then my room would be available if anyone else felt like staying the night?' Mar grinned sexily.

But Nat wasn't ready to talk about that sort of thing just now. He was relieved to see Will Nelson being wheeled back from his x-ray just at that moment.

'Now I have to wait again until the doctor's free to give me the results,' Will announced with a satisfied smile.

'Okay. So, Mar and I were just saying you can stay overnight with her if they don't want to keep you in. But we'll need to get hold of your Mum tomorrow, right.'

'Hey, cool!' Will grinned. He had been excited already to discover that Mar was one of the band members of *Raving*. The guys at school would be wild jealous, he'd told them. To actually stay overnight in a band member's apartment was the crowning touch.

So it was a very cheerful Will who hobbled out of Nat's car and made his way up to Mar's apartment, crutch and all.

'So, I'll say goodnight, Mar –' Nat began, but was interrupted.

'Not yet, you won't, mister. You come right in here and help me get this boy settled, see?'

Nat supposed that was fair enough. He set to work helping Mar to get the sofa bed arranged, and helped Will into Mar's bathroom while she fetched a spare duvet and pillow, and fished out an extra large T-shirt which she never used these days for Will to sleep in.

'And now, before you go,' she said eventually, 'wasn't there something about getting this boy's story in full detail, once we'd got his ankle seen to?'

'Hey, right! I nearly forgot.' Nat realised he'd been stupid. 'Okay, Will. Get yourself settled into bed. You'd better make sure the crutch is within easy reach, right? And then you can tell us everything you remember about this guy you saw, and what he was doing.'

'Anyone for coffee?' Mar interrupted brightly.

'Yeah, thanks,' said two voices.

'Not you, Will. It'll keep you awake all night. You can have some juice.'

Mar was amazingly quick with the juice and coffee. She didn't want to miss anything.

'Now, Will,' Nat began, as he and Mar pulled up comfortable chairs as near as possible to Will's bed. 'What can you remember?'

And Will, wrinkling his forehead in an effort to think hard and leave nothing out, told them everything he could.

Chapter Thirty-Seven

Wednesday night/Thursday morning

Seri felt as if she had been living in the hospital for days now. Except for the two meetings, on Monday night and then again on Tuesday, she hadn't left it. Fitz lay, white faced, eyes closed, unable to communicate. Seri was almost in despair. It was only the knowledge that people were praying that kept her from giving up hope.

On the Wednesday night she took a brief time out to go down to the canteen and drink another of the endless cups of coffee and crumble another sandwich without really eating it.

When she came back to the room where Fitz lay, Nurse Eileen was on night duty, and recognised Seri at once. She hurried forward to meet Seri and took both her hands in hers.

'Serena, you can go in and sit with him now, if you like, for a while. And –' she hesitated, then beamed. Seri saw that she was looking much happier. 'Now, I don't want to raise your hopes for nothing, but I think it's very possible – well, let's just say, it might be – that your boy friend is out of his coma now. He's still sleeping, and he'll go on sleeping for a good long while now, but I think it's just a natural sleep. Now, don't be telling anyone I said so! It's not official until the doctor says it is!'

'Oh, Nurse!'

Seri burst into tears of joy.

'Does that mean he's going to get better?'

'Ach, away now, it's not for me to be telling you that! That's the doctor's job. He's the one that knows.'

Then she saw Seri's face fall, and hurried into comforting speech. 'Mind you, I've never seen a patient recover so quickly, and if he doesn't get completely better very soon I'll – I'll – I'll burst my knicker elastic!'

Seri couldn't help laughing. She seized Nurse Eileen in her arms and gave her a warm hug. 'You're a darling! And please call me Seri – all my friends call me that, and I couldn't have a better friend than you.'

Nurse Eileen's face went very red. 'And I'm usually called Lena!' she confided.

'Lena! Thank you so much for everything!'

'Ach, don't be thinking we're out of the woods yet,' Lena said anxiously. 'Heavens, I'll get a quare tellin' off if they find out I've told you this! Now, away you in there and sit with your boy and see if he's ready to wake up and speak to you!'

Seri rushed on into Fitz's room. He was lying in the bed, just as before. But as she sat and took his hand, her eyes, searching his face carefully, told her that there was a definite change. Fitz was no longer the white, ghost-like figure of the last three days. She was almost sure she could see some colour in his cheeks, and he looked peaceful rather than worn out.

'Thank you, Lord,' Seri said. Then she settled down to wait for Fitz to wake up.

Hours later, since he was still sleeping, she crept outdoors to message her friends on her mobile, to give them the wonderful news.

Chapter Thirty-Eight

Thursday

Angel's interview with Sir Marshall O'Neill on the following day went without a hitch. She turned up at the studio lent for the purpose by BBC London in plenty of time. The camera men and the floor manager were there setting up, and Angel found them both friendly and helpful.

The studio was a wide room with two comfortable chairs and a coffee table with a decanter of water and two glasses arranged on it at one end of the available space. The cameras, three of them, were positioned to take shots from the front and the two sides, and they could move about within their own space to give plenty of variety, as well as zoom in for close-ups.

Angel and the camera crew discussed the sort of shots she particularly wanted with the Floor manager. Then it was time to collect Sir Marshall O'Neill from reception.

Sir Marty, as everyone called him, was a tall, broad man with a high coloured complexion and short, bristly fair hair with a touch of red to it. His eyes were the most striking thing about him. They were very blue and piercing, and his eyelashes were thick and long. Angel thought it was a pity he wasn't a girl, for in that case they could have been dyed, or coloured with mascara, to look black, and the eyes would have been even more amazing. But they would do as they were, she decided.

She had a preliminary chat with the great man. 'Call me Marty,' he suggested to her more formal beginning. 'Everyone does. It makes me feel weird to be called by this title all the time.' So Angel did.

As soon as the floor manager was ready for them, they went straight ahead with the interview.

'You were born and brought up in Belfast, Marty,' was Angel's first question after the introduction, 'so whereabouts was that? And what are your first memories of the place?'

'I was born in East Belfast,' said Sir Marty easily. 'Just off the Raven-hill Road. My earliest memories are of playing footer (football) with my mates in the street, or in the Ormeau Park, and being chased by the Parkie (the park keeper, right?). We were destroying the grass, he said.

'Nowadays there are proper football pitches for the kids, but when I was a youngster we played where we could. And mind you, it was dangerous enough playing in the street. The traffic was increasing all the time. By the time I'd reached my teens, it just wasn't possible any more. A mate of mine was knocked down and had his leg broken – after that we kept to the park.'

The interview went on easily, with the actor telling stories of his first performances in school plays and the bit parts on TV that had given him his start. He was funny, clever, and charming, and he managed to plug his forthcoming appearance as Macbeth in the Opera House without seeming self-centred. Angel felt that she had only to feed him the cues. Then he did the rest.

At the end, she said, 'Sir Marshall, I'd really like to ask you a favour. Could you possibly give us an excerpt from the play? The tomorrow and tomorrow speech, for preference – but I'll leave it up to you.'

'No problem, Angel my dear. Give me a moment to get myself together.'

Sir Marty closed his eyes and was very obviously concentrating. Then he opened his eyes and spoke. The great actor's voice, full and sonorous, rolled round the studio in one of the most moving speeches Shakespeare ever wrote,

'Tomorrow, and tomorrow and tomorrow
Creeps in this petty pace from day to day,
To the last syllable of recorded time;
And all our yesterdays have lighted fools
The way to dusty death...'
Angel caught her breath.

The actor ceased, his voice dropping on the final words,

'... it is a tale
Told by an idiot, full of sound and fury,
Signifying – '

he paused, and the silence in the studio was palpable –

'nothing.'

Angel could not speak for a moment. Then she said simply, 'Thank you.' She left another brief gap, then said, 'Sir Marshall O'Neill, one of Belfast's greatest sons.'

The cameraman deputed to do so was, she knew, taking close-ups. Others were taking further off views of Angel and Sir Marty chatting again.

Their words would not be audible. Instead, the closing music would override them.

The footage would be flown back to the BBC studios in Belfast to be edited, with the inclusion where appropriate of shots of the places referred to, clips from Sir Marty's previous roles, and whatever else the director might consider appropriate. Not Angel's responsibility, she reflected thankfully. But she was certain it would make a first class programme.

'Come and have a coffee with me, Angel,' invited Sir Marty when Angel had finished thanking him, thanking the studio staff, and checking that the footage would be sent to the right person. 'I've enjoyed talking to you about Belfast – it would be nice to talk some more.' He glanced at his watch. 'I have to be elsewhere in an hour or so. But that gives us half-an-hour coffee time, if you're free yourself?'

'Lovely! Thanks, Marty.'

They went to the BBC canteen, convenient and familiar to them both, and sat at a corner table with their coffee, chatting in a happy, relaxed, post interview mood.

'I hear bad news about Frankie Fitzgerald – Fitz,' said Sir Marty presently. 'Know anything about it, Angel? What's the latest? Is he going to be okay?'

Angel found herself pouring out the whole story into Sir Marty's sympathetic ears.

'We're all quite sure Fitz didn't take stuff himself,' she finished up, 'and the medical info confirms that. It was the sort of prescription drug Fitz just wouldn't have had, even if he'd been back on the hard stuff – which he wasn't. But we need to find out more about how it got into his drink – or where else it was. Mixed into his coffee, even?'

'I think you're right – Fitz wouldn't have had anything like that,' Sir Marty said. 'I don't know him personally, but I follow your logic. It makes sense.'

'Thanks for the encouragement,' Angel smiled.

'I don't think I can do much to help you,' Sir Marty went on, thoughtfully stirring the remains of his coffee. 'I won't be over there for a couple of weeks, and then I'll be up to my eyebrows in rehearsals and performances.'

'Yeah, of course. I didn't expect you to help, Marty. Just answering your question – at rather too much length.'

'No, no. I've been really interested. But what I was thinking is, I know someone who's a good friend of Fitz. Speaks very highly of him. And has a lot of influence. I guess he'd be a great help – and he'd love to, I'm sure. Dinger Bell. The MLA. You should get in touch with him and tell him what you've told me.'

'Of course!' Angel could have kicked herself. Why hadn't she thought of that? Richard Bell, affectionately known as 'Dinger' Bell. The Member of the Legislative Assembly whose card she'd seen in the cottage when she'd searched it.

'Great idea, Marty!' she exclaimed enthusiastically.

'Here, I'll write a message on one of my cards and you can use it as an introduction, if you like.' Sir Marty took a card out of his wallet and scribbled on the back.

'Hi, Dinger. Angel Murphy needs your help re Fitz. I'm sure you'll be delighted! Marty.'

He thrust the card at Angel, and hurriedly swallowed his last mouthful of coffee, brushing aside her fervent thanks.

'Gotta run now. Been great meeting you, Angel. Looking forward to seeing the interview when it gets broadcast. Don't bother to take me down – I really need to rush. Bye bye!'

He dived across the room and was gone by the time Angel had got to her feet. She stowed the card carefully away in her inside pocket. What a great idea of Marty's! As soon as she got home, she'd get straight down to it.

Chapter Thirty-Nine

<u>Thursday</u>

Angel had told Robbie Mallet to come to her hotel, the *Sinclair*, at seven o'clock. That meant that when she finished at the BBC, which only took a couple of hours longer, she had the late afternoon in front of her to spend with Josh Smith.

She would have liked to meet up first with John Branagh, her friend Mary's brother, who'd helped her to get her start at BBC Northern Ireland. But Mary had told her that John would be on location training, out of the studio, for the two days she was in London, so that wasn't going to happen. Pity.

Angel hurried back to her hotel room, and changed out of her working clothes – tailored suit in bright red over a creamy blouse, matching red high heeled shoes – into more casual gear – jeans, a pale green T-shirt, and trainers. Then she texted Josh on his mobile, *'R U up 4 a picnic?'*

'U bet!' Josh texted back.

'Hyde Park – by the Serpentine?'

'See U there pronto!'

So Angel took the lift down to the hotel's shopping area, and called in at their delicatessen. She bought all the nicest things she could see – melon slices, grapes, chicken and roast beef, olives, potato salad, mixed salad – and then from other shops she collected paper plates, knives and forks, spoons and cups, and a bottle of wine. She packed them all into a hamper supplied by the hotel, and then took a taxi to Hyde Park and walked across the grass to the river.

The sun was shining, the beds were full of spring flowers, white and yellow daffodils, multi coloured primulas in reds and blues and whites and yellows, beds of early tulips in reds and pinks and one of light purple. Angel sang as she moved lightly through the flowers and trees, swinging her hamper as she went. Her mobile buzzed. Another text message. Josh.

'I'm beside the river, where are you?'

'Just coming. Wave so I can see you.'

A small figure in the distance waved wildly. Angel broke into a run and saw as she drew nearer that Josh was running too. As they reached each other Angel dropped the hamper at her feet and was gathered happily into Josh's arms.

'Wow,' Josh said softly when their kiss came to a reluctant end.

Angel picked up the hamper. 'Let's find somewhere to sit,' she suggested.

Josh pointed to a nearby chestnut tree, its widespread branches already lit with bright green leaves and newly blossoming candles. 'That looks perfect,' he said.

Lifting the hamper and carrying it easily by the strap with one hand, he took Angel by his free hand and led her across to the tree.

They settled down on the daisy sprinkled grass, and Angel unpacked the hamper, first of all spreading out the blue and white checked cloth which came with the rest, and then taking out the various items and placing them carefully one by one on the cloth.

'Melon – for starters, if you like. Then chicken or beef with the olives and the salads. And finishing with grapes.'

'No. First of all,' corrected Josh, 'a glass of wine.' He lifted the bottle from the hamper, unscrewed the top, and poured some into one of the paper cups, which he handed to Angel. Then he poured another for himself, screwed the top back on the bottle before setting it down, and lifted his cup to her. 'To the brightest star in the universe.'

'And the cleverest cop,' Angel murmured in return.

When they were almost done with the beef and chicken course, Josh popped a grape into Angel's mouth, and said, 'So how did it go this morning?'

He had already heard everything about the previous evening after he'd left Mallet's flat. When Angel had got back to her hotel on the night before to find him waiting there, she'd poured it all out.

'Fine. The guy's unbelievable. But, Josh, we had a coffee afterwards, and he came up with a really useful idea.'

'Yeah?'

'Yeah. He says he knows the MLA, Richard Bell – you know, Dinger Bell – and he's sure Dinger would help us, because he thinks a lot of Fitz.'

'Leaving aside that I've never heard of this guy, Angel – I'm guessing he's a big name in Belfast, right? – what exactly could he do that you and the gang aren't doing already?'

'Oh, he's a big name all right, Josh. Not just in Belfast. But I suppose you've got a point. What could he actually do? I guess I was thinking of getting him to pull some strings for us, get the police moving –'

'But I thought you didn't want the cops brought into it? I thought you wanted to sort it all out yourselves first?'

'Do you know how annoying it is, Josh Smith, to be always right?' Angel asked severely. Then she laughed. 'Hey, let's forget it for now! We have the rest of the day before us!'

'Until seven o'clock!' Josh reminded her, and dodged away grinning as Angel pretended to bounce the empty wine bottle off his head. 'So what would you like to do now?'

'Let's stay here for a while. It's so lovely.'

'Okay.' Josh put his arms round her and drew him down beside him on the fresh, sweet grass, his lips finding hers again.

They were interrupted by Angel's ring tone.

'It's Mar,' she said, glancing at the sender ID. 'I'd better take it.'

Josh rolled over onto his front, propped himself on his elbows and plucked a piece of grass to chew as he listened resignedly to Angel's end of the conversation.

'Angel, thought you should know,' Mar began. 'Nat and I didn't take the bottle of Bushmills to the twins' chemist friend.'

'That's a relief,' Josh heard Angel say briskly. 'It wasn't the greatest idea, actually. If you'd taken it, the court would never have accepted it as evidence. Did you guys work that out yourselves?'

'No, Angel, listen! Someone else had been into the cottage and taken the bottle before we got there!'

'No! Wow!'

'And we found Billy Nelson's kid, Will, outside, and he told us he'd seen someone coming out.'

'Okay.'

Mar rushed on, pouring out the whole story. 'So then,' she finished, 'we got the details from the kid. He thinks the guy he saw coming from the cottage was the one who put his Dad in hospital. He thinks he'd recognise him again.'

'But it must have been far too dark at the cottage to recognise anyone.'

'Yeah, but he says he saw his face in the moonlight. And he says anyway he was the same shape and size as the guy who beat up Billy.'

'Mar, Will told me he didn't see that guy – just heard the voices.'

'Well, he's changed his story now. Says he wasn't sure at first how much he should tell you – how far he could trust you. And afterwards, when he believed you were on his side, he didn't like to let on he'd sorta lied.'

'Okay, I can buy that,' Angel said slowly. 'So he did see the guy at his Dad's flat?'

'So he says, now. And he thinks when his Dad called him Hammerhead, it must have been a nickname for Robbie Mallet. Mallet – hammer, get it?' Mar spelt it out unnecessarily.

'Yeah, yeah, I get it. But, listen, Mar, the kid's got it all wrong. Maybe it was Mallet who beat up Billy. But it can't have been the same man at the cottage. This was last night, you say? Around eight or nine?'

'Around that. Maybe a bit later.'

'So, Mallet has an eyewitness who puts him in London too soon after that for it to be possible. Even Superman could hardly have made it from the wilds of Country Antrim to London in an hour or so.'

'So maybe this eyewitness is lying?'

'I don't think so. It was me, Mar!'

There was a moment's silence.

Then came Mar's voice. 'That's messed it up rightly, girl.'

'It just means Will was wrong when he thought it was Mallet – if it was the same guy both times. Hammerhead could mean something else. Or else it was Mallet at Billy Nelson's apartment, and someone else at the cottage. I think that's probably the way of it. And, as we've thought all along, that means there's someone else involved in all this.'

'Right,' agreed Mar. 'But who?'

'That's what I'm hoping to find out tonight,' Angel said grimly. 'I'm seeing Mallet at seven. And I think he's going to come across with the name.'

Chapter Forty

Thursday

That same day, early in the afternoon, Nat and Mar had agreed to take Will Nelson to the hospital where his Dad, Billy, was still being kept in until he was considered fit enough to go home after his concussion.

Since Will was only twelve, Mar thought it wouldn't be good to let him go through the experience of seeing his Dad in such a state on his own. Especially with his damaged leg. It would be pretty hard for him to get around alone. The hospital might not allow them to go with Will to his Dad's bedside, but at least they could be there when Will was going in and when he came out again. Maybe they could offer him some comfort.

'And as well,' Nat observed while Will was in the bathroom just before the visit, 'it would be good to be on the spot and hear if Billy has anything useful to tell Will. Like, did he know the guy who beat him up? And who was he?'

'And there was something about 'Christine' or some name like that, wasn't there?' Mar added thoughtfully. 'Might be really helpful if Billy knows stuff he can explain about the whole thing.'

Then Will came hobbling out of the bathroom and it was time to go.

Billy Nelson was in the Antrim Area Hospital, the nearest one to his flat. Nat found a space to park not too far from the entrance, and he and Mar helped Will to get out and get propped up on his crutches.

'Do you know which ward?' Mar asked.

'Yeah, they told me when I rang. But I'm to check at reception in case he's been moved.'

So they went inside the building, waited for someone to appear at the reception desk, and asked for Billy Nelson. Then they followed the instructions and went up in the lift.

'He'll be fine, Will,' Nat said gently, noticing the worry on the boy's young face. 'Take it easy.'

'Yeah.'

'We'll wait for you outside.'

'And, Will, don't if you think he's not up to it, but if you could ask a few questions – like, who was it, and what about Christine, see? – it might help catch the guy and get him stopped.' Mar didn't want to upset Will, but it seemed silly for him not to take the opportunity of asking, if Billy was well enough to answer.

'I know. I'd love to help catch that scumbag, Mar.' Will spoke grimly. 'If Dad can answer questions, don't worry, I'll ask everything I can.'

'Good.' Mar smiled encouragingly. 'Okay, can you manage? Away you go, then.'

They watched Will swing rapidly off into the ward on his crutches, and retired to sit on the places provided for waiting.

Nat took a book out of his pocket and occupied himself by reading.

For Mar, the time dragged. She amused herself at first by studying Nat's beautiful profile, his dark hair curling down over his ear, his firm chin. Then Nat, looking up for a moment as he turned a page, caught her eye and grinned. Mar's cheeks burned and she looked away.

It seemed forever before Will appeared again out of the ward.

'Hi, guys. Dad wants to say thanks. The nurse says you can come in for five minutes, if you want to.'

They stood up and followed Will into the ward and over to where Billy Nelson, pale and bandaged, was grinning at them in welcome.

'This is Nat and this is Mar,' Will said.

'Hi. Just wanna say thanks, guys, for looking after this wee pest and taking him to the doctor and all.'

'No problem,' Mar muttered.

'Will says you and Angel Murphy are trying to find out what's been going on. Fitz. And Cindy.' Billy's face twisted when he mentioned the murdered reporter Cindy Baron. 'And me, as well.'

'We thought you probably know some useful stuff,' Nat said.

'Not a lot.' Billy was clearly growing tired. His eyes half closed, then opened again with what seemed an effort. 'The guy had a stocking over his head and face. I thought it might be Robbie Mallet, but when I called him by his nickname – Hammerhead – all the media crowd call him that – his name, see, and him being, like, a right snake – well, he didn't seem to know what I meant.'

'Did the guy say why he'd come, Billy? Why he beat you up? What he wanted from you?'

'It was something about me knowing Cindy was meeting Mallet that evening. About keeping quiet, not letting on to the cops or anyone. I think. And there was something about Kirstin – the singer, right? At least I think that was what he said. I wasn't hearing too clearly by then, see?' Billy grinned wryly.

'Kirstin – not Christine, then.' Nat was about to ask another question when he was interrupted by the nurse bustling over.

'Okay, say your goodbyes, you two. Will can stay for a minute longer – but that's all.' She ushered them firmly out of the ward, leaving Will an extra minute alone with his Dad.

But Nat and Mar had no sooner regained their seats in the waiting area when they saw Will following them out, the nurse behind him.

'Enough's enough,' they heard her saying. 'I'm sure it did your father good to see you, but we don't want him getting over tired, now do we?'

Will smiled and nodded politely. He limped over to the others.

'So, no time to ask anything more,' he announced briefly.

'No problem.' Mar smiled at him.

'Hey, I'm starving now!' Will said.

'Me, too,' agreed Nat. 'Let's go somewhere and eat. And think about what Billy told us.'

Chapter Forty-One

Thursday

'So, who's this Kirstin, then?' Nat asked, when they were sitting round a table in the nearest fast food café with burgers and chips in front of them.

'You must be joking!' Will said through a mouthful of burger. 'Kirstin? You must have heard of Kirstin!'

Only his good manners, Mar thought, prevented him from asking which planet Nat had been living on.

'Kirstin is a pop singer,' Mar explained to the puzzled artist. 'She's got really popular, recently. One of *Raving*'s chief rivals, you might say.'

'And what's she got to do with Robbie Mallet?'

'Oh, right, Mallet thinks she's great. It was because Mallet backed her when she was on his show '*Who's On Top?*' that Kirstin got her first break. He said she was the only person he'd ever seen on the show who shouldn't be taking singing lessons in a Kindergarten, or something pleasant like that. Then he actually said some positive stuff about her and gave her a ten.

Everyone else was so impressed that they thought she must have something, so they all voted her up too. She charged on through the semis and the final, and won. Then she got signed up by one of the big labels – *Marvel Records*, I think it was. Her first CD with them should be out soon.'

'Oh.' Nat said nothing for a moment. 'I'm just wondering,' he said presently, 'how this ties up with the attack Mallet masterminded on Fitz. It's the first thing we've come across that suggests any sort of motive, right?'

'Huh?' Will stared at him.

'Well, think about it,' Nat said. 'If this Kirstin is someone Mallet is trying to push for whatever reason, maybe he thinks it would help to knock *Raving* out of the picture.'

'Hey, he can hardly go round attacking every band that might be a rival of Kirstin!' Mar protested.

'I guess not. So, is there anything coming up that might be special? Some deal or some award where both Kirstin and Fitz are the frontrunners?'

Mar frowned, thinking hard. But it was Will who suddenly came up with an idea. 'What about the *New Music Awards*? I heard both Kirstin and *Raving* were nominated for that?'

'Yeah, that's right,' Mar nodded. 'They're way out ahead of the competition. If Fitz's reputation was damaged badly – even more if he was killed – Kirstin would walk it. It would put her right on top.'

'*New Music Awards?*' Nat asked.

'Oh, it's a thing *New Music* set up,' Mar explained. 'This is its first year. *New Music* is a music magazine – the music magazine, I should say. They're offering a gigantic prize and the opportunity to be the lead group in some fabulous American tour they're organising, and to do the soundtrack for the new film about John Lennon and I don't know what all else.

'Amazing package! *Raving* would certainly love to win it, and I suppose Kirstin would too. It's sorta funny that the two acts in the lead for it are both from here! People have been making lots of jokes about that.'

'Kirstin's from Belfast?'

This time, Will couldn't prevent himself from starting to ask, 'Hey, what planet are you living on?' but Mar cut in firmly before he could get it out properly.

'But what's in it for Robbie Mallet? Is she his girlfriend or what? I never heard that!'

'Hardly. She's way too young for him,' scoffed Will. 'He must be as old as my Dad!'

Mar and Nat exchanged glances over Will's head, and decided not to explain to this boy, who clearly still retained some of his innocence, that age had very little to do with what Kirstin might do, if she was that type of person. They both knew that if Kirstin expected to get something out of it, she might well be sleeping with Mallet, who in any case was still somewhere in his thirties. But then, so was Will's Dad, Billy Nelson.

'Well, leaving that aside,' said Nat briskly, 'we know Mallet often wrote scurrilous attacks on people in return for money – so that's most likely what was in it for him this time too.'

'Fair enough,' Mar agreed.

'But would Kirstin be paying him herself?'

'No way!' protested Will. 'She's not like that!'

'Oh, you're a fan, are you?' teased Mar.

'Leave it out! I sorta like her, okay?'

Mar hastily changed the subject. 'Kirstin wouldn't have the money to pay Mallet, I'm pretty sure. She has her record deal, but she can't be making all that much in hard cash just yet. The twins found out that Mallet was working for someone else, didn't they? His boss, right? So that's the guy with the money, I guess.'

'And we still don't know who he is.' Nat frowned. 'But, hey, at least we know now – or think, anyway – that he has some connection with Kirstin. If we work on that, we should be able to track him down.'

'Right,' agreed Mar. 'And we should give Angel this new info as soon as possible. She's coming home first thing tomorrow. We should arrange to get together, pool our results and plan out our tactics.'

Nat smiled admiringly. 'Wow, Mar, didn't know you were a tactician!'

Mar flushed. Was Nat laughing at her?

'I think that sounds good, Mar!' Will said loyally.

'Yeah.' Nat realised that he'd hurt Mar without intending to. 'It sounds dead on, Mar,' he said hastily. 'We'll do just that.'

Mar smiled at him.

'We need to find out as much as we can about Kirstin,' she suggested. 'Who her family are, what boyfriends she's had, all that stuff. See if we can come up with anyone who'd care enough about her career to wreck Fitz just to give Kirstin a push.'

'Her agent?' Nat asked.

'Yeah – but as far as I know, she didn't have an agent before she went on *'Who's On Top?'* and I don't think she has one yet. *Marvel Records* probably offered to act as her agent when they signed her. Clever, or what?'

'You mean they can do what they want if she doesn't have someone else representing her? Typical businessmen!' Nat looked disgusted.

'It happens.' Mar shrugged philosophically and swallowed the last mouthful of her coffee.

'Tell you what,' she added, 'I'm going to start ringing the rest of the guys now. The sooner we all get down to some research on Kirstin, the better. I'll try Angel first.'

But Angel's phone was unattainable. She had switched it off after Mar's earlier call had interrupted her picnic with Josh and still hadn't thought of switching it back on.

'I'm going to have to get to the Gallery now, Mar,' Nat said. 'The opening of my exhibition is only a few hours away.' He hesitated. 'I don't suppose you'd like to come with me? Then maybe we could go for a meal somewhere afterwards?'

'Love to!' Mar was delighted. 'But you'll have to drop me home first. I'll need to dress up for a special affair like this! And as for you, young Will, you can stay on at my place for another night, but after that, if your Da isn't home, or even your Mum, I'm going to drop you in at the Salvation Army!'

Later, when she had changed and was waiting for Nat to pick her up, Mar tried ringing Angel one more time. But Angel's phone was still switched off, this time for the sake of unobtrusiveness. At the time when Mar rang, she was just entering the dark alleyway where she was to meet Robbie Mallet.

Chapter Forty-Two

Thursday

It was a quarter to seven when Angel and Josh, happy and relaxed, after an afternoon spent wandering round central London, soaking in the atmosphere and re-visiting the sights, arrived back at the *Sinclair*.

'Did you give this Mallet guy your mobile number, honey?' Josh asked.

'No way,' Angel said in a firm voice. 'My mobile number only goes to friends. But I told him to come to the *Sinclair*.'

'Maybe check in case he's left a message?'

'Why not?' Angel approached the reception desk. The pretty dark haired girl on duty smiled at her. 'Can I help you?'

'Yes, I just wondered if there are any messages for me?'

'I'm afraid I've just come on duty, so I don't really know,' the girl smiled. 'But anything for you would be noted and left in your pigeonhole, Madam.'

'Thanks heaps.'

Angel followed the girl's pointing finger and found the rows of pigeon-holes where messages and post were left for hotel guests to collect. Her own, she saw, had a slip of paper which presumably reported a telephone message. Angel lifted it out and read the contents.

'Hey, look at this, darlin'!'

Josh looked.

'Phone message at 5.00pm. "Tell Angel Murphy I can't come to the hotel. Too obvious. I'll wait for her in *Sailors' Alley*, second on the left from the hotel's back entrance." The speaker gave no name, just said, "She'll know who this is from." End of message.'

'Okay. He's obviously frightened. Worried the boss man will notice if he comes to your hotel.'

'Not very logical.' Angel shrugged. 'Fear isn't always logical. But why should his boss be watching him all that closely in the first place? And how would he know anything about me, or where I'm staying?'

'Come to that, why should a dark alleyway be any safer?' Josh added.

'Five to seven already,' Angel said briskly. 'Let's move.'

'Maybe we should ask where the back entrance is first?' Josh suggested dryly.

The receptionist, although puzzled as to why they should want to know, since she hadn't seen Angel's message, obligingly gave them clear directions.

A few minutes later they emerged from the door near the kitchens into a large yard cluttered with rubbish bins, boxes, and goods still unpacked or stored away, plus a few cats on the prowl.

The yard entrance, wide double gates for the convenience of delivery vans and lorries, led out into a road much less respectable than the one where the front entrance of the *Sinclair* sat majestically. Angel and Josh turned left.

Some distance along they passed a fairly wide street, dark and dingy and lined with tall disreputable houses which might once have belonged to respectable, well-off people but which had evidently gone downhill. Probably cheap rentals, let out one room at a time, Angel thought.

'Do you think this is it, Josh?' she asked him.

'Naw. Second on the left. And this isn't the right name.'

Josh pointed to the name *Burton Street* attached at a height on the nearest house.

'Okay. But we turned left once already, out of the hotel. Still, wrong name.'

They moved on. Presently they reached a narrow alley leading off on their left. The street sign was in need of repainting, but it was still possible to identify it as *Sailors' Alley*.

'Not the place I'd chose for a meeting if I was scared already,' Angel commented.

'Still, not a place anyone would be likely to find you.'

'Unless they were following you to start with.'

'Come on. Let's slip in as quietly as possible.' Josh kept close to the side of the alley and moved slowly and cautiously along. Angel followed him.

The ground was rough under their feet. There was no pavement, only the one narrow strip of alleyway, and in the early May evening it was growing dark already. The high buildings, mainly warehouses and derelict shops, on either side of them, cast dark shadows and kept out the remains of daylight.

They were maybe halfway along when a deafening scream pierced their ears. Angel jumped, and then pulled herself together.

Ahead of them through the dim light they could just about see two figures struggling desperately. One seemed bigger and stronger than the other. Both looked like men.

Angel and Josh threw caution to the winds and rushed forward.

Angel grabbed one man by his right arm and twisted him round. Josh had the other, larger one by the throat, putting on enough pressure to force him to release his grip on the smaller man. They fought on, all four letting out grunts and gasps but saying nothing, until Angel's victim let out another of those horrible shrieks and suddenly collapsed at her feet.

Josh, his attention momentarily distracted, looked down. Instantly the big man twisted frantically, kicking out at Josh's leg as he did so, and somehow managed to tear himself from Josh's grasp. A second later he was thundering away down the alley, with Josh directly behind him.

The man had very little start. Josh felt confident of catching him up. He was reaching out his hand, almost within reach of the man's jacket, when suddenly the world turned upside down.

The rubbish which littered Sailors' Alley had caught him out. His foot slipped from under him, sliding on something wet and slimy. Staggering wildly to regain his balance, he found himself tripping over a cardboard box packed with empty tins. Next moment he was flat on his back on the hard ground. He struggled to his feet. But the incident had taken just too long. He caught a glimpse of the man escaping round the corner of the mouth of the alley. By the time Josh had reached it, he was out of sight.

It was worthwhile exploring a few possible hiding places – doorways, another narrow passage. But Josh didn't take long about this. The most likely thing was that the man had crossed the road and disappeared down any one of the possible streets nearby before Josh had reached the corner.

Turning he retraced his steps back to where Angel was crouching over the other, smaller man.

As she heard Josh approach, Angel looked up.

'It's Robbie Mallet, Josh,' she said. 'He's been stabbed. Look out or you'll have his blood all over you.'

'How bad is he?'

Angel's hand was on Mallet's wrist, feeling for a pulse. 'I don't think he's gone yet,' she said. 'But he's unconscious. And I don't think he'll last much longer.'

As she finished speaking, Angel heard Mallet give a strange whistling sigh. Then his whole body relaxed, and she knew he was gone.

Chapter Forty-Three

Thursday

'Get back to the hotel and lie low in your room, honey,' Josh said. 'I'll ring in and report this. As a straight mugging. No need for you to be involved in it. You want to get home early tomorrow, right?'

Angel saw the sense in this. 'I didn't see the guy's face. He had some sort of balaclava mask over his head. You didn't see any more, Josh?'

'No. I could have ripped off the mask at one point if I'd tried, but I was thinking more of getting a good grip on him. He was off like a shot before I really saw much. Nothing I'd recognise again, for sure.'

'So now we know definitely that there was someone employing Mallet. Someone who got rid of him before he could tell us his boss's name,' said Angel thoughtfully. 'We were right when we thought someone might have been following him. Well, he'll never tell his boss's name now. Okay, Josh, I'll get out of here. Ring me when you're free, okay?'

Josh put his arms round Angel and kissed her. Then he took his mobile out of his pocket and rang the police.

Back in her hotel room, Angel stripped off her bloody T-shirt, put it to soak in the sink in her en suite bathroom, and changed. Later she would squeeze it out and hang it up to dry. Then she sat down to think. What exactly was the scenario they were building up?

Like a jigsaw, it was taking time and imagination to put the pieces together and get the full picture.

The story started with Fitz, alone in the cottage he'd been lent by Seri Smith. Alone, but surrounded by the paparazzi outside his walls. They knew now that this situation had been engineered by Robbie Mallet.

They also knew that Mallet was working for someone else, who'd bumped him off when his knowledge became dangerous.

But one thing they didn't know was why. Why had someone paid Mallet to stir up his media acquaintances and upset Fitz? Was the idea to make him ready to take some drug which would steady his nerves? And had they switched his harmless tablets for something lethal?

Or had this someone spiked his whiskey? The fact that Billy Nelson's son Will had seen someone leaving the cottage, and that Nat and Mar had found the Bushmills Whiskey bottle gone, pointed to that.

Angel realised how little they knew about the method.

And they knew even less about the motive. Fitz was popular. Who could hate him enough to plan this? Or was it a question of straightforward hatred? Was there something else behind it all?

And where did Cindy Baron and Billy Nelson come in? Did they, also, know the identity of Robbie Mallet's boss? And if so, how had they known? Did Mallet tell them? Did he ask them to help? He might have asked Cindy, Angel thought. She had admired him, apparently. And then she might possibly have leaked the info to Billy when she asked him to give her some back up at her meeting with Mallet.

So, had both murders, and the attack on Billy Nelson, been carried out by the same man, the boss? Or had Mallet killed Cindy and beaten up Billy, and then been killed in his turn by the boss?

Angel sighed. There was a lot of ground to cover yet, she could see.

Tomorrow when she got back to Belfast she would contact Richard Bell, the Member of the Legislative Assembly. It was a good suggestion of Sir Marty's. They didn't need his help to bring in the police, but there were other doors he could open, other people he could put them in touch with, she was sure.

Meanwhile, she hoped Josh was getting on okay with his own connection with the police. Unless he told them the whole story, they would put it down as a mugging for sure. Josh would have to make a statement, but it needn't take long. Angel brightened up at the thought that he should be ringing soon.

The night was still young. She switched off from the puzzle temporarily, and began to plan the next few hours with Josh. For a woman determined to stay clear from further relationships with men since the end of her disastrous marriage, she realised ruefully that she was getting dangerously attracted to this young American, Josh Smith.

Perhaps she should phone the guys back in Belfast with the latest developments, such as they were.

But perhaps not. All that could wait until tomorrow. But she wondered briefly what they were all up to. Especially Nathaniel Deane, now she supposed busy at the opening of his exhibition, which she hadn't been able to attend after all.

Chapter Forty-Four

<u>Friday</u>

Angel's flight brought her to the *George Best Belfast City Airport* early the next morning. Just in time to get to her apartment, shower, change and breakfast, and be round at the BBC building in Ormeau Road by nine.

The unedited interview with Sir Marshall O'Neill had arrived safely. Angel thought she could leave it to her director to get it into shape. Normally she would have liked to sit in with him and make suggestions, but right now there was too much going on for that.

Her immediate boss, Minerva Daley, was around, and Angel went over to her.

'Hi, Min.'

'Angel. Interview go okay?'

'Yip. He's a natural. Got some great answers. Phil is editing it as we speak. It'll be just right for next week's programme. Next Friday.'

'Good.' Minerva smiled briefly.

'Min, any chance of me taking the rest of today off? Going to London at short notice threw me out – I've a lot of personal stuff to catch up on.'

Minerva glared ferociously. 'Do you mean to tell me you have a life outside these studios, girl?' Then she switched off the glare and grinned. 'No problem. You've done some good work. Take the day – but don't forget your interview with Nathaniel Deane – the painter guy. Make sure everything's edited and finalised there for this week's show tonight, okay?'

Angel had almost forgotten. But she covered up her shocked reaction easily. 'Sure, I've checked the final cut. That's going to be another good one, Min. You saw the initial footage, so you know he talked very openly. You'll want to have a look at the final version, but unless you want to change anything it'll be ready to go out tonight.'

'Okay. See you, then. Have a good day.'

Angel promptly vanished from the studio.

Her first move was to message the gang. 'Can we meet for coffee asap?'

Back came the prompt responses. A 'No' from Seri – she didn't want to leave Fitz. The doctors thought he might wake up again some time soon. She needed to be there when he did.

But the others, Mar, Nat, Zig and Pete, The Diabolical Twins, Mary and Jonty Carson all said they could make it. Angel suggested the quiet branch of *Clements* in the Linenhall Library opposite the City Hall.

Twenty minutes later they were gathered round a table with coffee and pastry before them, all talking at once.

'How did the opening go, Nat?' was the first thing Angel asked. 'Really sorry I couldn't make it.'

'It was fine,' Nat said. 'And Mar here was a great support.'

'Oh. Good.' Angel wasn't sure what she felt about that. However, time to get down to business. Everyone seemed to have plenty to say. She listened for a moment and then cut in.

'Whoa! Let's take it one at a time. Any developments since we last met? Nat, you'd better tell the rest this stuff you've told me. About going to the cottage – the bottle gone – Will Nelson and then what his Da, Billy, said.'

Nat and Mar immediately jumped into a joint narrative, interrupting each other but getting the gist across.

'Sure, that takes us quite a bit further,' Angel said when they seemed to have steamed to a halt. 'I might as well put in my own share now.' And she ran quickly over her experiences in London, burglarising Robbie Mallet's flat, meeting him in Sailors' Alley, and his murder, presumably by the unknown boss.

'I copied a lot of stuff from his computer that I need to go through,' she finished. 'But meantime I'm planning to have a chat with Dinger Bell. Sir Marty O'Neill told me he thought that might be our best bet. Dinger knows Fitz quite well, Marty said. He'd want to be helpful, and he knows everybody. He should have some good ideas for us.'

'Okay,' said Pete doubtfully. 'But Dinger Bell – would you trust that guy? He was well in with the paramilitaries not so long ago.'

'Aw, be fair, Pete!' his twin Ziggy interrupted him. 'Dinger's moved on from that. He pushed for the peace process, and he's cut all his ties with any of those guys who still want to keep the violence going.'

'True,' Jonty Carson agreed. 'But do we really need him, Angel? What can he do that we can't?'

'Sure, how would I know before I meet him?' Angel asked. 'I'd just like to give it a go.'

'Why not?' Mary put in. 'But it seems to me we're getting on quite well so far. We know Mallet organised the paparazzi to try to push Fitz over the edge. We know he was working for a boss – someone who paid him. We know this boss has some reason to want Kirstin to do well – in particular to win the *New Music Awards* instead of *Raving*, we think.'

'Well, yes, we think this stuff,' Angel said.

'Yeah.' Jonty looked thoughtful. 'I guess our best plan is to find out as much as we can about Kirstin. Her background, who's likely to support her, that sorta thing, right? We have the contacts. They took us to Robbie Mallet. Let's try them again, only this time to check out Kirstin.'

'Mind, now, I don't think Kirstin herself has anything to do with all this,' Ziggy said. 'Pete and I know her. She's a great kid, wouldn't do a tap of harm to anyone.'

'No, Zig – but someone connected to her, someone maybe who wants to make money out of her – that's who we're looking for,' Pete explained seriously. 'No way it's Kirstin herself who's behind this. But she could maybe give us some ideas about who it is.'

'Okay, boys. But be careful. Don't let on to Kirstin what you're after. She'd maybe be annoyed at us suspecting any of her friends. And she might let it out to the wrong person. So just have a chat with her, get her talking about herself if you can, and don't push too hard.'

'Fair enough,' agreed the twins in chorus.

'And the rest of you guys, good idea of Jonty's to research Kirstin's background with your media stroke showbiz contacts. And I'll try to get hold of Dinger Bell, if everyone's happy about that?'

It wasn't clear that Pete, or even Mary were exactly happy. Their faces told Angel as much. And to be fair she greatly disliked Dinger Bell's background as the political mouthpiece for one of the Loyalist paramilitary groups. But he had put all that behind him, as Ziggy had said.

You had to give the man a chance. And apparently he'd been a good friend and supporter of Fitz. He would be willing to help, she was sure. And he was in a position to give them some powerful support with the authorities when they reached that point.

Angel pushed back her chair and stood up.

'Right, guys,' she said, as the rest of the gang followed her example. 'Let's get moving!'

Chapter Forty-Five

Friday

Outside the *Linenhall Library*, Angel took out her mobile and checked that she had the number Sir Marty had given her for the politician Richard *'Dinger'* Bell. Yes, there it was. She punched it in and as she listened to the ringing sound she began walking back to her car. She'd parked it that morning at the back of the BBC building.

'Richard Bell's Personal Assistant speaking.' The female voice which answered was markedly polite, very up market in tone and accent. Angel stopped walking temporarily. No way she'd cross a road while on her mobile.

A Personal Assistant. Okay, it would be. No one got straight through to an MLA. Not even his wife. Maybe his mistress, but no guarantees there either.

'This is Angel Murphy of BBC NI,' Angel said confidently. 'I'd like to set up a meeting with Richard Bell as soon as possible. This afternoon for choice. You can tell him it's about what happened to Frankie Fitzgerald – Fitz.'

There was a pause while the voice at the other end thought about it. 'I'll check with Mr Bell,' she said at last, sounding reluctant. 'Please hold.'

Angel held, and began walking again.

Presently a warm friendly voice came online.

'Angel Murphy? Hi, Angel! I love your show on the box!'

'Oh, thanks,' Angel murmured, feeling flattered and charmed in spite of herself. 'Is that Richard Bell?'

'Oh, please call me Dinger – all my friends do. And I'm sure we're going to be friends. I certainly hope we are!'

'Dinger.'

'So, Angel, is there something I can do for you?'

Angel put her thoughts into words. 'I really hope so, Dinger. Sir Marshall O'Neill suggested I should talk to you about this terrible business of Frankie Fitzgerald – Fitz. Sir Marty tells me you're a friend of Fitz?'

'Fitz! Yes, what a ghastly business! Fitz is a good friend of mine. Sure, I grew up in the next street to his mother and went to school with her and her brothers. Fitz is a great wee lad, and he's done Belfast proud with his success. I'll never believe Fitz took anything himself. Or if he did, he was driven to it by those vile paparazzi!'

'I'm quite sure he didn't, Dinger.' Angel spoke firmly and confidently.

'That's good to hear. But do you just want to believe that, or have you any reason?' Dinger sounded faintly surprised.

'Yes, there are reasons. But, you know what, it's a bit of a long story, and complicated, for talking on the phone. Look, Dinger, is there anyway you can fit me in for a short talk face to face any time today? I'd really appreciate it.'

'Let me check my diary, Angel. Just hold on there.'

Once again, Angel held. But this time the wait was shorter.

'If you can get round to my house, I'll be there for another hour. Then I have a meeting I have to get to. I've some stuff I need to brush up on before I go, so I can't give you the full hour, you understand. But I'll take half an hour out – I really would like to do anything I can if there's some way of sorting this business out so Fitz isn't left with a black eye, publicity wise. Okay? You know my address? Malone Road – the top end.'

'I have your address, Dinger. Sure, it's in the phone book, so your constituents can ring you, isn't it? I can be there in around fifteen minutes or less. And thanks – I really appreciate this!'

A couple more minutes took Angel to her car. If the traffic wasn't too bad, she could make it to Dinger Bell's house in another ten.

Richard 'Dinger' Bell had come a long way from his East Belfast roots. Yet, she'd heard, he still kept many of the friends of his early days, and a trace – no more – or his Belfast accent. His house just off the upper Malone Road was one of the type of houses Angel remembered being impressed by when, as a very young child, she'd been invited to Christmas parties there by school friends or by friends of her father's.

It was large, with high walls round its gardens and a tall gate. Its front gardens with their winding drive were bigger than was normal so near a city centre, and the back gardens, she knew, would stretch out even further. She left her car in the secluded road in front of the gate, and went up the drive on foot.

Dinger came to open the door to her himself. He was a man in his late thirties or early forties, running slightly to fat, with thick dark hair still untouched by grey or by any signs of loss, and with a round, chubby face where thin lines of red gave him a healthy seeming glow. He beamed at Angel with a natural seeming enthusiasm.

'Angel! Girl, you look just as great in the flesh as you do on TV! Come on in, pet, and tell me all about it!'

He took Angel by the arm and led her into a room to the left of the hallway, chattering as he went and leaving Angel no time for anything but a brief, 'Hi.'

It was a huge and very comfortably furnished room, with soft chairs and sofas, bookcases along one wall and pictures on the others. An attractive looking wood burning stove was positioned facing them as they entered, but currently, with the warmth of the spring day, it remained unlit. Angel could picture how it would look on a cold evening, the flames glowing, throwing out heat and comfort.

'You'll take a wee noggin with me, won't you now?' Dinger Bell left Angel no time to agree or refuse. Moving over to the cabinet at the end of the room opposite the huge patio doors which led to the front garden, he began to mix her a Scotch and soda. Which, to Angel, normally not a spirit drinker, seemed considerably too strong. He pressed the glass on her, still talking, and assembled one for himself, which looked even stronger.

'I love Fitz – like I said on the phone, his family and me grew up together. He's a great singer and he has a real knack with the song writing. That *'Snowball!'* I keep finding it going through my head, and mind you it's not really my sort of music. I'm more a Country and Western kind of man, so I am.

'Sit down, Angel, sit down.' He waved Angel to a huge comfortable chair on one side of a low coffee table and took the one beside it, still without stopping his conversation. 'Now, I want you to tell me the long, complicated reasons you have for believing Fitz didn't take an overdose himself. Well, here's to Fitz!'

He raised his glass, forcing Angel to raise her own out of politeness, took a large slug of his Scotch and at last gave Angel a chance to speak.

Sipping cautiously at her own glass, barely wetting her tongue, Angel began. She did her best to keep it brief, but there was a lot of ground to cover.

She told the politician about the doctor who had spoken to Seri. Who had said that Fitz had had an overdose of chloral hydrate – she had heard from Seri that the actual drug was now confirmed. About the doubts of all his friends about Fitz having anything like that with him. About the tracking down of Robbie Mallet, the murder of Cindy Baron and the attack on Billy Nelson.

Time was running on. She decided to cut the story short. 'So we know Mallet has a boss – but we don't know who it is,' she finished. 'Have you any useful thoughts? Or about who might want to damage Fitz?'

She realised, as Dinger began speaking, that she hadn't asked him if he knew anything about Kirstin, but by then it was too late.

'Angel, I'm fascinated by what you and Fitz's friends have done,' Dinger was saying. 'I wish I didn't have to rush off now. But I'll give all this a lot of thought and get back to you asap, okay?

'I can't help thinking of Fitz in that lonely cottage all by himself, with the paparazzi outside his walls, driving him to despair. All alone, except for that huge white teddy bear he called Yogi. It chokes me up, so it does. I really will try to come up with some ideas.'

He sprang up, seized Angel's hand and drew her to her feet. Shaking her hand violently in both his, he pulled her close for a hug, then led her to the door. The interview was over.

Angel wished she'd talked less and allowed Dinger more of a chance to think it all over and suggest something. But he'd get back to her. She was confident that he'd meant that.

Meanwhile, there was something he'd said which was already very suggestive. If she could only think what it was.

Chapter Forty-Six

Friday

The Diabolical Twins, Pete and Ziggy, were determined to contribute more to the investigation than they had done so far.

'Sure, we found out all about Robbie Mallet's part in the paparazzi attack on Fitz from what Simon told us,' said Pete. 'But that wasn't much help – everyone else had got info about Mallet from their own sources.'

'Yeah, well, it helped a bit – it was the consensus of opinion from all the guys people asked that convinced everyone that Mallet was behind the trouble,' Ziggy said. 'But it wasn't a big deal.'

'And Si told us that someone else was behind it. That story about what his friend Lisa overheard.'

'But he wasn't able to tell us exactly who.'

'And our chemist friend wasn't needed to analyse the whiskey.'

'Right, since the Bushmills bottle disappeared.'

'But listen, Zig, we've got a considerable advantage now. Of all Fitz's friends, we're the only ones who actually know Kirstin.'

'Okay,' Ziggy said, 'it isn't a competition, we know that, but still, I'd love us to be some real use, right, Pete?'

'Right, Ziggy.'

'So, you've got Kirstin's number?'

'Sure I have.' Not so long ago Pete had had a short fling with Kirstin. It hadn't lasted, but they were still good mates.

'So, ring her and see if she wants to get together for a drink or something.'

'Both of us,' Pete stipulated firmly.

'Sure, both of us. Don't want her getting any ideas, right, bro?' Ziggy grinned.

Kirstin answered her phone straight away, which was a good sign, since she would have known it was Pete ringing.

'Hi, Kirst. Zig and me wondered if you'd like to get together for a drink later? Long time no see, right?'

'Pete!' squealed Kirstin. Her high notes were the thing she was mainly noted for. 'Would I what! Definitely, big guy!'

'So, how about we pick you up in an hour or so? You're still in the same apartment?'

'No problemo! Give me time to wash my hair. Hour and a half, okay? Hugs and kisses, sweetie pie!'

With a final squeal, Kirstin rang off, leaving the twins grinning at each other. 'Just as well I'm coming too, bro!' Ziggy said.

'Leave it out!' Pete gave his brother a friendly push.

They rang the bell of Kirstin's apartment at the time agreed. Her voice squeaked at them through the answer phone.

'Come on up, boys. I'm nearly ready.'

The door buzzed, and they pushed it open and went up. Kirstin opened her door, wrapped in several towels and with a hairdryer in one hand. She was, however, very fully made up with rainbow coloured eye shadow radiating out from her eyelids, skin powdered white and lipstick in very bright red, twenties style.

'Come on in! Won't be a tick!'

She dived back into her bedroom to continue drying her hair, calling out to them as she disappeared, 'Beer in the fridge! Help yourselves!'

Pete, who was familiar with this routine, winked at Ziggy and they sprawled comfortably with their feet up on each of two enormous black sofas, drinking their beer by the neck.

Half an hour later, Kirstin appeared. She posed in the bedroom doorway, expecting approval, so the twins happily obliged.

'Wow, girl, some get up!'

'Love the colours!'

Kirstin was dressed to impress in multi-coloured see through layers of scarf-like drapery, her bright red hair, much the same shade as her lipstick, piled high and held in place with feathery clips.

'You like?'

'You bet!'

'Got a gig later, Kirst?' Pete asked.

'Not tonight, Petey. But I thought I'd try out my new outfit on you guys. It's for my gig in the Park tomorrow.'

'So, you don't think you'll spoil the effect by letting people see you in it now?' Ziggy suggested. 'We were only going to our local, but there might be some of your audience there.'

'You think I should change?'

'No!' howled the twins in unison. The prospect of another hour or two while Kirstin decided on a different outfit was a killer.

'You look great, Kirst,' Pete said hastily. 'Never mind if people see you – they'll be all the keener to get to the gig.'

'Well, the tickets are sold out anyway – have been for months,' Kirstin pointed out. 'So it can't make any difference either way. I just wanted you to see me at my best, Petey sweetie. See what you're missing!' She giggled happily.

Pete blushed slightly, but pulled himself together. 'Okay, then, let's head.'

They took her to the *Swan*, one of the quietest pubs they knew, on the bank of the upper reaches of the Lagan, and installed her at an outside table festooned with hanging baskets and with a heater overhead. There was a beautiful view of the river and a sweet smell of wild flowers and from the roses in the hanging baskets, and the atmosphere was romantic in the extreme – just right for getting Kirstin into a friendly mood, Pete thought hopefully.

When they were happily settled, Pete went up to the bar for their drinks, while Ziggy cautiously began to feel his way into the type of causal conversation which they hoped would bring results.

'So, Kirst, I guess you've told me before, but you were born in this part of the world, right?'

Kirstin looked at him. 'D'ye know something, Ziggy? I don't really know.'

She was unusually silent for a moment. Ziggy said nothing, waiting for her to explain. He sensed that this was a touchy subject for the young singer.

At the crucial moment, Pete arrived back from the bar with two pint glasses of Harp and a Cosmopolitan for Kirstin. He set them down carefully and slid in beside the girl.

Ziggy said, 'Kirstin was just about to tell me how come she doesn't know if she was born here.' His voice was relaxed, not specially interested, but pleasant.

'Oh?' Pete said.

'Yeah.' Kirstin took a gulp of her Cosmopolitan and made up her mind. These boys were her good friends, after all. In the music business, good friends could be few and far between, especially when you began to climb the ladder.

'Well, the thing is,' she said, continuing to sip her drink between phrases, 'I'm adopted. Did you know that?'

The twins shook their heads silently.

'Not a lot of people know that.' Kirstin laughed at her own joke.

'Get on with it, Michael Caine,' Pete said pleasantly. 'Cut the suspense.'

'Okay. Well, like I said, I'm adopted. Oh, Mum and Dad are great. I wouldn't swop them for any crummy natural parents who couldn't be bothered to keep me. And I never thought of myself as anything but Irish, both before and after I knew the story.

'They sat me down, when I was six, to explain to me that I was special because most parents had to put up with what they got, but they had actually chosen me from a whole lot of other babies. I was quite pleased at the time. It was only when I got into my teens that I began to wonder about my actual birth history. I could have been Vietnamese or mid European or anything, really, couldn't I?'

'Not with your colouring,' Pete said logically. 'You've got quite an Irish look about you.'

'Or Scots,' Ziggy suggested.

'Same thing,' Pete instructed them. 'The Scots and the Irish were one race for centuries if you go back a while. And they intermarried for yonks after that. In the north, that is. Go further south and it's the English and Irish who are interconnected.'

Kirstin clearly wasn't interested. 'You know, Pete, that's the main reason we broke up, did I ever tell you?' she said. 'You would keep trying to teach me stuff I couldn't care about. It wouldn't matter which or what I was. The thing is, I didn't know, and still don't.'

'Well, why didn't you ask your Mum and Dad?'

'Zig, I thought about it, but I sort of knew it would hurt them terribly. Especially Mum. Mum is my real mother in any real sense of the word. She'd hate to think I didn't believe that, I just know she would.'

Kirstin's lips trembled. She pushed her empty glass towards Pete and said, 'Hey, get me another of those. Here.' She fumbled in her handbag and produced a crumpled wad of notes. 'Take it out of this.'

Pete shoved the notes back at her. 'No way. What's a fiver to the likes of us?' He winked at them and disappeared towards the bar again.

'Kirstin, this is upsetting you too much,' Ziggy said. He leaned across the table and dabbed at Kirstin's eyes with a tissue from his jeans' pocket – luckily a clean one. 'Let's just forget it and talk about something else.'

Kirstin sniffed, then pushed the tissue away and grabbed for her handbag again. 'Hey, Zig, watch what you're doing to my eye make up!'

She produced a tiny mirror and a tissue of her own and made swift repairs. 'No, it's okay, I don't mind talking about it to you guys. I never do, right? I wouldn't share this with anyone else. But we go back a long time. School and stuff. Underage drinking on Bangor pier. The heap. So I know I can talk to you without worrying in case it goes any further.'

Ziggy felt bad. Here was Kirstin trusting them not to repeat what she told them, and the only reason they were there with her was to get information for Angel and the others. Okay, for Fitz. But Kirstin was a mate, too.

'You won't see it on the front page of the *Sunday Life*, pet,' he said lightly. 'But – well – ' He broke off in relief. 'Hey, here comes Pete with the drinks.'

Pete deposited the drinks and slid back into his seat. 'Next time, you get a beer and like it, girl,' he announced severely. 'Tears already, I see. We didn't bring you out here to get you maudlin drunk.'

'Pete,' Ziggy said nervously. 'I've just been thinking. Kirstin loves Fitz just as much as the rest of us, right? What I think is, maybe we should tell her just why we did bring her out here.'

Pete stared at his twin in disbelief. Kirstin stared in amazement first at Ziggy, then at Pete.

There was a frozen silence.

Then Pete recovered. 'You know, I guess you've got a point there, bro',' he said slowly. 'Okay, I hope this isn't going to upset you too much, Kirst. We were glad of the chance to hook up with you again. It's been too long. But, yes, Ziggy's blown it. We have another reason for wanting to talk to you. Don't know how you'll feel about this, but here goes. We're going to trust you.'

And trying to keep the long story to a minimum, Pete began to explain. He just hoped he and Ziggy were guessing right and that Kirstin would take it the way they wanted.

Chapter Forty-Seven

Friday

There was a long silence when Pete had finished speaking. Kirstin looked down at her almost empty glass, took the final sip, and then looked up at them again.

'Okay, boys. Time for that beer you promised me. Just one thing. Why didn't you come out with some of this – just enough to give me an idea of what was going on – when you rang me?'

Pete grinned with relief. 'Your turn for the bar, Ziggy,' he said briskly. Ziggy slid out obediently.

Alone with his former girlfriend, 'Should have done, Kirst,' Pete admitted. 'Should have done. But we'd sort of told the others – well, Angel especially – we wouldn't let anything slip.'

'But now you've told me the lot?'

'Yeah. Being with you, we both realised how crazy it was to treat you like an enemy. Hey, we're mates, we know you. You have to be on our side!'

Kirstin smiled, a sweet, natural smile unlike her professional beam. 'Yeah, I'm on your side, guys. Fitz! How could I not want to help Fitz? It was Fitz who gave me my first guitar lesson, who encouraged me to develop my high notes when everyone else thought I should sing in a lower key – where would I be without Fitz?'

'But you're in competition with *Raving* for the *New Music Award?*'

Ziggy came back and set three bottles down as Pete asked the crucial question.

'So?' Kirstin frowned angrily. 'Pete Carmichael, do you really think I would try to cheat my way to the top – especially against Fitz? Sure, I'll do everything I can to win – pull out all the stops, give a hundred and twenty per cent of a performance. But that's it. Nothing slimy! Did you really think I would?'

Pete, horrified, saw Kirstin's eyes begin to brim over with tears again.

'No! Hey, no way, Krist, man! We didn't think that! I put it all wrong!'

Kirstin produced another tissue from her bag and used it carefully.

'Okay, so what did you mean, then?'

'Just. Is there anyone connected to you who'd do the sleazy stuff? An agent? Or what? Somebody who'd stand to make a lot of money if you sail to the top?'

Kirstin stared thoughtfully at her bottle and took a swig. 'I don't know. I signed up with an agent when I won *'Who's on Top?,'* right? Morty Wilkinson. Don't know that much about him. *Marvel Records* recommended him. But I think he's an okay guy.'

'You signed up with an agent recommended by your record company?' Pete sounded horrified.

'Yeah? What?'

'An agent is supposed to be on your side, against everybody, especially the record company, if necessary, girl.'

'Oh. Yeah, I reckon. Didn't think of it. But he's okay, I'm sure of it. He's fought them more than once for me already. Got a better contract, better deal, than I'd have had without him.'

'Okay. But what sort of guy is he? Would he try to damage Fitz to get you a win?'

'No way.' Kirstin sounded decided. 'I tell you, he's okay. Not that sort of guy at all.'

Ziggy said, 'Sounds like we can forget about him, then, Kirst.' Over the young singer's head he winked at Pete, who understood that Ziggy was telling him that they could look into this Morty Wilkinson afterwards. No need to fight with Kirstin about him. 'But, hey, you were telling us about your own family background. Did you ever check into who your real parents were? I know you didn't want to tell your Mum and Dad you were doing that. But without them knowing?'

Kirstin looked ashamed. 'Well, okay, I did. But I didn't get anywhere. Next September, when I'm eighteen and of age, I can apply for information from the adoption society. But not until then. And I didn't know what else to do. Oh, I tried the Internet and posted on various 'Find your family' sites, but zilch, so far.'

'Okay. So you know nothing. But your biological parents know who you are, of course. Could be they – or one of them – is trying to help you?'

'That's a dreadful idea, Pete!' Kirstin said indignantly. 'I can't believe they'd do such a thing! Anyway, how does it help you? If you don't know who they are, how can you tell if they're involved in working against Fitz?'

And the twins had to admit that she was right.

Time to leave it for now. They would spend the rest of the evening with Kirstin simply catching up on old times and enjoying themselves.

Chapter Forty-Eight

Friday

Angel went back to her apartment after her talk with Dinger Bell, and tried to relax and get her head in order. She was lying back in a hot, scented bath, doing absolutely nothing, and allowing her mind to drift, when her mobile rang. It was Nathaniel Deane.

'Nat. Good to hear from you.'

'Hi, Angel. Look, I just wanted to check if you're still on for tomorrow night?'

'Tomorrow night?'

'Yeah. Meal and cabaret at *AM/PM*?'

'Oh.'

Angel realised too late that not only had she forgotten all about the date she'd arranged with Nat, but that she'd given away the fact by her response.

'Ah – yes. Yes, I suppose so.'

'Because, if you want to cancel, just let me know.'

'Do you know what, Nat, it would have been nice, but there's so much going on right now. And, hey, you and me – well, I'm not sure it's going anywhere.' She hesitated. 'Listen, why don't you take Mar instead? Sure, you and Mar seem to be getting on really well, aren't you?'

Nat was silent for a moment, considering the suggestion. Then he spoke, and his voice sounded much brighter and happier. 'Well, Angel, I actually think that would be a very good idea. No use me keeping on chasing you when you're not really interested, girl. Yes – I'll take Mar instead.' He put down the phone, and thought for a minute. Take Mar instead. Yes. He suddenly knew that that was a really good idea.

Angel lay back in her bath and firmly rejected the feelings of guilt which threatened to creep over her. Josh – he was the main man in her life just now. No use letting Nat get ideas which would never come to anything. When she'd left Josh, he'd promised to make it over to Belfast really soon. That was something to look forward to.

Angel in Belfast – *Gerry McCullough*

Presently, feeling happily free from worry, she found herself going over the events of the last few days and listing the information she and the gang had picked up.

She had got as far as the raid on Robbie Mallet's flat when something struck her. What a fool she was! She'd copied the contents of Mallet's computer files to her stick, and hadn't looked near it since!

True, she'd had a lot happening. The interview with Sir Marty to prepare for. The picnic with Josh Smith. The meeting with Mallet, and his murder. But she certainly had missed out on checking the information she'd picked up. Time she had a look at it.

Refusing to hurry herself, Angel stepped slowly out of her bath, dried herself and dressed. She made a pot of coffee and a sandwich. Finally, she moved into her living room, inserted the stick into her laptop, and began working on it.

There were email folders with emails Mallet wanted to keep saved to them. There were word processing documents, probably articles he'd written. And there were notes, some of them about articles, others a diary type of thing, where apparently Mallet had felt the need to unburden himself of his thoughts, and comment on the things that were happening in his life. Most people used blogs or their *Facebook* status for this, Angel thought cynically. It looked as if Robbie Mallet wanted to keep his 'diary' rather more private than that.

She worked steadily through the various files. It was getting late, nearly eleven o'clock, when she suddenly stiffened, scrolled back, and read one of the entries again.

Chapter Forty-Nine

Friday

Seri sat by Frankie Fitzgerald's hospital bed, waiting for him to wake up.

She knew he was no longer unconscious. He had come out of his coma, and had recognised her, and spoken her name, already. But that seemed a very long time ago, now. The doctor said it would do him good to have lots of good, natural sleep. They didn't want to wake him. Just let him take his own time.

But Seri, praying as she sat by Fitz's bedside, couldn't help worrying. She had heard of people who came out of a coma only to show that they had suffered brain damage. And no matter how much the doctor assured her that this wasn't going to happen to Fitz, she still wanted to hear him speak to her himself, more than just her name. To know for sure that he was his normal self.

Dr Quinn put his head round the doorway. 'Seri, I think you should go and get yourself something to eat. You've been sitting here for far too long. It won't help Frankie when he wakes up if you're so weak from hunger you can only weep over him!'

Seri smiled. 'I suppose you're right, doctor.'

'Go on down to the canteen and have a decent meal. If he wakes up while you're gone, so what? I'll tell him you're here and that you'll be back any minute. Right?'

Seri stood up. 'Right, doctor.'

'And don't rush! Take time to digest your food properly.'

Seri couldn't help laughing at the typical medical advice. She went over to the lift and pressed the button for the ground floor.

She'd been to the canteen before, during the terrible time before Fitz first recovered consciousness, when she still didn't know if he was going to survive. Hurried snacks and cups of coffee had kept her alive.

She hadn't dared to stay away from the Intensive Care Unit for more than ten minutes at a time, except for the two meetings in her apartment. Now she resolved to take Dr Quinn's advice and have a proper meal, not rushing it. She needed to be strong and fit for Fitz if she was to help him when he recovered.

She sat at the plastic topped table with a tray in front of her. On it were a bowl of vegetable soup, a roll and butter and a banana. It was all she had felt able to eat. And now that it was here, she didn't know if she could eat it, after all. But she must try.

Would Frankie be okay when he next woke up? Dr Quinn had said he would. No reason to disbelieve him.

And would he know anything about what had happened to him? Or would it all be a complete blank?

Maybe all the work his friends had done would prove to be unnecessary. Maybe Frankie himself would know exactly what had happened, and would be able to tell her.

But would it be a good idea to ask him to think back, just yet? Maybe he should be allowed to forget that awful night, until he felt like remembering it himself? Seri didn't know.

She tried to take spoonful after spoonful of the soup. It was nice. It reminded her of the soup her mother had made when Seri was a child. What were called soup vegetables – parsley, celery, leek and carrots – with dried barley and pulse vegetables as well. Thick and nourishing. But she could only manage a fraction of it. The roll was impossible. She pushed it aside, slipped the banana into her handbag, took one last spoonful of the soup, and stood up.

Time to get back to Frankie's room.

It was much later, and the dusk was falling outside the hospital windows, when Seri became aware of a change.

Fitz's eyes were still shut. But his hand, until now flaccid and still beneath hers, was stirring. Not exactly moving. But there was something happening. Some awareness that her hand was holding his.

'Fitz.' Seri spoke softly, determined not to shock or distress him.

Fitz's eyes fluttered open. His head turned very slightly. He was looking at her. He could see her.

Seri gave a moan of pure joy. 'Fitz,' she said again.

'Seri.'

Then his eyes closed again.

Seri didn't want to do the wrong thing. Instinct kept her from trying to wake him. Presently his eyes opened again, and he spoke in a stronger voice.

'Am I in hospital, Seri?'

'Yes, Fitz. You're okay. You're going to be fine.'

'What happened?'

Seri hesitated. 'You collapsed, up at the cottage. They flew you here by helicopter. But the doctor says you'll be fine.' She repeated the words not so much for Fitz's benefit as for her own.

'I don't remember.'

'Don't try. It'll all come back to you soon enough.'

Fitz's face twisted. 'The wolves. Howling outside the door. I remember that.'

'It's okay now, Fitz. They won't come back.'

'Good.' Fitz closed his eyes again.

The next time he woke, he seemed stronger, more able to talk. 'What's this thing in my arm, Seri?'

'It's a drip. So the doctors and nurses were able to feed you while you were unconscious.'

'Have I been here long, then?'

'Not very long. Four – no, five days.'

'I don't remember anything except the day at the cottage. I went for a walk in the woods. It was so beautiful. So peaceful. Something I really needed.'

'Yes.'

'I brought in a lot of wood and peat and built up a fire. I didn't light it until later. Not until about an hour before the wolves started howling. Two hours before my visitor came.'

'Visitor?' Seri looked at him. 'I didn't know you had a visitor.'

'Oh, yes. It was kind of him to come, but I would really rather have been on my own. But he didn't stay long.'

Seri waited.

'I knew who it was as soon as I heard the door knocker, of course. I hadn't told anyone else that I'd be there – only him and you. And you wouldn't have butted in on me, I knew that.'

'No.'

As Fitz continued to talk in a gentle rambling voice, Seri listened.

And as she heard what he had to say, she found presently that she was frozen in horror.

Chapter Fifty

<u>Friday</u>

Pete, Ziggy and Kirstin had been talking for hours, on the 'Do you remember when?' theme, when Kirstin unexpectedly yawned, sat up, and said, 'You know what, guys, I've just had a thought.'

'Surely not?' murmured Ziggy.

'Yeah, really. This stuff about my parents. Mum and Dad gave me a folder, when they were explaining to me how they'd chosen me instead of having to put up with what they got like most parents.'

'A folder?' Pete leaned forward, suddenly feeling excited.

'Yeah. It had some stuff from my biological mother in it. Mum thought I'd like to have it.'

'Kirstin Mackenzie, how come you're only mentioning this now?'

'Well, Petey sweetie, I sorta forgot. I mean, like, I haven't thought about it for years. It was nothing interesting, right? And I wasn't worried about anyone but Mum and Dad right then, see?'

'Cut to the chase,' Ziggy said. 'Do you still have it?'

'Oh, yeah.' Kirstin frowned and considered. 'Well, like, I think I should have. I stuck it in a drawer with some other private stuff. Letters and diaries, right? And when I moved into the apartment I'm pretty sure I brought it with me.'

'Yeah, you're not the sort of girl to clear things out, Kirst. Don't I just remember?'

'Don't be a meanie, Petey. I like to keep things that matter to me.'

'And all the old rubbish of the day, as well,' Pete added.

'So,' Ziggy said impatiently, 'the question is, can you find it?'

'Oh, yes. Well – I think so. But, mind you, I don't think there'll be anything useful there.' Kirstin looked confused. 'Sure, I don't even know why I mentioned it. Just something Ziggy said reminded me of it. But it didn't tell me anything at the time.'

'Never mind, Kirst. Even though it didn't tell you anything, it might tell us, see? For one thing, you were only a very young kid at the time, weren't you?' Ziggy tactfully didn't add, 'and not a very bright kid, at that.'

Instead he said, 'If Pete and I look at it with fresh minds we might see something you missed. Worth a try, anyway.'

'So, it's in your apartment?'

'Yeah.' Kirst brightened. 'Do you want to come back with me and look for it, Petey?'

'We'll both come back with you, Kirst.' Pete spoke firmly.

'Okay.' Kirst looked disappointed for a moment, then she brightened up again. 'It's been a lovely evening, boys. I'm glad it's not over yet.'

Pete and Ziggy drained their glasses and stood up. 'Come on, girl, get that down you,' Pete said. Kirstin obediently finished her drink. Pete took her by the arm, and the three of them made their way back out to the car park where they had left Pete's red Corsa.

It was only a short drive to Kirstin's apartment. They made their way upstairs amid giggles (from Kirstin) and vain attempts to shush her (from Pete), and with feelings of considerable excitement (from both twins). It looked as if they were getting somewhere at last.

An hour later, it was looking less hopeful. Kirstin's bedroom was, to put it bluntly, a mess. It gave the impression that she had never thrown out anything she'd ever owned. Pete, familiar with the syndrome, was less surprised, but Ziggy found it frankly unbelievable.

They sifted through piles of clothes and underclothes, heaps of magazines, and hundreds of letters, mostly brightly coloured advertising spam or unpaid bills, and were about to give up when Ziggy suddenly said, 'Hey. What's this?'

He was holding up a cardboard folder which had been buried beneath a pile of old free newspapers, clearly ones which had never been opened.

'Wow! You've found it!' squealed Kirstin.

'You think?'

'Well, Ziggy, it looks like it.'

Kirstin grabbed the folder from Ziggy's hand, retreated to the king size bed, and sat down on its edge to examine Ziggy's find.

The folder wasn't sealed. One flap was tucked under the other side. Kirstin ripped it open, to exclamations from Pete warning her to be careful, and the contents began to spill out onto the bed. Pete grabbed it from her, bundling up the scraps of paper and thrusting them back inside. Then he sat down beside her and began to sort methodically through them.

'A pink hair ribbon. Sweet.'

Kirstin lifted the ribbon, looked puzzled, then beamed. 'Yes, I remember seeing this. But it's for a baby. It was far too short for me to use when I got the folder. I'd forgotten it was there.'

'I expect your natural mother bought it to tie up whatever wisps of hair you had when you were a newborn. Mums do that, don't they?' said Pete.

Ziggy produced a birth certificate in an envelope. 'This might be something.'

They crowded round to read the certificate. It said, among other things such as the date of birth, 'Mother: Kaitlin O'Donnell.' Kaitlin's parents' name were left blank – unknown. Then came 'Father's name. Another blank – unknown. And his parents were also blank – unknown. Naturally.

'So, this doesn't tell us too much,' Pete said slowly.

He looked round at Kirstin and found that she was in tears. 'Oh, poor Kaitlin!' she sobbed presently. 'All on her own, with a baby girl to look after. Poor thing!'

Ziggy felt glad that Kirstin felt sorry rather than angry. 'There's another certificate here,' he announced, pulling out another brown envelope and opening it. 'Oh. It's a death certificate.' Silently he handed it to Kirstin.

Mopping at her tears, Kirstin squinted at the certificate.

'Is it for Kaitlin?' she asked doubtfully. 'I can never make head or tale of these forms, Petey. You read it!' She thrust the certificate to Pete, who took it and read it to himself.

'Yes, it's for your mother, Kaitlin O'Donnell, Kirst,' he said. He kept his voice as calm as possible, not to encourage more tears in Kirstin, though to tell the truth he found the document quite upsetting himself. 'She must have died shortly after you were born, pet. So no wonder you were adopted.'

Kaitlin snatched the certificate back from Pete. 'Date of birth: 6 June 1978. Date of Death: 12 September 1995. Cause of death: Post natal complications. Petey, I'm not that great at maths. What age does that make her?'

'Seventeen,' Pete said. 'Right, Ziggy?'

'Yeah.'

'And my natural father wasn't around. He just left her to get on with it! The scum! The dirtbag!' Kirstin's tears had dried miraculously, leaving her ragingly angry. 'If I could find out who he was, I'd kill him!'

Strength and energy flowed from her, the sort of emotion which made her glow and send out sparks on stage and made her performance so much more than just an amazing voice.

'Hey, calm down, kid!' Pete took her hand and sat her down on the edge of the bed. 'So far we haven't a clue who he was. Let's just see what else we have here.' He kept hold of Kirstin's hand and turned to Ziggy. 'What else is in that folder, bro'?'

Ziggy upended the rest of the contents on the bed beside Kirstin and Pete. 'Not a lot, I think.'

There was a letter, quite a short one. It seemed to be from Kirstin's natural father. 'Okay if I read this, Kirst?'

'Yeah, go ahead.' Kirstin's anger seemed to have turned to listlessness.

'Darling Kaitlin,' Ziggy read, 'sorry I haven't been around lately. I'll give you a ring soon. Let me know how things go with you and the coming baby. Lots of love, Richie.'

'It's dated 20 May 1995,' he announced. 'The rat knew about the baby, okay. I don't know if he ever rang, but if he'd written again, I'd guess the letter would be here. Looks as if he got offside. No proper name signed, only a shortened form of his first name. No help there.'

Pete released some of his anger in a gust of swearwords. 'Sorry, Kirst,' he said eventually.

'Feel free,' was all Kirstin said. 'You couldn't say anything bad enough about the guy.'

Ziggy picked up the remaining paper from the folder. He looked at it, and stiffened. 'Hey, people, look at this!'

It was a photo of a young man. Dark and good looking – maybe twenty or so. He was wearing what they all recognised as the uniform of a loyalist paramilitary organisation. The photo was signed on the back. 'See you when I get back. Love, Richie.'

'So maybe he died in the Troubles?' Kirstin suggested slowly. ' Maybe I haven't been very fair to him either?'

'The Troubles were mostly over by 1995,' Pete argued reasonably. 'Well, odd patches of stuff was still happening, I suppose.'

'And why would his name not be on the birth certificate, if that was how it was?' Ziggy burst out. 'No reason for Kaitlin not to give it, if he was dead!'

'True.'

Kirstin looked from one to the other of the twins, not sure what she was feeling. Was her natural father a cowardly villain or someone who'd been killed for what he believed – rightly or wrongly. Was he a snake or a sort of hero?

'I don't know, Kirstin,' Pete spoke again. 'Could be you're right. But I've got a strong feeling I've seen this guy somewhere before. In a photograph, maybe. Even on TV. Looking a good bit older. But if it's the same man, then there's no way he died in the Troubles. He's still around.

'And maybe he attacked Fitz because he wants to do something for you, Kirstin. Because he still feels guilty that he left your Kaitlin to manage on her own, nearly eighteen years ago.'

Chapter Fifty-One

Friday

Angel re-read the diary note she had copied from Robbie Mallet's computer when she broke into his apartment. She wished she'd taken time to read it before. It made many things much clearer.

April 30. So, he's now offering far more. For boosting Kirstin on 'Who's On Top?' it was £20,000. An okay amount. I was pleased with it. But now he's offering ten times as much. £100,000. Wow! But for slightly different work, right? Getting the media lined up against Fitz. Not so easy, he's their darling. I'm going to suggest another approach. Something I can make work. A paparazzi hunt down – like with Princess Di. Something that will get on Fitz's nerves and make him destroy himself.

May 2. So, he's pleased with this. But I think – just guessing – he has something else up his sleeve. I don't want to know!

May 4. He thinks he can bully me into doing some of his dirty work for him. No way! I don't need to get myself into deep trouble. Why can't he use his contacts from the UVF? Everybody knows he still has them.

May 5. He's going to use someone else for the really rough stuff. But he still wants me to rustle up the paparazzi attack. No problem. Especially for £100,000!

May 6. Today's the day! Fitz is moving up to the cottage this afternoon. I'll make sure the guys hear about it in time to cluster round tonight. Brilliant tactics!

Here the diary ended. Angel could follow what had happened easily enough. As they had thought, Robbie Mallet had been responsible for organising the media siege of Fitz's cottage. The siege which might have driven him over the edge. But there had been a further plan. And Angel didn't have to think too hard to realise what that was.

Something had been put in Fitz's drink. Something to knock him out, to make it look as if he had reacted to the paparazzi outside his walls by taking an overdose. The implication being that he was still on drugs and had plenty available. Which would leave his reputation in the mire.

Angel hesitated, then decided to take another quick look through the emails. There was a name which had caught her attention.

Ah. There was the folder she'd noticed with vague surprise. What was this particular guy doing, contacting Robbie Mallet?

She opened the folder and began to read, starting with the latest messages. Straightaway she struck pay dirt.

A message to Mallet, but with his own first message, and the answer to it, attached.

This kid Cindy I told you about, she found out what you hired me to do about Fitz. And she reckons she wants some money for her share, or she'll tell everyone. Make it go viral on Twitter, she says. Don't know if she can do that, but she can certainly make trouble. I'm supposed to be seeing her later tonight. What should I say to her?

The answer read.

Do nothing. Arrange to meet her up by Fitz's cottage. It's nice and quiet there. But don't show up. I'll get Artie to deal with her.

And Mallet's final response.

Okay. But you won't do anything to hurt her, will you?

But for the really rough stuff, someone else, Mallet had said in his diary note. Someone with a paramilitary background, used to killing, from the sound of it. For the murder of Cindy Baron, for beating up Billy Nelson, and finally for killing Mallet himself? Wiping out anyone who might know too much, Angel thought. The only question which had occupied her mind for the last few days seemed clearly answered. Who was the big boss? It was the man who'd sent Mallet that email. There was one more question – how had he managed to get the chloral hydrate into Fitz's glass?

Angel sat back for a moment and pressed her fingers to her temples. And thought.

Someone had said something to her that didn't make sense. Something, if she could remember what it was, that would give her the answer to the puzzle.

She sat quietly for a long time, running over in her mind everything she had heard or been told in the last few days.

Presently she sighed. It wasn't coming to her.

She stood up, stretched, and went over to the cabinet on the far wall of her living room where she kept a supply of drinks. There was a bottle of red wine already opened. Carelessly Angel lifted it, twisted off the patent bottle closer, and poured herself a small amount in one of her cut glass goblets with the long stems.

She stood sipping the liquid slowly, savouring its bouquet. Angel made no claim to being an expert in wines. One aroma was much like another to her. But she especially liked this *Mavrodaphne* which she had brought back with her from her recent holiday in Crete. A sweet, very pleasant wine, but strong in spite of that.

Suddenly her head jerked and she almost spilled what was left in her glass. A thought had come to her. Something someone had said. Yes. Someone had let his tongue run away with him unnecessarily. Someone had said something he didn't need to say. Had spoken about something there was no way he could have known about. Unless ...!

It was at that moment that she heard her phone buzz and begin the ringtone for text messages.

It was Ziggy.

'Angel, do you think you could recognise a photo for us? Sending it now.'

Angel waited patiently.

More quickly than she expected, the photo was there. The wonders of modern technology. Angel stared at it for a moment. It meant nothing to her.

The ringtone again. Pete this time.

'My idiot brother should have told you to add at least eighteen years to the guy.'

Ah! That was different. Angel stared at the photo, trying to add the requisite number of years. And found her brain spinning.

Yes! Of course!

It was at that moment that her phone signalled a message yet again.

Seri.

'Angel, Fitz just woke up and told me someone visited him at the cottage that night. I'll not say who – it doesn't seem fair. I'm going to see this guy now, just to ask him a few questions and see if he's okay. Or not. Let you know.'

Angel read the message a second time. And groaned.

Sweet, innocent Seri, heading off on her own to tackle a man who was at the very least someone who'd attempted murder. And more than likely someone who'd hired thugs to carry out not one, but several murders for him.

How could Seri think she could deal with a guy like this on her own?

Angel frantically messaged Seri back.

'Seri! Don't go! Wait for me!'

But Seri's phone was switched off. There was no way of reaching her.

Chapter Fifty-Two

Friday

Okay, the first thing was to message Pete and Ziggy. It would certainly do no harm to have them as back up. And maybe they could let the rest of the gang know whom she suspected and where she was going.

This done, Angel took time to dress for the part.

First of all she stripped and showered. Put on simple underclothes with no frilly bits to catch on anything, and black tights. Then she pulled on a pair of close fitting, stretchy black trousers which gave her the maximum of freedom of movement. She followed this with a thin black tee shirt in a flexible artificial fabric, and sat down to pull on her boots.

These were the ones recommended by her kick boxing instructor. Not for the practices. They were too dangerously strong for that and might inflict serious damage on her boxing partner. No, these were boots which her instructor said were perfect for situations where she might have to defend herself for real.

Finally, she smeared her face with a dark cream which had been supplied to her by Josh Smith from his *Interpol* kit.

She had learnt a lot from her kick boxing instructor over the last year. But even more from Josh, the professional *Interpol* policeman and fighter. On their holiday in Crete, she had picked Josh's brains, learned from him how to disarm someone who had a gun, among other skills. Not by kicking the gun, which might easily go off, but by kicking the nerves in the arm to numb the hand holding the gun, as she'd done with Robbie Mallet. And how to dress and darken her face for dangerous exploits like this. She was very grateful to both Josh and her instructor.

Time to go.

Angel drove as fast as she thought safe through the dark streets. The streetlights gave her plenty of help while she was still within the city centre. But before long she had left the centre of Belfast behind and the light from the street lamps was less powerful.

But she knew exactly where she was going, and before long she had reached her goal.

High walls surrounded the house and grounds. Angel had already decided not to go in by the gate and drive. Instead she took the car out of sight to the rear of the grounds and parked it close to the high wall. She had a thin rope secured around her waist. Now she uncoiled it and fastened one end to the steering wheel. Springing athletically onto the roof of her car, she stretched up to grasp the top of the wall. A strong push and she had hauled herself up astride it.

There was no car to help her on the inside. Instead, she pulled up the rope, giving it several tugs to make sure it was securely fastened. Then she dropped it down inside the wall, and swarmed down it. She was standing at the foot of the wall in minutes.

Angel planned to take the rope with her. To do that, she had fastened it with a clove hitch with two long ends. It would come unfastened when she gave it a tug on one end. Now, she gave a sharp tug to the knot on the steering wheel and jerked it free. She took a moment to coil it carefully back round her waist. It would be useful later in helping her climb anywhere she needed to.

She stood for a moment, getting her bearings. The smell of night stock came to her faintly from a nearby flowerbed. Early roses, too.

There was no moon. The darkness inside the grounds was absolute. She was glad of the advice Josh had given her about always carrying a torch. She pulled it from her pocket and switched on its narrow pencil beam. Feeling her way cautiously by its light, she made her way through the trees and bushes. She rounded a corner of the house and knew she was at the front. A faint light ahead told her she was nearing one of the windows of the house.

A crashing sound in the bushes nearby warned her that someone or something was approaching her. Angel switched off her torch and ducked down behind the nearest shrub. She was confident that no one could see her there.

But the crashing sound kept on coming closer.

Angel felt in the right hand pocket of her trousers for the cosh she carried there. The sounds came even closer. Then she heard a bark.

So, the noise came from a dog. A watch dog, she supposed.

Angel stood up. No use hiding from an animal which was tracking her down by smell rather than sight.

'Good boy,' she said coaxingly.

To her surprise and pleasure the dog gave another woof, came bounding up to her, and began to lick her extended hand.

It was a large black and white Newfoundland, very furry and friendly and absolutely useless as a watchdog – provided it didn't make enough noise to alert the people in the house. Angel breathed a sigh of relief and, crouching down again, began to make a fuss of the dog, patting it and rolling over with it in a cordial game.

When she felt that she had done enough to make sure of the dog's friendship, she stood up again and took hold of the dog's collar in one hand.

'All right, boy,' she said firmly. 'Hush, now! You and me are going for a little walk.'

Pulling the dog along with her, she made for the house. The light she had seen came from the set of patio windows giving onto the front garden. Angel slipped carefully along the wall of the house until she was in a position to put one eye, no more, round the edge of the window.

There were Venetian blinds, of course, but it seemed that no one had thought of closing them. Angel could see a small segment of the room, and could hear the voices of two people inside, could catch a glimpse of the wood burning stove, now lit and throwing out a cheerful gleam.

'I just want to understand,' one voice was saying. 'It seems as if you must have been responsible. But if you tell me you weren't, of course I'll believe you. If you can explain to me just what did happen.'

It was a girl's voice, and Angel recognised it at once.

It was Seri.

Angel knew even before she heard his voice that her guess had been right. The man talking to Seri was Dinger Bell.

Chapter Fifty-Three

Friday

'I'm confused, Seri. Seri? Is that right?'

'Yes. Short for Serena.'

'Lovely name.' Angel could hear the politician putting all his practised charm into his voice as he spoke. 'What exactly is it you think I did?'

'I thought I explained.' Seri sounded puzzled. 'Frankie told me you were there at the cottage with him that night.'

'Fitz said that? Well, now, I think he must be a bit mixed up. I've never been near the cottage. Wouldn't even know where to find it. The poor boy is suffering from confusion and memory loss from the sound of it. Not unusual after what he's been through, don't you think?'

'No.' Seri's voice had become firm again. 'He told me you were there. He wasn't confused. And he says the last thing he remembers is you pouring him a drink from the bottle of whiskey. Telling him it would calm him down.'

'I'm sorry, Seri, but he must have dreamt it.' Dinger Bell laughed ruefully. 'What can I say? Okay, I wasn't at the cottage that night or any time. I didn't visit Fitz. And I certainly didn't pour him a glass of Bushmills, whatever that has to do with it.'

'Someone put something in that glass,' Seri said. 'That's what it has to do about it. And, Mr Bell – how did you happen to know it was Bushmills whiskey?'

There was a stark silence. Then Dinger Bell laughed. 'Why, my dear girl, I knew it would be Bushmills because that was what Fitz always drank!'

'No, he didn't,' said Seri calmly. 'Fitz doesn't much like whiskey. He never drank it by choice. But a fan gave him that bottle not long before he left for the cottage. He showed it to me. He wasn't taking anything else to drink with him, but he said it was a very kind gift, and he'd take it along, and might even try it. So you still haven't explained how you could have known the whiskey he had at the cottage was Bushmills?'

'Good heavens, I didn't know anything about it!' Bell said in an exasperated voice. 'I just assumed when you mentioned whiskey that Fitz would have only the best!'

'Story number two,' said Seri. She laughed. 'Is there a third one coming up?'

Angel, listening outside the window, was impressed. She hadn't expected Seri to handle the politician so calmly and expertly. However, time she took a hand herself, perhaps. Dinger Bell might get ugly soon.

And indeed, as she thought this, she saw the man take a step forward and grab hold of Seri's arm. 'Now listen, that's just enough!' he growled at her. 'As a matter of fact, I was with a friend that evening. Artie Flanagan, my bodyguard. And as it happens, he's here tonight. We're normally together, as you might expect. Tell you what, I'll call him in now, and he can confirm what I'm telling you.'

Seri looked angry. 'I'm not sure your bodyguard's word is all that reliable, Mr Bell. Won't he be happy to support you in most things?' She stepped back, pulling her arm loose from Bell's grasp.

Angel decided not to wait any longer. She inspected the windows carefully. As she had feared, they were securely locked. And being a politician, Bell probably had them alarmed. Yes, she could see the wires running down the sides of the patio doors.

Better find another way in. Maybe an upstairs window. It was less likely that the alarm system would cover that.

Angel backed quietly away from the window and began to circle the house, looking for a way in. It was a tall building and one that had been there for a couple of hundred years, probably, Angel thought. The walls were in the typical Belfast style of red brick. It had been modernised in parts – the patio windows she had just left, for instance – but much of it remained as it had always been. The sort of house which had been built in Victorian days to house a family of maybe thirteen, plus servants.

The servants, of course, had pigged it out in the attics and the basement. There were numerous windows, mostly tall and opening with sashes. Angel reckoned she could get through one of these, especially one on the top storey. Provided there were no alarms. But it seemed likely that the security system had been confined to the first couple of floors, and the rooms in use.

To one side of the house, a garage had been converted from former stables. Angel pushed open the wide doors cautiously. A gleaming BMW. And behind it, tucked away out of sight, a Yamaha motorbike. Possibly – indeed, probably – the bike used by Cindy Baron's murderer. Things were beginning to come together.

Angel slipped quietly out of the garage again and made her way on round to the back of the house, until she found a secluded spot directly in front of a series of windows, each placed just above the others, one to each storey of the house.

Running down the wall of the house, not too far from the windows, was a downpipe. Angel noticed that it was fastened to the wall at intervals by what looked like very secure brackets, a couple to each storey. Near enough to the windows for easy access.

She uncoiled the rope from around her waist and attached one end to a strong metal hook which she had carried in one pocket. Then, standing well back to get as good a view and as correct an aim as possible, she hurled the end with the hook towards the nearest bracket above the first floor window immediately over her head.

She needed several tries before she was sure it had caught. Even then, she took the time to tug the rope firmly more than once until she knew beyond doubt that the hook was securely attached over the bracket. Then, bracing her feet against the wall, she took a firm grip on her end of the rope and began to climb, surely, cat-footed, making no mistakes.

It was only a minute or so before she reached the windowsill and was sitting on it. She drew her legs up beside her. Then she stood up cautiously, unhooked the rope, and threw it accurately towards the bracket over the window on the floor above.

Once again, after a few tries, she knew that the hook had caught safely. Not omitting the precaution of preliminary tugs to make sure the attachment was firm, Angel swarmed on up to the second floor level. Then she moved up another storey to the attic level, and there rested for a moment on the sill to get her breath and to explore her prospects.

There seemed to be no sign of an alarm system. Good.

The window, like most of the others she'd seen, operated on a sash. Angel took out a small penknife and worked it carefully along the place where the top half of the window met the lower half. This was where the window was fastened. She knew what she was doing. She'd spent some time not long ago practising how to slip the knife in and push back the catch, under the instruction of Big Hughie. Around the same time that she'd learnt how to work a picklock on a door.

She remembered only too well how she'd longed to be able to open a locked door during her adventure in Crete. She smiled grimly to herself. Her friend Big Hughie had been really helpful, both in showing her where to buy the picklocks and in teaching her how to use them. It was amazing what you could find on the Internet these days. And what you could buy. Her set of picklocks hadn't been cheap, but at the same time they hadn't been hard to purchase.

Five minutes careful work and she felt the catch give. Angel withdrew her knife blade and knelt to push up the lower pane of the window. The only question remaining was, would she find the room empty?

But she was ninety-nine per cent sure that she would. Even Dinger Bell didn't have a crowd of live-in servants these days. And any he did have would be accommodated in much better rooms than this.

She put the knife back in her pocket, coiled up the rope again, and began to slide through the window. Then, as her feet touched the floor, she froze.

Immediately inside the room a dark figure, which seemed more than life size, loomed up in her path.

Chapter Fifty-Four

<u>Friday</u>

For a moment Angel stood completely still, hardly daring to breathe.

Then she recovered herself, caught her breath again, and laughed.

The figure which had alarmed her so much was nothing more than an old fashioned dressmaker's dummy, the type of thing women used to keep at home, at a time when making your own dresses was more common. No longer in use, it must have been relegated to this remote attic to be out of the way.

The room had clearly also been in use as a place to store everything else that wasn't to be thrown out. Piles of books, a couple of broken chairs, some dusty paintings, a good many boxes and trunks, some securely fastened, but others gaping open with lids flung back and out-of-date clothes tumbling over the edge.

Angel checked that she had everything in place, everything she needed, after the scramble up the walls of the house. Hook back in her pocket. Rope coiled round her waist. Rubber gloves in one piece – no nicks to reveal her fingerprints through the tear. Yes, it all seemed to be okay.

She moved cautiously towards the attic door, her pencil torch in one hand. The beams of moonlight shining through the window where she had just entered made it unnecessary for the time being, but when she went out of the attic through the door and began to make her way down through the house it would be a different matter.

Reaching the door, she pushed it slightly open and paused to listen.

No sound of anyone around. Good.

Angel slid carefully through the door, looked in every direction, and switched on her pencil torch. The tiny beam lit up a winding staircase directly before her feet. Moving slowly, Angel went down the stairs.

The landing below her was as dark as the stairs above. Without the torch, Angel would have been groping in the dark.

She stood there for a few moments, getting her bearings, her ears alert for information. What had been happening in the room where she had watched Dinger Bell trying to convince Seri of his innocence?

A sudden clamour smote her ears, making her jump with alarm. Voices – sounds of furniture bumping or falling. A high voice which she was almost certain was Seri's calling for help.

Angel started for the next flight of stairs, intending to charge down it helter-skelter. Then she stopped. Abruptly she drew herself back into the shadows of the upper landing.

Below her she could see vague figures. Two people, men from their appearance, dragging a third. A third who seemed to be a woman and an unconscious woman at that. Seri, instinct told her.

The men, grunting and groaning, pushed open a door on the landing below. Then they made their way through it, with considerable effort, hauling their helpless prisoner with them. The door slammed shut.

Angel hurtled down the stairs. By her over-careful decision to enter the house somewhere that wouldn't set off the alarm, instead of bursting in on Bell straightaway, she had exposed Seri to goodness knew what sort of violence.

As a past victim of violence herself, during her unhappy marriage, Angel was only too aware of the horror of this sort of thing. She blamed herself furiously as she moved to Seri's rescue. Then she took a hold on her emotions, and made a cold decision to stop this self-blame. It was pointless. What she needed to do now was to be calm and clear about her next move.

She wished passionately she had brought her gun with her. It would have made everything so easy. But she remained reluctant to use a gun except in extreme circumstances. She hadn't expected to need it tonight.

Standing outside the door of the room where Seri was imprisoned, she listened carefully. She could hear voices, not very distinct but clear enough to understand.

'You fool, what possessed you to hit her so hard? I was talking her round nicely. No need for you to butt in.' The grumble came from Dinger Bell, the politician. Angel drew in her breath as she took in the callous nature of his question. He wasn't worried about Seri's pain, only about himself and the position he was in.

'Well, boss.' The second voice was more of a whine. 'What did I know? I came in and there you were with the girl lashing out at you. Punching your face, it seemed to me. I hit her over the head because it seemed the way to stop her.'

'In future, think first.' Dinger Bell had regained his self-control. 'She'd lost her temper with me. But what does a smack from a wee girl like that mean to me? She'd have backed down – been ashamed of losing her temper and hitting out. Gone away happy enough by the time I'd talked her round. And now look at her!'

'She's okay, boss.' The second voice sounded anxious in spite of his cheerful words. 'I only gave her a light tap. She'll come round in no time.'

'Well, help me get her onto this bed,' ordered Bell. 'We'll leave her to recover. I've a few words to say to you, Flanagan. You've been going berserk – not just tonight, but did you need to bump off that reporter girl, Cindy Baron, or Robbie Mallet? I know I told you to deal with them – but that wasn't what I meant, for any sake!'

'Wasn't it, boss? I got you wrong, then. I thought that was what you wanted. It always used to be when we were working together during the Troubles.'

'Yeah, but sure things have changed now, ye eedjit! Murders aren't two a penny any more!' Bell's voice grew louder in his increased exasperation. 'And there was no need for you to go back up to the cottage and steal that Bushmills bottle. Sure, the chloral hydrate was never in it at all. I put it in the glass.'

'Did you, boss?' Artie Flanagan's voice sounded humble. 'But I thought there might be your fingerprints on it?'

'Well, maybe you have a point there. Okay. But what about Robbie Mallet? I sent you over to London to keep an eye on Mallet just in case he was in contact with anyone. Not to bump him off!'

'But, boss, I told you he was meeting this Angel Murphy girl. She was at his flat, and the next day he called her hotel and left a message! I heard him speaking on his mobile! He was up to no good, I'm telling you!'

'Maybe. Well, it's too late now. You gave him the works. No use moaning about it, I suppose. But in future you've got to start thinking before you hit out, Artie boy. Come on. Let's get you out of here before this Seri girl comes round. If she doesn't see you maybe I can persuade her it was an accident – that she tripped and banged her head, or something. Thank goodness you came on her from behind, so she may not even have realised there was someone else there.'

There were sounds of the two men moving towards the door. Angel drew back out of sight and slipped into the next room.

She took a good look at the man with Bell as they came through the doorway. Her eyes were used by now to the semi darkness. There was enough moonlight to light up Artie Flanagan's face. A hard, brutal face, the face of someone who had lived with violence for too long and had no intention of giving up on it now.

Angel wanted to be sure that she would know this man who had attacked Seri so pointlessly. Not even because his boss had wanted him to. Just because it was ingrained into his own vicious nature.

The men headed off down the stairs. Angel allowed them a few moments to get out of sight round the bend in the staircase, then she approached the door of the room where they had left Seri.

Chapter Fifty-Five

Friday

As she had half hoped, half expected, it was unlocked. She had heard no sound of a key being turned in a lock when the men came out.

Angel turned the handle quietly and slipped inside, drawing the door gently shut behind her.

Seri was lying, comfortably enough, on a large double bed, a pillow beneath her head and a duvet drawn up round her. As Angel entered the room and crossed to her, she stirred slightly, moaned, and opened her eyes.

'What happened? Where am I?'

'It's okay, darlin'. You're still in Dinger Bell's house. But you're all right.'

'Am I?' Seri sounded doubtful. 'My head feels sore.'

'Yes. Well. I suppose there's no point in not telling you. One of Dinger's ex paramilitary yobos hit you over the head. You've been unconscious. But if it's any consolation to you, Dinger was pretty mad with him for doing it.'

'I don't understand.' Seri sounded very weak. 'Why are you here, Angel? I didn't tell you where I was going, did I?'

'No. But I'd just found out from reading Robbie Mallet's emails that Dinger Bell was the man. And he made a stupid mistake when he was talking to me. He said he hated to think of Fitz all alone in that cottage, 'with only his big white teddy bear for company.'

'You guys had told me Fitz was given that bear just before he went up to the cottage. So how did Dinger Bell know about it, unless he'd gone there to see Fitz and had seen the bear himself? The man's a fool.'

'Yes – he made another mistake, the same sort of thing, when I was talking to him. He referred to the whiskey at the cottage being Bushmills. He'd no way of knowing that either, unless he'd been there.'

'I heard him. I was outside the window, Seri. I should have come in then, but I thought you seemed to be doing very well without my help and maybe I could find some hard evidence if I prowled around the house – and I thought it'd be better not to set off the alarm. Sorry about that – I could have saved you a nasty blow.'

'No worries.' Seri grinned. 'Come to that, if I hadn't lashed out at Bell, I don't suppose anyone would have thought of hitting me. But what a fool that man is, Angel.'

'I know. He talks too much for his own good – like all politicians. Gives himself away over and over just by not shutting up.'

Seri sat up cautiously. 'I think I feel a bit better now. Should we go?'

'Might be best.' Angel wondered if she should mention that Ziggy and Pete ought to be weighing in any time now. Better not, perhaps. Seri would want to stay if she did. She thought she'd just get Seri safely away and then wait for the boys before tackling Dinger Bell and his hard man Flanagan.

'I think our best plan is to sneak downstairs and get you out to my car, darlin', she said. 'You can rest there. I want a doctor to have a look at that head. And the police, of course. I think tonight is the time we bring them in on this. We have a clear picture now of what happened, and some evidence. Come on, I'll help you downstairs.'

She put an arm round Seri and helped her off the bed. Then they made their way across the room and moved quietly down the stairs. They had reached the front of the house and were about to cross the entrance hall, and Angel was wondering if the alarms would go off when she opened the door from the inside, or if they only worked when someone tried to come in, when they heard a thunderous knocking.

'Open up!' bellowed a voice Angel recognised. 'Open up in the name of the law!'

It was Ziggy. A moment later she heard Pete say distinctly, 'Shut up, ye eedjit! We aren't the police!'

'No, but we might as well be! And we can get them here any moment now if we want to. Open up, Dinger!' He resumed his bellowing. 'We know your guilty secret!'

Angel found herself laughing in spite of everything. She pulled Seri back out of sight as the sound of quick footsteps told them that Dinger Bell was on his way to answer the front door.

'What's going on, you hellions?' he roared at the twins as he pulled the door open. Either the alarm didn't work when the door was opened from inside, Angel noted, or else he had switched it off, for there was no ringing. 'What d'ye think you're doing, shouting the place down at this time of night? Are you drunk or what?'

'Us? Drunk?' Ziggy began indignantly. Then remembrance of the many pints he and Pete had drained with Kirstin earlier in the evening pulled him up short. 'Well. Maybe slightly. But,' he went on sternly as he and Pete pushed their way past Dinger Bell and stood foursquare in his entrance hall, 'that's not the point. We want to talk to you, Bell. About your daughter Kirstin. And about what happened to Fitz in the cottage in Cushendall.'

Bell stood for a moment, unable to speak. The mention of Kirstin's name seemed to have knocked the stuffing out of him.

He staggered backwards. Then he seemed to recover himself. 'Listen, we can't talk about that sort of thing here. Come in. Come in. And shut that door for any sake before the neighbours hear you.'

'You're not in the Newtownards Road now, Dinger,' Pete said cheerfully. 'Your neighbours here are miles away. How are they going to hear anything?'

'You'd be surprised,' muttered Bell. With a furtive look round, he pulled them into the front room and pushed the door shut. They were in the room where Angel had heard him talking to Seri earlier.

'Sit down,' he said. 'Now, what on earth are you talking about? My two daughters are neither of them called Kirstin. And right now they're on holiday with their mother in America. Well for you – coming out with scandalous rubbish like that! If they were here to listen to you it'd be a lot more serious.' He was beginning to get back into gear, Angel saw, trying to talk his way out of whatever the boys had found out.

'No, Dinger,' said Pete coolly. 'We're talking about your daughter Kirstin, the one you had back in 1995 with Kaitlin O'Donnell. We've seen the birth certificate, you know.'

'Birth certificate? My name wasn't on the birth certificate!' Once again the politician had opened his mouth too wide.

'Aha!' crowed Ziggy triumphantly. 'And how do you happen to know anything about it, Mister Dinger Bell?'

'I – I mean, it couldn't be on any certificate because I never had such a daughter!' Bell stammered. He was beginning to look green.

'But that's not all,' Pete went on. 'We have Kaitlin's photo of you with your name on it. But even without the name, it would be easy to recognise anyway. You haven't changed a bit, Richie! And how you suit the uniform!'

He made the mistake of holding out the photo for Bell to see. Next second, with a wild cry, Dinger Bell had leapt forward, snatched the photo from Pete's hand, and was charging off with it up the stairs as fast as he could go.

Pete and Ziggy were left standing with their mouths open, thunderstruck.

But Bell had hardly rounded the first bend of the stairs before Angel was on his heels.

Chapter Fifty-Six

Friday

'Flanagan!' howled Dinger Bell as he thundered upwards. 'Get her!'

A door opened on the next landing above them. Artie Flanagan burst out of his room and stood staring down at his boss and the pursuing Angel.

Bell pushed past him and on up. Angel reached the landing just as Flanagan took in the situation and moved forward to grab her.

Balancing firmly on one leg, Angel kicked out sideways with the other. She caught Flanagan behind the knee, making him trip forward. Her hands flashed out, the edge of one catching him across the bridge of his nose and the other using his arm to twist him round and down.

Flanagan, balanced now precariously on the edge of the top landing stair, found himself unable to recover. With an angry wail he went headlong down the stairs. Pete and Ziggy, coming up behind Angel by now, were just in time to seize hold of him as he came hurtling towards them. Angel left them to it. She was already moving swiftly again after her main target.

She took time to wonder why Bell had headed upwards. If he wanted to get rid of the photo, surely the wood burning stove in the front room would have been the ideal place? Was it because he knew Flanagan had gone up there? Or was there another reason?

Bell pounded on, up another flight and another. They were at the top of the house now, on the attic floor where Angel had made her entrance a short time ago. The Flanagan episode, brief as it was, had given Bell a lead. He had time to dive into one of the attic doorways before Angel could catch him. It was the room she'd been in earlier. The door slammed in her face and a key turned in the lock just as she reached it.

Angel got out her picklocks without any waste of time. It wasn't a difficult lock to open, she could see. Nevertheless it would take her a minute or so. Meanwhile, what would Bell be doing with the photo? There was nowhere here that he could burn it, surely?

She concentrated on the lock, speaking to Bell as she worked. 'Dinger! Don't be a fool! We know the truth now – you may as well admit it! Come on out!'

No answer. Angel could hear the sound of things being dragged across the floor. She remembered that the room had been used as a rubbish store, and thought Bell must be moving the trunks and boxes about, searching for something. She hoped it wasn't a gun.

The lock gave a satisfying click and Angel breathed a sigh of relief. Pushing the door open she went in with a rush. Nothing to be gained by caution. Bell knew she was there.

He was crouched in the middle of the room, bending over one of the trunks she had noted before, one which was securely fastened. In his hands was a bunch of keys and he was trying one after the other in the lock.

The photo which he had snatched lay on the dusty floor beside him. As Angel crossed to him he succeeded in opening the lock, and thrust open the lid of the trunk. Inside Angel could see a bundle of letters, a number of press clippings, and a photograph album.

Dinger Bell looked up at her with an expression on his face of what seemed like fear. 'Back off!' he snarled. 'None of this is anything to do with you.'

'What you did to Fitz is to do with me,' Angel said. 'I intend to see that the truth comes out.'

'No! No, you can't do that to me! I'll be ruined!'

'You tried to ruin Fitz – as well as kill him. That has to be put right.'

'I never meant to kill Fitz. It was only a dose of chloral hydrate. Okay, I put a small dose in his whiskey – but it wouldn't kill anyone except in huge doses!'

'Not so huge, Dinger. The doctor said it was touch and go.'

'All I wanted to do was knock him out of the *New Music Awards!*'

'And ruin his career afterwards.'

'No! He'd have got over it. The press would have a new victim in another week. I didn't mean Fitz any harm – I like the boy. But I had to help Kirstin. I left her and Kaitlin on their own – I needed to make up for it.'

Dinger Bell buried his head in his hands and groaned. 'It's only this last year or so that I started to realise what a terrible thing I'd done to my two girls. Poor little Kaitlin. She was so young. I loved her so much. But how could I marry her? It was against everything I was fighting for!'

'You mean because she was a Catholic and you were a Protestant?' asked Angel slowly.

'Yes.' The answer came in half a sob and half a whisper.

'You realise that it's that attitude that tore our country apart for nearly forty years? That caused thousands of deaths and even more heartbreak?'

'Yes. But how could I tell my followers that I was in love with a Catholic? That she was expecting my child? How could I ever dream of marrying her?'

He looked up at Angel hopefully, wanting some degree of understanding, even sympathy. 'Here.' He took a handful of letters from the trunk and held them out to her. 'Read these. Then maybe you'll understand how much we loved each other. But it had to be a secret.'

Angel glanced briefly at the letters. Letters from Bell to Kaitlin and from Kaitlin to him. She read enough to see that although Bell had written regularly to Kaitlin, he had asked her always to send his letter back with her reply, so no one else would ever see it.

Angel found it impossible to give him the sympathy he wanted.

'I see no real love here, Dinger Bell. Only selfishness and cruelty.'

A cry burst from the man's lips. 'I know! I know! That's what I've come to realise. That's why I want to help Kirstin! I made it my business at the time to find out what had happened to her. I had connections, it wasn't difficult. And so I knew she'd been adopted by some good people. But I realised not long ago that I should have done much more for her. I paid Mallet to promote her. And I paid him to gather up the media and use them to break Fitz down.'

'And you thought that would make what you did to Kaitlin all right? You don't have the first idea, Dinger. Yes, I'm sorry for you in a way – sorry that your ideas have always been so mixed up. But it all has to come out now. You've made it impossible to keep it a secret any more. Fitz's reputation has to be saved. You have to admit that you visited him at the cottage and put the drug in his whiskey. And I don't see the press letting up until they work out your motives for doing that.'

'Angel, wait!' Dinger Bell stood up eagerly and reached into the inside breast pocket of his jacket. 'Look, here's my chequebook. I'll write you a cheque that'll turn your life around. Just promise that you won't tell anyone the truth!'

Angel pushed away the chequebook which Dinger Bell was thrusting towards her.

'Don't be such an eedjit, boyo! Even if I would ever dream of taking your dirty money, Bell, there's a whole group of us, Fitz's friends, working together to sort this out, and they all know by now that you're the one responsible – and they're all out for your blood! Face it, the secret's out!'

Dinger Bell stood for a moment, the chequebook dangling from one hand, the letters from the other.

Then he gave a wild cry, and sprang for the window.

Chapter Fifty-Seven

Friday

Angel leapt after him. She wanted Dinger Bell alive and convicted of his crime. Fitz mustn't be left under the stigma of being one more junkie pop star who'd overdosed. It would wreck his career. Wreck his life.

Bell was struggling to open the window. He had the catch unfastened and was pushing up the lower half of the sash when Angel reached him. She caught him round the shoulders, squeezing the upper part of his arms tight to his body, and began to pull him back into the room.

'No way, Bell!' she panted. 'You're staying here!'

The room was full of old toys, chairs, pictures, books. They were piled everywhere. Dinger Bell's arms were helpless, but he could use his feet. He kicked out viciously, backwards, and caught Angel on her shin. For a moment she reacted by staggering back. Bell's foot caught against something else and pushed it towards Angel. It was a Jack-in-the-Box. And now it was under her right foot.

Angel felt the Jack-in-the-Box slip beneath her weight. She put out all her strength and managed to remain upright. Dinger Bell was still struggling to free himself from her grip.

'Pete! Ziggy! Can you come?'

She knew the twins were dealing with Bell's hard man, Flanagan. But maybe they had him tied up and under control by now? She could do with any help that was going.

If all that was needed was to knock Dinger Bell out, she could have done that. But if she took one hand away from the grip she had on him for long enough to deliver a sideways slash at his neck, she knew he would slip out of her grasp and would end up by falling out of the window. He was out on the sill by now, the lower sash raised, and they were struggling precariously. One more slip from her, she knew, and she would let him slide away from her to plunge down to his death.

She held on grimly, finding a part of the floor which was uncluttered to brace herself against.

Bell was a strong man, with years of violent action behind him. He didn't have Angel's skills, but when it came to a straight trial of strength between them, he had the edge.

'Let me go! Let me go, Angel! I can't live on and face this disgrace!' He was groaning, struggling hard to escape her.

Angel hung on with all her strength.

She heard, dimly, the sound of feet thundering up the attic stairs.

'Coming, Angel!' called one of the twins – Pete, she thought. She heard the voice. Without meaning to she relaxed slightly and felt Dinger Bell tear himself out of her grip. The impetus of his heave was enough. A second later he was hurtling headfirst out of the window.

As he fell, Angel heard him scream.

She was shuddering, her hands over her ears, when Pete and Ziggy arrived. The twins moved past her and gazed down out of the window.

'I think he's had it,' Pete said.

'But we should go down and check,' Ziggy said soberly. 'There might still be a chance for him.'

They went down, all three, and stood looking at what was left of Dinger Bell, the great politician and ex paramilitary leader.

Pete knelt down beside the bloodstained body and felt for a pulse. Nothing.

'He's gone, I'm afraid.'

Dinger Bell had been a bad man throughout his life. But seeing him lying dead before them had a sobering effect, nevertheless.

'We'd better ring the police and the ambulance services,' Angel said. 'And they can arrest Flanagan at the same time. I heard Dinger Bell say he was the one who stabbed Cindy Baron and Robbie Mallet, to say nothing of beating up Billy Nelson and pinching the Bushmills bottle for Dinger Bell. And I think he has the knife he used on them in his pocket now. Where's Seri?'

'Lying down inside. And keeping an eye on Flanagan. We tied him up securely.'

Seri sat up when they came into the room.

'What happened?'

They told her.

'So,' she said slowly, 'we have nothing to prove that Bell drugged Fitz?'

'Oh, I wouldn't say that.' Angel recovered herself sufficiently to smile at Seri. 'As it happens, I had my pocket recorder with me. And I had it switched on. It would be better if Bell was alive to make a confession. But listen to this.'

Chapter 57

She took the mini recorder out of her pocket, and pressed a switch. Listened for a moment, then fast forwarded it. Turned up the volume. Dinger Bell's voice sounded loud in the quiet room.

'I never meant to kill Fitz. It was only a dose of chloral hydrate. Okay, I put a small dose in his whiskey – but it wouldn't kill anyone except in huge doses!'

'Not so small, Dinger. The doctor said it was touch and go.'

'All I wanted to do was knock him out of the New Music Awards!'

The conversation went on. Presently Angel switched the machine off.

'So, we have all the evidence we need, Seri. Tomorrow I've promised my boss, Minerva, to let her have the recording if, as I hoped, I got something worthwhile. And she's planning to work with a colleague on the news programme, and get it broadcast tomorrow.'

'But you can't do that to Kirstin!' It was Ziggy who burst out, sounding very unhappy.

'Don't worry, darlin'. Kirstin won't come into it. I'll edit the tape so she isn't mentioned. Dinger's motive won't be public knowledge. But everyone will know that Fitz was set up. That he doesn't do drugs any more. That was what we wanted, wasn't it?'

'Yeah.' The agreement was mutual.

'Okay. Then I think we have a right to celebrate, once the authorities have wrapped this up. Let's get the whole gang together, as soon as we can. I have a couple of bottles of champagne back at mine. What say we go round there?'

'Hey!' responded Ziggy enthusiastically, while Pete and Seri smiled and nodded assent. 'You're a great girl, Angel Murphy! You couldn't have a better idea! Let's go for it!'

And, eventually, they did.

About the author

Gerry McCullough has been writing poems and stories since childhood. Brought up in north Belfast, she graduated in English and Philosophy from Queen's University, Belfast, then went on to gain an MA in English.

She lives just outside Belfast, in Northern Ireland, has four grown up children and is married to author, media producer and broadcaster, Raymond McCullough, with whom she co-edited the Irish magazine, *Bread*, (published by *Kingdom Come Trust*), from 1990-96. In 1995 they published a non-fiction book called, *Ireland – now the good news!*

Over the past few years Gerry has had more than sixty short stories published in UK, Irish and American magazines, anthologies and annuals – as well as broadcast on *BBC Radio Ulster* – plus poems and articles published in several Northern Ireland and UK magazines. She has read from her novels, poems and short stories at several Irish literary events.

Gerry won the *Cúirt International Literary Award* for 2005 (Galway); was shortlisted for the 2008 *Brian Moore Award* (Belfast); shortlisted for the 2009 *Cúirt Award*; and commended in the 2009 *Seán O'Faolain Short Story Competition*, (Cork).

Belfast Girls, her first full-length Irish novel, was first published (by *Night Publishing*, UK) in November 2010 (re-issued July 2012 by *Precious Oil*). *Danger Danger* was published by *Precious Oil Publications* in October 2011; followed by *The Seanachie: Tales of Old Seamus* in January 2012 (a first collection of humorous Irish short stories, previously published in a weekly Irish magazine); *Angel in Flight* (the first Angel Murphy thriller) in June 2012; *Lady Molly and the Snapper* – a young adult novel time travel adventure set in Dublin (August 2012) and *Johnny McClintock's War* (August 2014) – a historical novel set during WWI and early 20th century Ulster.

The *Cúirt Award*-winning story, *Primroses*, and the *Seán O'Faolain* commended story, *Giving Up*, will be included in a new collection of twelve Irish short stories written by Gerry – Deams, Visions, Nightmares – to be published shortly. Also in the pipeline are; and *Not the End of the World* – a humorous, futuristic, adult fantasy novel.

Johnny McClintock's War:

One man's struggle against the hammer blows of life

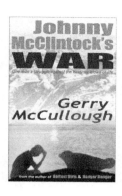

Gerry McCullough

The story of one man's struggle to maintain his faith in spite of everything life throws at him.

As the outbreak of the First World War looms closer, John Henry McClintock, a Northern Irish Protestant by upbringing, meets Rose Flanagan, a Catholic, at a gospel tent mission – and falls in love with her.

When Johnny enlists and sets off to fight in the War he finds himself surrounded by death and tragedy, which pushes his trust in God to the limit.

After more than five years absence he returns home to a bitter, war torn Ireland, where both he and Rose are seen as traitors to their own sides.

John Henry and Rose overcome all opposition and, finally, marry. But a few years later comes the hardest blow of all. Can John Henry still hang on to his faith in God?

> *"brilliant .. this book had me captured from the start .. moves at a fair pace throughout"*
> **Tom Elder**, *Amazon.com*

> *"characters you will truly care about ..*
> *a gut-wrenching emotional ride .. a must read"*
> **Tom Winton**, author, USA

> *"Gerry McCullough's best book yet ..*
> *a powerful tribute to those who died for their countries and what they believed"*
> **Juliet B Madison**, author, UK

> *"an emotional roller coaster ride .. an epiphany .. highly recommended*
> *.. a book that will make you think about how wonderful life truly is"*
> **Thomas Baker**, Amazon.com, Santiago, Chile

> *"will hold you spellbound until the very last sentence*
> *.. I love this book"*
> **Sheila Mary Belshaw**, author, UK, Menorca, Cape Town

Belfast Girls

The story of three girls – Sheila, Phil and Mary – growing up into the new emerging post-conflict Belfast of money, drugs, high fashion and crime; and of their lives and loves.

Sheila, a supermodel, is kidnapped.

Phil is sent to prison.

Mary, surviving a drug overdose, has a spiritual awakening.

It is also the story of the men who matter to them –

John Branagh, former candidate for the priesthood, a modern Darcy, someone to love or hate. Will he and Sheila ever get together?

Davy Hagan, drug dealer, 'mad, bad and dangerous to know'. Is Phil also mad to have anything to do with him?

Although from different religious backgrounds, starting off as childhood friends, the girls manage to hold on to that friendship in spite of everything.

A book about contemporary Ireland and modern life. A book which both men and women can enjoy – thriller, romance, comedy, drama – and much more ..

"fascinating ... original ... multilayered ... expertly travels from one genre to the next"
Kellie Chambers, Ulster Tatler (*Book of the Month*)

"romance at the core ... enriched with breathtaking action, mystery, suspense and some tear-jerking moments of tragedy.
Sheila M. Belshaw, author

"What starts out as a crime thriller quickly evolves into a literary festival beyond the boundary of genres"
PD Allen, author

"a masterclass, and a vivid dissection of the human condition in all of its inglorious foibles"
WeeScottishLassie

Belfast
Girls

Gerry McCullough

Published by

Chapter One

Jan 21, 2007

The street lights of Belfast glistened on the dark pavements where, even now, with the troubles officially over, few people cared to walk alone at night. John Branagh drove slowly, carefully, through the icy streets.

In the distance, he could see the lights of the *Magnifico Hotel*, a bright contrasting centre of noise, warmth and colour.

He felt again the excitement of the news he'd heard today.

Hey, he'd actually made the grade at last – full-time reporter for BBC TV, right there on the local news programme, not just a trainee, any longer. Unbelievable.

The back end shifted a little as he turned a corner. He gripped the wheel tighter and slowed down even more. There was black ice on the roads tonight. Gotta be careful.

So, he needed to work hard, show them he was keen. This interview, now, in this hotel? This guy Speers? If it turned out good enough, maybe he could go back to Fat Barney and twist his arm, get him to commission it for local TV, the Hearts and Minds programme maybe? Or even – he let his ambition soar – go national? Or how's about one of those specials everybody seemed to be into right now?

There were other thoughts in his mind but as usual he pushed them down out of sight. Sheila Doherty would be somewhere in the hotel tonight, but he had plenty of other stuff to think about to steer his attention away from past unhappiness. No need to focus on anything right now but his career and its hopeful prospects.

Montgomery Speers, better get the name right, new Member of the Legislative Assembly, wanted to give his personal views on the peace process and how it was working out. Yeah. Wanted some publicity, more like. Anti, of course, or who'd care? But that was just how people were.

John curled his lip. He had to follow it up. It could give his career the kick start it needed.

But he didn't have to like it.

* * *

Inside the *Magnifico Hotel*, in the centre of newly regenerated Belfast, all was bustle and chatter, especially in the crowded space behind the catwalk. The familiar fashion show smell, a mixture of cosmetics and hair dryers, was overwhelming.

Sheila Doherty sat before her mirror, and felt a cold wave of unhappiness surge over her. How ironic it was, that title the papers gave her, today's most super supermodel. She closed her eyes and put her hands to her ears, trying to shut everything out for just one snatched moment of peace and silence.

Every now and then it came again. The pain. The despair. A face hovered before her mind's eye, the white, angry face of John Branagh, dark hair falling forward over his furious grey eyes. She deliberately blocked the thought, opening her eyes again. She needed to slip on the mask, get ready to continue on the surface of things where her life was perfect.

"Comb that curl over more to the side, will you, Chrissie?" she asked, "so it shows in front of my ear. Yeah, that's right – if you just spray it there – thanks, pet."

The hairdresser obediently fixed the curl in place. Sheila's long red-gold hair gleamed in the reflection of three mirrors positioned to show every angle. Everything had to be perfect – as perfect as her life was supposed to be. The occasion was too important to allow for mistakes.

Her fine-boned face with its clear translucent skin, like ivory, and crowned with the startling contrast of her hair, looked back at her from the mirror, green eyes shining between thick black lashes – black only because of the mascara.

She examined herself critically, considering her appearance as if it were an artefact which had to be without flaw to pass a test.

She stood up.

"Brilliant, pet," she said. "Now the dress."

The woman held out the dress for Sheila to step into, then carefully pulled the ivory satin shape up around the slim body and zipped it at the back. The dress flowed round her, taking and emphasising her long fluid lines, her body slight and fragile as a daydream. She walked over to the door, ready to emerge onto the catwalk. She was very aware that this was the most important moment of one of the major fashion shows of her year.

The lights in the body of the hall were dimmed, those focussed on the catwalk went up, and music cut loudly through the sudden silence. Francis Delmara stepped forward and began to introduce his new spring line.

Chapter 1

For Sheila, ready now for some minutes and waiting just out of sight, the tension revealed itself as a creeping feeling along her spine. She felt suddenly cold and her stomach fluttered.

It was time and, dead on cue, she stepped lightly out onto the catwalk and stood holding the pose for a long five seconds, as instructed, before swirling forward to allow possible buyers a fuller view.

She was greeted by gasps of admiration, then a burst of applause. Ignoring the reaction, she kept her head held high, her face calm and remote, as far above human passion as some elusive, intangible figure of Celtic myth, a Sidhe, a dweller in the hollow hills, distant beyond man's possessing – just as Delmara had taught her.

This was her own individual style, the style which had earned her the nickname 'Ice Maiden' from the American journalist Harrington Smith. She moved forward along the catwalk, turned this way and that, and finally swept a low curtsey to the audience before standing there, poised and motionless.

Delmara was silent at first to allow the sight of Sheila in one of his most beautiful creations its maximum impact. Then he began to draw attention to the various details of the dress.

It was time for Sheila to withdraw. Once out of sight, she began a swift, organised change to her next outfit, while Delmara's other models were in front.

No time yet for her to relax, but the show seemed set for success.

* * *

MLA, Montgomery Speers, sitting in the first row of seats, the celebrity seats, with his latest blonde girlfriend by his side, allowed himself to feel relieved.

Francis Delmara had persuaded him to put money into Delmara Fashions and particularly into financing Delmara's supermodel, Sheila Doherty, and he was present tonight in order to see for himself if his investment was safe. He thought, even so early in the show, that it was.

He was a broad shouldered man in his early forties, medium height, medium build, red-cheeked, and running slightly to fat. There was nothing particularly striking about his appearance except for the piercing dark eyes set beneath heavy, jutting eyebrows. His impressive presence stemmed from his personality, from the aura of power and aggression which surrounded him.

A businessman first and foremost, he had flirted with political involvement for several years. He had stood successfully for election to the local council, feeling the water cautiously with one toe while he made up his mind. Would he take the plunge and throw himself whole-heartedly into politics?

The new Assembly gave him his opportunity, if he wanted to take it. More than one of the constituencies offered him the chance to stand for a seat. He was a financial power in several different towns where his computer hardware companies provided much needed jobs. He was elected to the seat of his choice with no trouble. The next move was to build up his profile, grab an important post once things got going, and progress up the hierarchy.

In an hour or so, when the Fashion Show was over, he would meet this young TV reporter for some preliminary discussion of a possible interview or of an appearance on a discussion panel. He was slightly annoyed that someone so junior had been lined up to talk to him. John Branagh, that was the name, wasn't it? Never heard of him. Should have been someone better known, at least. Still, this was only the preliminary. They would roll out the big guns for him soon enough when he was more firmly established. Meanwhile his thoughts lingered on the beautiful Sheila Doherty.

If he wanted her, he could buy her, he was sure. And more and more as he watched her, he knew that, yes, he wanted her.

* * *

A fifteen minute break, while the audience drank the free wine and ate the free canapés. Behind the scenes again, Sheila checked hair and makeup. A small mascara smear needed to be removed, a touch more blusher applied. In a few minutes she was ready but something held her back.

She stared at herself in the mirror and saw a cool, beautiful woman, the epitome of poise and grace. She knew that famous, rich, important men over two continents would give all their wealth and status to possess her, or so they said. She was an icon according to the papers. That meant, surely, something unreal, something artificial, painted or made of stone.

And what was the good? There was only one man she wanted. John Branagh. And he'd pushed her away. He believed she was a whore – a tart – someone not worth touching. What did she do to deserve that?

It wasn't fair! she told herself passionately. He went by rules that were medieval. No-one nowadays thought the odd kiss mattered that much. Oh, she was wrong. She'd hurt him, she knew she had. But if he'd given her half a chance, she'd have apologised – told him how sorry she was. Instead of that, he'd called her such names – how could she still love him after that? But she knew she did.

How did she get to this place, she wondered, the dream of romantic fiction, the dream of so many girls, a place she hated now, where men thought of her more and more as a thing, an object to be desired, not a person? When did her life go so badly wrong? She thought back to her childhood, to the skinny, ginger-haired girl she once was. Okay, she hated how she looked but otherwise, surely, she was happy. Or was that only a false memory?

"Sheila - where are you?"

The hairdresser poked her head round the door and saw Sheila with every sign of relief.

"Thank goodness! Come on, love, only got a couple of minutes! Delmara says I've to check your hair. Wants it tied back for this one."

* * *

The evening was almost at its climax. The show began with evening dress, and now it was to end with evening dress – but this time with Delmara's most beautiful and exotic lines. Sheila stood up and shook out her frock, a cloud of short ice-blue chiffon, sewn with glittering silver beads and feathers. She and Chrissie between them swept up her hair, allowing a few loose curls to hang down her back and one side of her face, fixed it swiftly into place with two combs, and clipped on more silver feathers.

She fastened on long white earrings with a pearly sheen and slipped her feet into the stiletto heeled silver shoes left ready and waiting. She moved over to the doorway for her cue. There was no time to think or to feel the usual butterflies. Chloe came off and she counted to three and went on.

There was an immediate burst of applause.

To the loud music of Snow Patrol, Sheila half floated, half danced along the catwalk, her arms raised ballerina fashion. When she had given sufficient time to allow the audience their fill of gasps and appreciation, she moved back and April and Chloe appeared in frocks with a similar effect of chiffon and feathers, but with differences in style and colour. It was Delmara's spring look for evening wear and she could tell at once that the audience loved it.

The three girls danced and circled each other, striking dramatic poses as the music died down sufficiently to allow Delmara to comment on the different features of the frocks.

With one part of her mind Sheila was aware of the audience, warm and relaxed now, full of good food and drink, their minds absorbed in beauty and fashion, ready to spend a lot of money. Dimly in the background she heard the sounds of voices shouting and feet running.

The door to the ballroom burst open.

People began to scream.

It was something Sheila had heard about for years now, the subject of local black humour, but had never before seen.

Three figures, black tights pulled over flattened faces as masks, uniformly terrifying in black leather jackets and jeans, surged into the room.

The three sub-machine guns cradled in their arms sent deafening bursts of gunfire upwards. Falling plaster dust and stifling clouds of gun smoke filled the air.

For one long second they stood just inside the entrance way, crouched over their weapons, looking round. One of them stepped forward and grabbed Montgomery Speers by the arm.

"Move it, mister!" he said. He dragged Speers forcefully to one side, the weapon poking him hard in the chest.

A second man gestured roughly with his gun in the general direction of Sheila.

"You!" he said harshly. "Yes, you with the red hair! Get over here!"

Danger Danger

Two lives in parallel – twin sisters separated at birth, but their lives take strangely similar and dangerous roads until the final collision which hurls each of them to the edge of disaster.

Katie and her gambling boyfriend Dec find themselves threatened with peril from the people Dec has cheated.

Jo-Anne (Annie) through her boyfriend Steven finds herself in the hands of much more dangerous crooks.

Can they survive and achieve safety and happiness?

"starts with a bang and never quite lets up on the tension ... it will hook you from the beginning and keep you spell bound until the very last sentence."
Ellen Fritz, Books 4 Tomorrow

"The emotional intensity of the characters is beautifully drawn ... You care for these people."
Stacey Danson, *author*

an amazing, page turning, stunning novel ... equal to Belfast Girls *in every respect. I can't wait for her next novel to be published.*
Teresa Geering, *author*

an attention-grabbing plot, strong writing, and vivid characterization, ... fast-paced and highly addictive
L. Anne Carrington, *author*

Danger Danger

Gerry McCullough

Published by

www.preciousoil.com/publications

Prologue

The shining red car hurtled across the road towards them.

'Dec!' Katie shrieked.

Declan swerved to the left, jammed on his brakes, and felt the Honda bike skid to a shuddering stop. Then it toppled over. There was a blinding pain in his left leg, then nothing.

Katie felt herself flying through the air. She landed on her left arm. The black leather jacket ripped apart. She felt her head crash into the hard surface of the railing in the centre of the road. Her helmet tore loose. It wasn't attached to her head any more. It flew across the road, landing far away from her. Then darkness, and silence.

* * *

The motorbike had come up out of nowhere. Steven saw it vaguely out of the corner of his eye. He'd thought he could make it across, in the last moments after the lights changed, just before any traffic came from the other direction. But here came this bike, way before anyone could have expected it. He dragged on the wheel, tore the Mazda round away from the bike, towards the right. Had he managed to miss it?

He felt the car wheels squeal across the wet slippery surface of the road. The car was spinning, out of control. He heard a scream which pierced his ears agonisingly. Out of the corner of his eye, he saw Annie's shoulder bang against the passenger door, saw the door burst open, saw her shoot out of the car. He wrenched at the wheel, trying obsessively, passionately, to regain control of the car. But it was too late.

He was crashing into something – he wasn't even sure what. The concrete bollard with the blue direction arrow in the middle of the road, perhaps. A moment later, his head hit the windscreen. And then there was nothing more.

Chapter One

Time – 14 May 88, twenty-three years ago.

Place – St. Austin's Maternity Hospital.

Marie Sinclair, aged seventeen and single, lay in a hospital bed, struggling through the first stages of childbirth.

She had been to the ante natal clinic, had learnt how to relax, had learnt all about the second stage, about panting like a dog and not pushing until the doctor or the midwife told her to push.

She had hoped that Jamie would be with her when all this was happening. She had to admit that she was scared.

Natural childbirth, that was the thing to go for, everyone had said. But right now, there were only two things she wanted. One was a hefty dose of some helpful drug, something, anything, to take away the pain.

The other was Jamie.

If he had been here to hold her hand and tell her he loved her, it would have been so much better. But he had chickened out. He'd been horrified when he found that she was pregnant. Had never suggested marrying her, even moving in with her. Didn't want a baby. And when the scan showed that there were actually two babies, he was even more reluctant.

Marie groaned loudly again. The pains were coming more strongly than ever.

The doctor offered an injection of pethedine. Marie gratefully agreed.

Everything was further away now. She could still feel the pain of the strong contractions. But it felt as if they were happening to someone else. Someone miles away. Then suddenly she could hear the midwife calling out to her loudly.

'Marie! Marie!'

She listened with an effort.

'Don't push! Don't push!'

It was almost impossible to obey. The urge to push was almost overwhelming.

Marie remembered her ante-natal training. Pant like a dog.

She panted. Panted some more. Went on panting.

Then, 'Good girl!' It was the midwife, speaking from so far away. 'One more effort, now. Push!'

The second baby came flying out, fielded dextrously by the midwife. Then the afterbirth.

And then peace, and a time of rest.

Marie slept.

When she at last surfaced, there were two tiny babies in two cots, one on either side of her bed.

Marie gazed at them in awe. How beautiful they were. But how could she look after two?

She remembered that she had arranged that one of the babies should be adopted. She couldn't bear to think of giving up both. Now, with a pang, she realised that she didn't want to give up either.

Her mum had offered to help, so that Marie could go back to school, get qualifications for a decent job in the future. But only if Marie didn't keep both babies. Mum could only help if Marie only kept one. Mum had made it clear that two babies were a bit much for her to look after.

Jamie didn't want to get involved.

Marie was frightened. She had been set against abortion. It was murder, nothing else. But here she was with two beautiful babies, and a decision to make. She didn't even know if they were boys or girls.

If they were one of each, she would keep the girl, she thought suddenly. It seemed, somehow, as if that would be easier.

A nurse peered round the bed curtains, and pulled them back enough to be able to come in.

'Awake, now?' she asked pleasantly. 'Have you held your babies yet?'

'No,' said Marie weakly. 'I'd like to.'

The nurse came round to Marie's left side, scooped a tiny bundle out of the cot, and placed her carefully in Marie's arms.

'A little girl,' she said, flicking back the blanket which was wrapped round the baby, to demonstrate. 'Isn't she beautiful?'

Chapter 1

Marie gazed at her daughter. 'She's so tiny.'

An overwhelming love for the baby swept through her.

'I'll keep this one, nurse.'

The nurse looked surprised at the suddenness of the decision. But it wasn't a good idea for her to rock the boat, so she said nothing.

'I decided I'd keep the girl,' Marie said. She knew she didn't need to explain, but somehow she wanted to justify herself.

'Right,' said the nurse briskly. 'So this other one is for adoption. You have six weeks to change your mind, you know.'

'No!' said Marie. 'No! I can't keep them both. Please take the other one away now, nurse! I'll sign the forms when the six weeks are up, but I couldn't bear to have him here all that time, and get to love him. Please!'

The nurse felt that she understood. It would be better if the baby was looked after away from the new mother until the adoptive parents could legally take it. Silently she wheeled the cot out from the cubicle.

Marie continued to hold her little daughter. She would call her Catherine. Katie for short.

She felt that she had made the right decision. A girl was more helpless. A girl needed her mother.

No one had told her that the other baby was a little girl, too.

The Seanachie:
Tales of Old Seamus

Gerry McCullough

A humorous series of Irish stories, set in the fictional Donegal village of Ardnakil and featuring that lovable rogue, *'Old Seamus'* – the Séanachie.

All of these stories have previously been published in the popular Irish weekly magazine, *Ireland's Own*, based in Wexford, Ireland.

"heart warming tales ... beautifully told with subtle Irish humour"

Babs Morton (author)

"an irresistible old rogue, but he's the kind people love to sit and listen to for hours on end whenever the opportunity presents itself"

G. Polley (author and blogger – Sapporo, Japan)

"This magnificent storyteller has done it again. Each individual story has it's own Gaelic charm"

Teresa Geering (author – UK)

"evocative characterisation brings these stories to life in a delightful, absorbing way"

Elinor Carlisle (author – Reading, UK)

Other (non-fiction) books from

A Wee Taste a' Craic:

All the Irish craic from the popular
***Celtic Roots Radio** shows, 2-25*

Raymond McCullough

> *I absolutely loved this! I found it to be very informative*
> *about Irish life culture, language and traditions.*
> **Elinor Carlisle (author, Reading, UK)**

> *a unique insight into the Northern Irish people*
> *& their self deprecating sense of humour*
> **Strawberry**

Ireland – now the <u>good</u> news!

The best of *'Bread'* Vols. 1 & 2 –

personal testimonies and church/fellowship
profiles from around Ireland

Edited by:
Raymond & Gerry McCullough

"...fresh Bread – deals with the real issues facing the church in Ireland today"
Ken Newell, minister of Fitzroy Presbyterian Church, Belfast

The Whore and her Mother:

9/11, Babylon and the Return of the King

Raymond McCullough

Could the writings of the ancient Hebrew prophets be relevant to events taking place in the world today?

These Hebrew prophets – Isaiah, Jeremiah, Habbakuk and the apostle John, in *The Revelation* – wrote extensively about a latter day city and empire which would dominate, exploit and corrupt all the nations of the world. They referred to it as Babylon the Great, or Mega-Babylon, and they foretold that its fall – 'in one day' – would devastate the economies of the whole world. Have these prophecies been fulfilled already?

Is Mega-Babylon the Roman Catholic Church?
A world super-church?
Rebuilt ancient Babylon?
Brussels, Jerusalem, or somewhere entirely different?
Should this city/nation have a large Jewish population?
Why all the talk about merchants, cargoes, commodities, trade?

Can we rely on the words of these ancient prophets?
If so, what else did they foretell that is still to be fulfilled?
Do they refer to other major nations – USA, Russia, China, Europe?
What about militant Islam?

"AMAZED when I read this book ... in awe of your extensive knowledge on so many levels: Christian, Jewish, and Muslim culture; the Jewish diaspora ... Greek & Hebrew; ... thought-provoking and troublesome ... many will be offended, but you consistently build your case instead of being sensationalistic."
James Revoir, author of *Priceless Stones*

More info from: *preciousoil.com/publications*

Printed in Great Britain
by Amazon

29264794R00145